THE MANDARIN'S
VENDETTA

WES LOWE

AUTHOR'S INTRODUCTION

China, the once-sleeping dragon, has awoken. Airborne and spreading its wings wide, its energy and influences are global and formidable.

And yet, it is still an enigma, full of inconsistencies and contradictions. Transparency and openness remain elusive and despite brash, fantastic displays of pageantry - who could ever forget the dazzling opening of the Beijing Summer Olympics or Shanghai's pronouncement as a "great world city" when it hosted the World Expo - there is still the mystery and reality of the "inscrutable Chinese.

The Mandarin's Vendetta shows us a bit of the dragon's hidden underbelly. Mixed in with the breakneck, unrelenting action is illumination into the dark world of corruption, crime and desperation of both sides of the Pacific.

The world is a dangerous place to live, not because of the people who are evil, but because of the people who don't do anything about it.

Albert Einstein

INTRODUCTION TO MODERN CHINA

China. One of the most fascinating, complex and unpredictable countries in the world. With a history of more than five thousand years, the "Middle Kingdom's" population is approaching a billion and a half people that speak one or several of the over two hundred dialects of Chinese. Tectonic shifts politically, socially and economically are the norm, especially since Chairman Mao declared the formation of the People's Republic of China. The proverbial China, governed by dynasties, warlords, emperors, autocratic monarchs and regional kings, is no more.

After the assumption of power by the Communist Party in 1949, Chairman Mao ruled China with a reign of terror while he transformed China from an agrarian society to an industrial one. Despite mistakes, abuses and an inability to control corruption, there was one factor that endeared him to the people—Mao stood up to foreign imperialist powers and ended a century of humiliation.

China's desire to establish itself on the world stage continued after Mao's death with subsequent generations of leaders—but with a radically different approach. While never stated as official policy, the older Communist ideal of all people being equal was replaced by a more capitalist approach of letting the cream rise to the top, economic advancement and opening the "Bamboo Curtain" to enter the global economy.

Since 1977, it's been a constant tug of war between traditional and contemporary, Communist and capitalist, laissez-faire and government control. What has made it more difficult for the Chinese and anyone or any country trying to establish business or diplomatic relations is an inconsistency in application of rules. Some bureaucrats and party officials ignore them; others follow them to the letter of the law. That doesn't mean the system is broken. It just means that playing the game has to be approached from multiple perspectives. (As an example, in Beijing, one can visit Tiananmen Square where, in 1989, pro-democracy protesters were mowed down by soldiers. Yet, in the midst of the square, is the mausoleum of China's dictator for twenty-five years, Chairman Mao Zedong. And, mere steps away, is the Forbidden City, the imperial palace for twenty-four emperors during the Ming and Qing dynasties.)

With no strong guiding hand of governance, towns and cities have become mishmashes of economic, cultural and social environments, often co-existing virtually side by side. Bright megastores are steps away from street hawkers with carts; European designer houses are footfalls from little shops with cheap knock-offs hidden behind the counter; turn the corner from a luxury apartment and there may be cardboard and sheet metal shacks.

This current generation, with the emergence of capitalism, has seen an explosion of millionaires and even billionaires. While China under Communism is largely atheistic, that doesn't mean there is no God. He's just been replaced. With money as the new center of worship, there has been a stampede toward materialism, any for many, the desire to flaunt their new wealth. In major cities around the world, designer shops cater to mainland Chinese. China today is the single most important market for Mercedes Benz and Porsche. Chinese buyers account for one quarter of the world's luxury goods sales. From single malt scotch to expensive French wines, the Chinese have become the most important purchasers.

How did so many Chinese get their wealth? Of course, there are many honest, hardworking citizens who grew their businesses, paying attention to regulations, standards and ethical business practices. But, like everywhere else in the world, advancement's wheels are oiled by willing officials who will bend or ignore the regulations when bribes are offered. The preponderance of corrupt administrators, civil servants, officials and party members has grown astronomically and periodic crackdowns have been unable to stem the tide.

There are also many for whom rules and honesty are nuisances to be ignored. No different from anywhere else in the world but, with such a preponderance of those who have entered the category of the *nouveau riche,* it is clear that corrupt government officials often collaborate with criminals or fraudsters in the private sector.

But, as Abraham Lincoln allegedly stated, "You can fool all the people some of the time and some of the people all the time, but you cannot fool all the people all the time."

And, even if you don't get caught, the consequences can still be dire.

PART ONE
INTERNATIONAL TRAGEDY

ONE

PRISON LEPER

Corruption and Shoddy Construction Behind School Collapse in China Earthquake (*China Daily Tribune - English Edition*)

Guangzhou

After a three-month investigation, a committee investigating the collapse of two primary schools in the city of Zongtian during a mild earthquake that measured only 4.2 on the Richter scale has concluded that shoddy workmanship, substandard materials and shortcuts in construction were the root causes.

The four-story schools, less than five years old and located three miles apart from each other, crumpled within sixty seconds, crushing hundreds of children beneath a sea of bricks and concrete. Three hundred schoolchildren were crushed to death and close to two thousand children, ages six to eleven, suffered injuries ranging from minor bruises to fractured skulls. Frantic rescue workers and wailing parents searched overnight in pouring rain, clawing through tons of mud, rubble and debris.

With many older buildings surviving the earthquake, outraged parents demanded an investigation. (In most cases, an earthquake of this magnitude causes only slight shaking and minimal damage.) At that time, Chen Bigao, the Housing Minister for China's Guangdong Province, stated, "It is unacceptable that we put the lives of our children into the hands of property developers who care only about lining their pockets with money obtained through the blood of our children. We will not stop until we have all the answers and imprison all those who are guilty of murdering our children."

Today, the results of that inquiry were released:

The vertical columns in the Zongtian primary school had inadequate reinforcing rods—a critical structural flaw. The concrete was substandard with a high percentage of sea sand instead of the legally required river sand. The untreated sea sand contained chlorine and salt that corroded the steel girders. In addition, an oversupply of the cheap sand was mixed with the concrete, making the structure less sturdy. To cut costs further, illegal and inexperienced migrant workers, mainly farmers or "rural refugees," made up the construction crews instead of experienced construction workers. They were recruited from "shanty towns," impoverished slum areas in major urban areas. These unskilled laborers worked for a fraction of what properly trained workers cost... but the amounts paid by the government to the contractors was at the top of the pay scale for the best workers. (*In China, people must have permits, or hukou, to be allowed to work, live or go to school in an area outside their place of birth.*)

School Planning Director, Wen Jiang, who okayed all the major contracts, has been arrested. His explanation was that he was given an "impossible" budget to complete the project and that Zongtian, which has never experienced significant tremors, was in an "earthquake-free zone."

A deeper examination revealed that his record-keeping was abysmal—there was little in the way of a proper paper trail. Many transactions were done with cash and without receipts. Other "contracts" were made with fictitious companies, or companies that have gone out of business and cannot be tracked down. While all of Wen's assets have been seized in China, it is suspected that the corrupt official laundered millions into hidden overseas accounts. Wen has been arrested for corruption, negligence and homicide, and justice officials plan to seek the death penalty.

THIRTY-SEVEN-YEAR-OLD WEN TRIED to sleep on the concrete floor in the Western Mountain District Detention Center in the city of Guangzhou. It wasn't easy because he shared the moldy, dank cell the size of a classroom with thirty other men. He had no blankets, no pillows, and was wearing only the clothes he had on when he was arrested. His luxury condominium was seized and his wife and the love of his life, his one-year-old son, were evicted. He had no idea where they were or how they were doing.

For the week he had been detained, he'd had the crap beaten out of him almost daily. Sometimes it was a guard; sometimes it was one of the other inmates. For this, his money was of no help and he knew no amount of bribes would ever gain him freedom again. Even though there was no proof of his direct involvement, that mattered little. Public outcry was too much for someone everyone felt was responsible for the deaths of so many innocents.

He was a leper. Other than to use him as a human punching bag or as an ashtray to butt out illicit smokes, no one associated with him or wanted to talk to him. It really didn't matter if anyone did or not. Festering pus around an untreated stab wound in his arm was growing. It would only be a matter of time before no one paid any attention at all to him.

Which was why it was surprising that someone requested to speak with him.

In a small interrogation room, Wen watched as a sixty-something-year-old man entered. He looked like so many other bureaucrats around the world: cheap suit, tie that was tied too long, and a disinterested attitude that told you he was counting the seconds before retirement. As the man sat, his cell phone fell out of his pocket. He snarled, picked it up and placed it on the table.

"What do you want?" asked Wen.

"You know what I want. The same as the rest of us

that have come. We want to know who your accomplices are," droned his bored interrogator, going through the motions. He glanced at the tiny window in the door and saw the guard staring in. The man lifted his hands in exasperation. His body language declared—*WTF. He's not going to say anything, but it's a job.*

"I have told you all a million times. I don't know anything. I was just hired to do a job. I never asked questions."

The official discreetly kicked Wen subtly under the table and with the slightest of motions pointed at his cell phone. "Yeah, same as me. I have a job to do, too." He stood up, took a quick, firm hold on Wen's head and banged it on the table. The guard watched with interest, not noticing that the man had directed Wen's head at the cell phone screen.

There was a message on the cell that flashed for a second. *Act normal. I have saved your family.*

"There's not a chance I'll get out," snapped Wen, yanking himself up. "Even if I knew anything, what's in it for me?"

For a second time, Wen's head was hammered against the hard metal table. This time it was face down so that when Wen's head lifted, his nose was broken and bleeding. Again, the guard was more interested in what was happening with Wen than looking at the cell phone.

Wen glanced at the phone's screen. There was now a picture of his wife and son smiling under a sign in an airport, "Welcome to Vancouver. *Bienvenue* à *Vancouver.*"

Wen's eyes fixed on his visitor. He thought he saw the

tiniest of an acknowledging head movement. "Maybe I can get you some better food once a week."

"If I do that, they'll kill my wife and son."

"Who are 'they?'"

"I... I don't know their names..."

"You're useless."

"I told the other guy and the other guy and the other guy that."

The bureaucrat rolled his eyes and made ready to leave.

As he stood up, Wen barked, "Wait!"

"For what? I've got to get to my next prisoner."

"May I send a message to my wife... please?"

The man shook his head in disgust. "Just make it fast." He handed his cell phone to Wen.

Wen typed in about thirty words, then handed the phone back to his anonymous questioner. "Thank you."

"Maybe your memory will improve next time." With that, the bureaucrat took his phone and walked to the door.

After letting the man out, the guard at the door accosted him. "I want to see what he wrote."

"Suit yourself."

He handed over his cell to the guard. A cursory check revealed nothing other than some brief inanity to his wife.

The guard glared at the civil servant. "You're not supposed to do this."

"I know. I did it to try and butter him up. Like I told Wen, I'm hoping next time he'll say something I can use. Truth is, I'm not going send it. You think I'm going to risk losing my job because of him? I'm a week away from retirement and no way do I want to jeopardize that." The official motioned his head in the direction of the interrogation room. "No way... You can keep the phone if you want." He walked away.

TWO

MESSAGE DELIVERED

Outside the prison, the nameless bureaucrat took out a cell phone identical to the one the prison guard had taken. But this one contained the real notes that Wen had typed: seven names and three of the companies that Wen had dealt with during the school building fiasco. Because the official was physically abusing Wen, he knew the guard would be so focused on the prisoner that he wouldn't notice that he was actually the one typing the love note. With practiced deftness, he exchanged the phones after Wen handed the phone back to him.

He sent off the text. He then opened the cell, took out the SIM card, and replaced it with another. He broke the old SIM card in two and placed one of the halves in a bucket of dirty water that a food hawker used to rinse dishes. He walked half a block, then tossed the other half of the SIM into a garbage can.

HALFWAY AROUND THE world in a secluded resort in California, in a concrete bunker fifty feet below ground equipped with state-of-the-art-and-beyond computers and electronic wizardry, super-geek Julio Ibanez was on the receiving end of the digital message. The multi-tasker's fingers flew across a keyboard as he made a phone call to a secure private line.

"I guess this call means you got it," said Arthur Yang, the real name of the person who had visited Wen in prison.

"Yeah, yeah, yeah," gasped Julio as the first bits of intel flew onto a monitor.

Both Arthur and Julio were part of the shadowy, covert self-funded vigilante organization, *Fidelitas*. The younger super-geek Julio was head of intelligence while Arthur, a former field operative, was a current board member. Julio's intel skills were legendary, or would have been had anyone been allowed to know about them.

The illegal Mexican immigrant nodded his approval. "This is good stuff, Arthur. I'll have something ready for you in two hours."

"That long?" chided Arthur. "Are you losing your touch? I've already given you thirty seconds."

"Problem is that almost everyone on this list has a small or non-existent digital presence. Makes tracking down any kind of data about them, including financials, really hard but hey, what's life without a few challenges? But, from what I've seen already, I would start making plans."

"We'll talk in two hours. Thanks, Julio."

Arthur ended the call and started another one.

THREE

DEVILS

Pyongyang, Capital of North Korea

North Korea's General Park Daesoon and the Mandarin had been doing business together for almost twenty years. When they first started, North Korea was heavily involved in the manufacture and sale of heroin and pure, potent meth. Those were the glory days, with their high quality illegal drugs in demand from criminal organizations around the world. With North Korea needing foreign currency, the government, through its front companies and reps, including military officials like Park, happily sold its product to anyone who paid them a buck.

This included the Mandarin, who had a ready supply of users from the illegal migrants in his old shanty town in Guangzhou. Even though the inhabitants had little money, everyone wanted something to take their minds away from the numbing reality. Ice was cheap.

While the Mandarin was a small customer, about five kilos a month, he was steady and paid in cash. What made him even more desirable to Park was that the Mandarin gave him an additional kickback, hidden from his superiors. While the military commander constantly tried to get the Mandarin to increase the volume of his business, the Mandarin rejected Park's entreaties. Yes, he could make more but that would be dangerous for the Mandarin's core business of supplying construction workers. Stoned and high workers were even less reliable than unskilled ones on a construction job, and there was no way the Mandarin would jeopardize that cash cow.

Business between the two became much more difficult in 2005 when the North Korean government made a sudden change of policy—the manufacture and distribution of heroin and crystal meth was shut down. That didn't mean the drug business ceased operations. It just meant that the government could sanctimoniously claim they had no involvement in the industry. Any statements or accusations that the DPRK was connected to drug-related crimes were due to the "reptile Western media and the South Korean puppet regimes."

But official position and reality are two different animals. The drug industry in the Hermit Kingdom did not abate; it just went underground.

For businessmen like the Mandarin, it meant costs went up. If he didn't pay, someone else would. The business was still there—it just needed to be more creatively accessed.

Park kept his DPRK military title but his income was slashed. That he didn't mind at all because he "went indie." Even with the bribes that he now had to pay, he made more money—Park was very good at hustling business.

It was more work, though. Instead of ordering drugs directly from the state factories, Park had to hire the now-unemployed chemists to manufacture the drugs, coordinate the raw materials and book the factories. Delivery became messier. Instead of sending a fishing vessel into North Korean territorial waters, Park hired drug mules who swam or waded across the Yalu River at the China/North Korean border to deliver the packages to the Mandarin's representative at the river bank, who arranged delivery in China.

For the Mandarin, Park wasn't the cheapest way to achieve results but more important than cost was reliability: the general always delivered first class product.

Not to mention the perks.

———

IN STARK CONTRAST to the dreary and dilapidated buildings surrounding it, Pyongyang's majestic Paek-dusan Hotel stood out like Goliath in a leprechaun colony. In addition to fine dining and luxury spas, their female masseuses had an international reputation for beauty and exceptional creativity. Park had just treated the Mandarin to the pleasures of a smokey-eyed beauty with oval eyes, luscious lips and legs for days. Session completed, the two of them were relaxing in the heat of burning pine wood in one of the hotel's igloo-shaped kiln saunas.

"Mandarin, why don't you expand into America?"

asked his host, sweat beading profusely out from his skin. "I can easily get you more product. You know my goods are much better than the shit from Myanmar or Burma or the Philippines."

"I make a good living in China. Don't need the headache of dealing with blacks, Russians, Hispanics and the whites. They're all cheats and cheapskates."

"Well, of course they are. But they will give up their firstborn in order to feed their addiction. Easy money."

"You need to have distribution... connections. All mine are in China. If there were somebody Chinese I could trust, I might consider it."

"You should not be such a racist," chided General Park. "Some of my clients ship product every month to Vancouver or Los Angeles. Prices they get are much higher than in China. "

"I'll think about it."

Park sighed. "Thinking about it means 'no.' I tell you, it is an opportunity."

"More money means more headaches."

"Those are good kinds of headaches," laughed Park.

What the Mandarin didn't tell his business associate was that he had floated a trial balloon in America and had partnered with the China Red Gang, the Asian gang with the greatest success in penetrating the American market, on a small shipment of ice to Los Angeles.

The experiment was a great success and the Mandarin was waiting for Danny, the head of China Red, to return to China so they could meet and plan out their next phase.

"Talk to me about something other than making money. What's new?"

The military man was pensive. There was something he was thinking of saying but...

"Just spit it out, Park. After that, I'll treat for the next round," growled the Mandarin.

The general inhaled a deep gulp of the scalding air. "There's something else we're working on, too. A lethal synthetic drug. N115. It's got a similar chemistry to crystal meth but the rush, the high... it's better than anything else. When people try it, they just gotta have more, the kick is so good. Because it hasn't been released yet, no one knows about it. One kilo is enough to kill twenty-five to thirty thousand people with typical dose sizes. Interested?"

"I don't have that many enemies," chuckled the Mandarin. "Besides, if I want somebody dead, I'll just pay some gangbanger fifty bucks."

"Yes, but just a few milligrams is all you need to do the job. Good enough for hundreds or thousands of people. Two million a kilo."

"I don't have that many enemies, General. But if I do, you'll be the first person I call." The Mandarin slapped Park on his sweaty back.

FOUR
WAKEY WAKEY

Dawn was just breaking as the sun peeked through a crack in the heavy drapes covering the huge glass windows in Rayna Tan's San Francisco condo. At four a.m., clad only in her underwear and sports bra, the athletic Asian woman had already gone through a brutal Special Operations level workout and black belt level martial arts routine.

Hers was not the living space of a normal person. Her bedroom and living room had more resemblance to NASA than Better Homes and Gardens. There were at least twenty-five video monitors, all that were turned on to news feeds from a dozen different countries in a dozen different languages, six business channels that had up-to-the-second analysis and quotes from major and minor stock markets. This was not particularly unusual for anyone involved in financial management, planning and investing.

What was not normal were the half dozen monitors filled with the rantings of ethnic and religious terrorists.

Rayna had recently thwarted a new terrorist group, the American Muslim Militia, which had threatened to blow up Safeco Field in Seattle. That threat had been neutralized but, in any situation like this, there were always loose ends that needed following up on. At any given time, there were not just major organizations, but thousands of cells around the world plotting world domination, jihad. The hard part was to determine which were real and which were hot air. One of Rayna's tasks was to determine how valid any of these threats were.

One of her concerns was *Hukm* (Arabic for *Judgement*), an obscure apocalyptic Islamic cult that seemed to have its origins in the U.S. Midwest. As her family had a strong Christian background, she was fascinated by doomsday cults of all religions. She knew well the rantings and writings of Christian leaders like David Koresh and Jim Jones. Somewhere along the line, their knowledge became corrupted, but their natural charisma led to fanatic believers who followed these flawed leaders to their deaths.

Rayna was peeling away the layers of the surface web and delving into Hukm's anonymous network on the dark web. Her research was sounding frighteningly familiar. "Judgement is imminent," and "America's sins must be accounted for," were two prominent themes.

She was working on her second espresso when a voice from one of the video monitors greeted her.

"Good morning, Rayna," smiled Barry Rogers, her boss at Fidelitas. With the screen showing a San Francisco morning skyline, it was obvious he was already at his office.

"Good morning to you too, Barry. To what do I owe this early morning pleasure?"

"Hold on. I don't want to repeat myself."

On another monitor, another familiar face. In a decrepit, dark room, Chuck Hanson, a muscular black man and retired Navy SEAL 6 member, was swinging a shovel at Assam, a former Islamic terrorist, trying to decapitate him. Assam dodged the deadly broad blades by leaping, ducking and backflipping. During a vicious thrust to Assam's throat, Chuck's cell phone started honking loudly—this could come from only one source and when it did come, it meant drop everything to answer.

Chuck immediately dropped the lethal garden tool and answered the phone, giving Assam a thumbs up.

"Hey, Barry, what's up?"

"Smile. You're on Candid Camera. Rayna and Arthur are here, too."

"Damn. If I knew that, I would have killed the bastard."

Rayna saw Chuck swatting off a blow to the head from Assam. "So, what's the purpose of our gathering?"

Arthur, from another monitor, spoke up. "We want you to come to China. Now."

FIVE

HOMELAND

Rayna took a sip of her second espresso. This was not what she was expecting but then again, there wasn't much with Fidelitas that was predictable. "What's the story?"

"Did you hear about the two schools in China that collapsed a few months ago during a mild earthquake?" asked Arthur.

Rayna and Chuck shook their heads simultaneously. "Nope."

Arthur sighed. "Most people didn't. Not newsworthy enough—which means it's a fit for Fidelitas. We did our own due diligence and discovered that, while one mid-level official took the fall, there were at least a dozen or more contractors that had levels of directs responsibility. Short cuts in construction led to defective buildings. More than twenty-five hundred deaths or injuries from a quake that measured only 4.2 on the Richter."

"That's unconscionable," stated Rayna.

"Any idea who's responsible?" asked Chuck.

Arthur nodded. "Yes, I'm taking care of the low-hanging fruit right now but we need you, Barry and Rayna to knock some heads together and flush out the rats. I'm organizing a special lunch in Guangzhou to bring some of them out."

"What makes you think they'll come?"

Arthur grinned as a photo of Rayna in a yellow bikini pointing an AK-47 directly at the camera came onscreen.

Rayna rolled her eyes. It was an old photo taken when she was in JTF2 that she never should have agreed to. "Are you going to hold that against me forever? What angle are you peddling now? Cupcake with a cannon? Babe with a bayonet? Fox with a firearm?"

Arthur shrugged. "Don't flatter yourself. You can't compete with the teenage goddess bimbos that surround these powerful pricks. But you are smart, you are lethal and you can get any job done... that is the turn-on. I'm going to tell them enough about Fidelitas to make them want to know more. My pitch is about getting them and their cash out of the country."

A certain segment of Fidelitas' clientele—high end criminals and wealthy corrupt scum— engaged the corporation to conduct sensitive, illegal transactions. In many instances, white-washing clients' funds was part of the job. As for personal exit strategies? Fidelitas' connections could get anyone, anywhere.

"How do you plan to do that?" asked Chuck.

"Haven't figured that part out yet. All I know is that we just got the intel an hour ago and we've got to act fast.

So Chuck, the jet's picking you up in an hour. Two hours later, it'll be in Frisco, then we take off to China. Got it?"

Chuck nodded on the other screen.

Noting Rayna's sudden thoughtfulness, Barry queried, "Rayna. You good?"

China. The country she was born in. The country of which she had so many unanswered questions. Rayna asked quietly, "Do you think I might be able to take a personal day while I'm there? And is it okay if my father comes along?"

Barry cleared his throat. He immediately figured out the reason. Rayna was adopted at birth, but he had been unable to find out anything when he did his background check on her. If Fidelitas couldn't find out, it would be hard for any normal mortal to discover anything, either— unless he had a personal connection, which Rayna's father definitely had. "We can arrange that. We'll take a detour and pick him up, too. Now, let's get ready."

With that the conference ended and the monitors resumed pumping out the news.

Rayna cradled the phone as she punched in a familiar number.

"Hello. Pastor Henry here."

"Hi, Dad, it's Rayna. Got a sec?"

"Of course. I'd much prefer talking to my daughter instead of being planted at my desk and working on sermon prep." Rayna could sense the smile on her father's face at the other end of the line. She felt his warmth oozing through. "You think you could take a few days off with me, like starting in like... four hours?"

"Of course," said Henry without hesitation.

"You didn't even ask why."

"I don't need to. If you need me, I'm there. I'll just call up Jordan and ask him to preach this Sunday instead. What is it we're doing?"

"The company is sending me on a business trip to China to Guangzhou. I recall you saying that is close to where I'm from... I... I want to go back to the village where I was born and see if I can find anything out about my birth family."

After a few thoughtful moments, Henry broke the silence. "I was wondering when this day would come. Tell me what flight you're going on so we can coordinate."

"Don't worry about that. I will pick you up in our company jet. Why don't you start packing?"

"Did you say, 'company jet' as in 'private jet for just those you're working with?'"

"Yeah."

A whistle was heard over the phone. "Who are you working for, Rayna?"

"I told you before, Dad. Don't ask me. We'll get a driver to pick you up when it's time to go."

"I can catch a cab," protested Henry.

"He wouldn't know where the private airfield is. See you soon."

"Wait!" Henry's tone became serious. "I don't want you to get your expectations too high. The circumstances of our adopting you were unusual at best. Your mom and I respected the wishes of the birth mother for anonymity and not to tell us anything..."

"I understand, Dad. I just thought it would be nice to have you around... as my tour guide."

Henry squinted. "I think I should have recorded that."

"Just start packing."

SIX
BLACKMAIL

Vancouver

Jackson Lam was the Mandarin's son, one of those Chinese that Canadians loved to hate. The eighteen-year-old emigrated to Canada with his parents eight years earlier under Canada's Immigrant Investor Program, a program where qualified investors could get Canadian landed immigrant status (the Canadian equivalent of the American Green Card), in exchange for investment into the Canadian economy.

There was no doubt that this was a "win win" situation for both sides of the investment equation. Canada would get much desired private investment and the immigrants could gain access to what most considered a better quality of life than the country they were from, as well as a multitude of new investment opportunities. For three decades, Canadians were happy with the system. The value in their homes went up, retailers had new shoppers willing to buy everything from top-of-the-line appliances to automobiles, and restaurants welcomed thousands of new customers.

But, in recent years, attitudes of some long-time Canadians began to change. Homes became unaffordable in certain prime areas; signs in stores were no longer in English; and with the study ethic of immigrant students and hushed bribes (or "donations") by their parents, getting into the best schools seemed an impossible wall to scale.

It was during this time of nascent resentment that Jackson and his parents emigrated. If the press or mainstream Canadians found out what Jackson's family had been doing, resentment would have changed to outrage... or even an uprising.

The family purchased a brand new luxury home of over five thousand square feet with a sticker price that was double that of Beverly Hills—paid for in cash. While none of the family was that conversant in English, the universal language of money ensured Jackson's entry into an elite private school. Of course, the Mandarin rarely spent time in Canada; there were businesses to run in China.

Within two years, Jackson's mother, Kitty, a former actress in Chinese television shows, decided Vancouver was too "boring." She moved back to China to hang out with her fellow washed-out starlet friends, trying to find ways to spend their unfaithful husbands' money. Sadly, two days after she returned to the Middle Country, she was the victim of random violence—she was raped, then strangled in her new apartment. It was whispered that a heavyset Chinese man in her husband's employ was seen leaving her residence in the early hours, but no one would substantiate the claim.

The Mandarin asked Mary Wu, his executive assistant, to help supervise the needs of his son. Not to take charge—he needed her on the job, but at least to make occasional phone calls and pay any of his bills.

In other words, young Jackson was left in Vancouver to be raised by a Filipino nanny whose sole qualification for taking care of children was a three-month course in housekeeping. Mary made sure there was a monthly deposit of fifteen thousand dollars spending allowance into Jackson's bank account. There were no restrictions placed on how the boy spent it. About the only parental guidance he had was his father's admonition, "Make sure you pass everything." Not the greatest student in the world, Jackson learned that passing was easy—make sure you took care of your teachers and they would take care of you.

Jackson hated Filipino food, which was the only thing the nanny knew how to cook, so he hung out in the Chinese malls in nearby Richmond, where the Chinese population was so large that it was ignominiously nick-named, "Hongcouver." There, he ate too much fast food, played too many video games and bought a new cell phone almost every other month when he wasn't buying the most useless knick knacks in the world. Online, he managed to find custom basketball shoes at ten grand per pair—he bought six pairs.

As Jackson became more accustomed to North America, his spending habits and outlook transformed. He fell in love with NFL football and thought nothing of hiring a limo for the three-hour ride to bring himself and a few buddies down to Seattle to watch a Seahawks game.

When Jackson turned sixteen, and even before he got his driver's license, his father gave him a Ferrari convertible. While it seemed ostentatious and extravagant to the average working stiff, it wasn't the most expensive car owned by students at the school Jackson attended.

Even with high-priced tutors and bribed teachers marking his tests, Jackson was a marginal student at best —he couldn't buy everything. There was no way he was going to get into any Ivy League or any top tier school, no matter how much money his father was willing to donate. Jackson was about to hire a Mensa-gone-wrong type to masquerade as himself to write the SATs but then the idiot got caught—he'd pulled that trick one too many times. A good SAT score wasn't that important, though. Jackson didn't need a degree from a fancy school. He would never have to work a day in life and a degree wouldn't be much more than a piece of paper hanging on a wall.

But the Mandarin did want his only son to have a college degree of some kind.

This resulted in the first serious argument that father and son ever had. Jackson had no interest in college and wanted his father to bankroll the opening of a high end karaoke bar. His father knew that Jackson had no business mind and just wanted a place where he could be a big shot with his buddies.

This fueled further argument until Jackson asked poignantly, "What's in it for me if I get a degree?"

Without hesitation, his father answered, "One hundred million American dollars."

"What do I get if I don't get a degree?"

"Nothing. I will give it to Annalee's children."

"She doesn't have kids."

"She's pregnant."

It wasn't true but Jackson didn't know that. His father's mistress was just a year older than him. But Jackson knew this was not an idle threat.

Now the pressure was on. He had Mary help him with filling out forms. There were thirty-two rejections but ultimately Jackson found himself enrolled in the obscure, lower tier Pacifica College, an hour and a half south of Los Angeles in an equally obscure town, San Roca.

SEVEN

TELL ME A SECRET

As the Fidelitas jet smoothly winged its way over the Pacific, Barry sat staring intently at his laptop, Henry had been watching Chuck and Rayna go at each other for forty-five solid minutes with a combination of martial arts, boxing and old-fashioned street fighting. He could not believe his little girl could not only absorb the pounding that Chuck administered but more than retaliated with her fair share of sidekicks, forearm smashes and whatever it was that they did on television's MMA. And then they began individual workouts. Pushups that fired like engine pistons pumping up and down. Lightning fast squat jumps... alternating jump lunges... killer shadow boxing blows.

Finally, the two collapsed on their backs, staying still for half a minute before beginning the cooling down with leg stretches that exhibited ballerina-like flexibility. Henry saw Rayna's facial intensity unknotting until she lay still on the jet's carpeted interior. Even though Chuck was more than twice Rayna's age, Henry could see the bond between them. Not as lovers but as warriors who had been at each other's side in battle.

This is what she did for years as part of Special Ops... but she's no longer part of them... Maybe I can find out now.

Glowing with exhilarated exhaustion, the two athletes high-fived. Chuck plopped himself down beside Barry while Rayna sat with her dad.

Henry knew that Rayna was sworn to secrecy about her history. But damn it, he was her father and he wanted to know. Unable to hold himself back, he nonchalantly ventured, "So what was it like, Rayna?"

"What was what like?" responded Rayna evasively.

"You know. Being part of the most courageous group of soldiers that Canada has ever put together. Joint Task Force 2. JTF2. The only time I heard from you was when you were in the heat of some battle or other and wanted me to pray about saving your bacon."

While Rayna felt that her father was a little overzealous in terms of his Christian faith—what could she expect? He was a pastor, after all—she respected, loved and appreciated him. "You know I can't tell you, Dad."

Henry stretched out his fingers as hard as he could. It was a habit of his whenever he was uptight about something. But this time it didn't work. He just had to say something.

"Rayna, I don't know anything about you anymore. We haven't had a conversation of more than five minutes since you graduated from high school. During your breaks, you were hanging with your friends or working out with your mom. Summers? You spent every one of them training with other soldiers. Then, after you graduated, you went directly into full time military service and rarely spoke about anything you did. After you joined Special Forces, you clammed up completely. I want to know what is happening with my daughter. Can't you say something other than, 'Hi. Having a great time," or "Pray for me?"'

"You know, Dad, that JTF2 is crazy mad over secrecy of personnel and operations."

"I know more about American Navy SEALS or British SAS or the CIA than I do about anything you've done. Surely there's something you can tell me."

There was a suspenseful pause, and Rayna caught herself stretching her fingers in the same way her father had just done. *Like father, like daughter?*

Rayna blew out a puff of air, trying to think of something to deflect the question. Avoiding her father's probing eyes, she asked, "Why don't you ask me something else? Something that I'm allowed to answer."

"Like what?"

"Like why I finally wanted to find out about my past. I've never asked before."

"Okay. Why do you want to find out now, Rayna?"

Rayna glanced toward Barry and Chuck. "

"I don't really know. It's just that..." The sentence lingered in mid-air as Rayna swallowed. "It's just that, with this new company I'm working with, there's this married couple, Julio and Helena, who have adopted at least half a dozen kids or more... kinda made me wonder about myself."

"Wow, six? You were a handful at one!" smiled Henry. "Why do they have so many?"

"They were orphans. Some were adopted at birth. A couple of sisters were older. They were in bad situations."

"What kind of bad situations?"

"Umm... that's classified."

Henry looked over to Barry and Chuck, Rayna's co-workers. Chuck was built like the Great Wall of China and Barry? The man sitting across the aisle was about the same age as him, but he had the physique of a professional athlete who kept his fitness level up.

Who is Rayna working with?

EIGHT

CHINESE COWBOY

Fourteen hours later, the Fidelitas group arrived at Guangzhou Baiyun International Airport. Despite the more than a million millionaires and billionaires in China, the private jet and airfield market continued to be almost non-existent. Which meant there was an extra couple of hours of red tape and processing.

After passing the security clearance gates, Barry, Chuck, Rayna and Henry strode through the automated terminal doors into the crisp, arid heat.

Barry turned to Henry. "I've got a limo for you and our luggage. Rayna, Chuck and I will meet you at the hotel. We have some business to do."

Before Henry could reply, Rayna jumped in. "Absolutely not. I'm not going anywhere without having a shower and blow-drying my hair."

All the men stood dumbfounded except Henry. He chuckled, "Guess you boys aren't used to having daughters, are you?"

"Why didn't you take a shower on the plane like me?" grumbled Chuck. "You had hours to do it."

"Too small and I prefer to have my own bathroom."

There was no point in arguing. Barry knew they had enough time to allow Rayna to do her little "quirk."

A YOUNG MAN wearing a dark chauffeur's uniform stood outside one of the exits of the Guangzhou Baiyun International Airport's exits. Like fifty other drivers, most more casually dressed than him, he carried a little sign that he held up for all the exiting passengers to see. His sign read, "Smith" but, even though Smith was the most common English surname, no one bothered to approach him.

Which is exactly what he wanted. Glancing periodically at the lot with the limos, he saw what he was looking for—a Mercedes Maybach sedan was pulling in. He walked discreetly toward the car. When the chauffeur, a lanky Chinese wearing a black suit and Stetson stepped out and walked to the terminal, he made his move.

Putting away his sign, he stepped to the German luxury sedan and discreetly fastened a small tracking device under the rear bumper. He then walked over to his own car, an older Audi sedan, got in and drove away.

BARRY LOOKED AROUND and spotted the tall, skinny man wearing a Stetson and looking smart in his black suit. A shade under six feet, he carried a small placard that read, "Barry."

Barry flagged him down and the cowboy scurried over.

"Hello, I'm Barry Rogers. There's been a change of plans. Can you bring us all to the hotel first?"

The wiry man offered his hand. "Welcome to Guangzhou. I'm Tex and I am delighted to be your chauffeur for as long as you need me."

"Thanks, Tex," said Barry as airport porters gathered their suitcases.

Tex led them out of the terminal area to the limo parking area. He dropped the bags in front of the luxurious black Mercedes Maybach.

He turned to his new customers, opening his arms expansively. "Congratulations! You are the first passengers in our company's new car. We got it just for you." The bright-faced Tex swung the door open.

"What did you say to the company when you booked the car?" whispered Henry to Barry. "This car's got a sticker price of at least two hundred and fifty thousand dollars."

"Nine hundred and fifty," corrected Tex, overhearing Henry. "We charge more for our services than anyone else so we had a few things done to upgrade. More gold! More glitz!"

AFTER EVERYONE WAS SETTLED IN, Henry queried, "Tex is a pretty cool name. How did you get it?"

That's Dad. Diplomatic. Straight to the point. Rayna shook her head and smiled.

Tex beamed. "It's short for Texas. You should know. Dallas Cowboys. The Mavericks. Selena Gomez. The best steaks in the world. And, of course, my hero, Chuck Norris, the Texas Ranger!"

"You got taste, Tex. Chuck's my favorite, too. That's why I changed my name." Chuck bobbed his head in total agreement.

"You're a Chuck, too? Awesome. Awesome."

Rayna was flabbergasted. She was about to open her mouth when Henry interjected, "Chuck Norris is the best, Tex. He's a brother to me!"

"You got it, bro! You even look like him!" exclaimed Tex.

It was definitely weird and a little humorous listening to someone trying to talk like a Texan with a Chinese accent.

RAYNA HAD NEVER BEEN to Guangzhou before and didn't mind Tex taking the scenic route to the hotel. The driver gave a running commentary as he drove by the Buddhist Temple of Six Banyan Trees and through Guangzhou's *Yuexiu Park* with its pretty artificial lakes, foothills and cultural relics. Unfortunately, Tex's remarks had nothing to do with the scenery but everything to do with Chuck Norris. Chuck, the martial artist. Chuck, the Texas Ranger. Chuck, the man of God. By the time they reached the thirty-foot concrete statue of Five Rams, they were thankful that Tex took a break so they could hear the musicians play their lilting melodies on traditional Chinese instruments.

The Mercedes' passengers craned their necks looking outside to the modern heights and sights of the Tianhe district. Surrounded by skyscrapers and symbols of international commerce, the Oceania Hotel was an impressive, modern, international six-star hotel, inspired by the shape of a lotus flower. As the Mercedes limo pulled into the lavish circular driveway, its occupants marveled at the glass fountain with its shimmering blue green water.

"Welcome to Guangzhou," greeted Arthur as Rayna, Barry, Chuck and Henry entered the immaculate lobby, an architectural masterpiece combining Chinese elegance with European contemporary luxury. Every item in the hotel and every person on staff were carefully chosen to help achieve a singular goal: to make their guests feel special, pampered and wanted.

He handed the guests their room cards.

"Thanks for having me," spoke Henry softly, his eyes not hiding the fact that he was trying to figure out who exactly the stately gentleman in front of him was.

"I'm Arthur Yang. Forgive me for not entertaining you, Reverend Tan, but the four of us have some things to discuss. After Rayna's had a chance to shower and freshen up, of course." Arthur pointed at the concierge, who immediately sent two bellhops over. "However, I'm sure Tex will be quite entertaining, and Tex..."

"Yes, Mr. Yang."

"Make sure you take Mr. Tan to the best seafood restaurant in Guangzhou."

"Yes, sir!"

It was subtle but clear to Henry that he was being dismissed. "I'll see you later, honey." He planted a kiss on Rayna's cheek.

"Make sure they use low sodium soya sauce and tell the cooks to go easy on the oil and fried foods," warned Rayna.

"Not a chance," Henry beamed.

NINE

THE BOONIES

Jackson got the shock of his life when he arrived in the booming metropolis of San Roca, population 11,429. He never bothered doing any research on the town before he came, assuming, because it was California, everything was going to be hip; everything was going to be cool.

Not. San Rosa was Hicksville.

And, worse than that, almost everyone was either white or Hispanic. About the only Chinese he met were other students who couldn't get in anywhere else.

Poor babies. Jackson and his Chinese buddies hated Mexican food. Tacos, burritos, refried beans... Much as they would have liked, it was impractical to drive to LA every time they wanted a plate of chow mein or barbecued pork.

A Google search revealed that the easiest major in college was education, so that's what Jackson chose. But, even though there were only twelve hundred students in the whole school, passing was not going to be a slam dunk, especially as his preferred method of passing courses—bribing teachers—was not going to work. In his limited research, Jackson didn't pay any attention to the line where the college described itself as having "moral values." Within two weeks, he discovered this meant the profs were ethical and he learned the hard way—with the threat of expulsion—that they couldn't be bought off.

Which meant Jackson actually had to study, something he never had to do before.

To take away the stress of using his brain, Jackson decided he needed diversions. This was where life dealt him another harsh blow—there was almost a complete absence of anything that he found remotely interesting. In Vancouver, he could go to a karaoke bar, drink bubble tea, play the latest video games, but in San Roca? Everything shuttered down by nine o'clock at night except the bars.

Jackson and his Chinese student buddies began to partake of the demon rum. "Bangers" was their favorite hangout. With its 1970s-era wood paneling, burgundy vinyl-covered bar stools, and an unending supply of stale peanuts, its chief attraction was that the bar staff didn't bother to check their fake IDs. After all, the kids tipped big.

Still, alcohol didn't agree with Jackson. Puking his guts out two or three times a week was definitely not fun but, for a hundred million dollars of Daddy's money, he was willing to put up with Pacifica and San Roca for a few years.

After all, he was young. Indestructible. Even if something blew up, he could bail at the last second and survive and thrive.

A MONTH LATER, Jackson was starting to sweat—his grades were dropping to the point of expulsion, no easy feat for a school with such low academic standards. To compound the young man's angst, the professor in the "Understanding Young Children" course announced there would be a midterm in two weeks.

"I'm gonna flunk out," confessed a much-worried Jackson to his best bud, Sonny Lin.

"You'll be fine. You just need medicine," asserted Sonny. "I been watching you and you are like my crazy sister. Can't sit straight. Always zoning out. No attention to detail."

"That's just who I am. I've always been that way," argued Jackson defensively.

"I guarantee, if you don't take meds, you'll always be like that. You got attention deficit problems, man."

"Huh?"

"ADD or ADHD. Same deal. Attention deficit hyperactivity disorder."

"You're making me sound psycho. I don't want any pills."

"What planet do you live on? Everybody uses them to focus. Finance guys. Lawyers. Brain surgeons. Musicians... Here, take some of mine. Ritalin and Adderall. I guarantee you're not as stupid as you think you are."

Sonny gave Jackson a Ziploc bag with thirty green and white pills. "Take one of each every day."

IT WAS AMAZING. No, it was miraculous. Not only did Jackson pass but he aced the midterm as well as two surprise quizzes. With the pills running out, it was time to get a new stash.

"Hey, Sonny. Gotta buy some more of those pills. I'll get two hundred each."

"Whoa, I only got enough for myself. For those numbers, you got to go ask Dougie. He's the main man for that kind of stuff."

"I HAVE no idea what you're talking about," said the brash know-it-all, sophomore Dougie Brownside.

Jackson shrugged. He knew it was part of the game. "That's too bad, Dougie, because I was going to offer you ten bucks a pill for two hundred pills. Or I'll take more if you got them."

Dougie's eyes popped. He was used to fifty and a hundred dollar purchases but two thousand bucks? At double his regular price? "You got that kind of moolah? On you?"

"Maybe." Jackson reached into his pocket and extracted a wad of bills and counted off five thousand dollars. "You got five hundred, I'll take them."

Holy shit! Dougie put his knapsack on the cement statue of some long-forgotten school president and opened it. With his hands hidden from view, he began making shuffling noises. A minute and a half later, he pulled out a plain paper bag and handed it to Jackson. "I guarantee these brain boosters will help you improve at least one full grade point."

"As long as I pass, that's all I want." Jackson immediately popped five pills and washed them down with water from Dougie's bottle.

"Hey, hey. That's too much," cautioned Dougie.

"Relax. I'm totally chill."

"Whatever you say, boss." Dougie wandered away.

A HALF HOUR and another half dozen pills later, Jackson's body was tingling. He hadn't eaten and was feeling really damn good—maybe the best he had ever felt. Definitely not the time to go home yet. After all, he was going to pull an all-nighter and study all the next day. Jackson pulled out his cell phone and punched in a number. "Hey, Sonny. Whatcha doin'?"

"Studying. What else?"

"Take a break. Bangers for a quick drink. Okay? Then we can go back to prison."

"Twist my arm."

TEN

BOTTOMS UP

Of course, it wasn't a quick drink. Or actually, it was, but then there was another quickie, then another, then another... Added to that, Jackson and Sonny were indulging in Jackson's newly bought bag of goodies. Amazingly, despite the equivalent of almost a mickey of pure alcohol in their blood streams, the two underage boozers were holding their own without the slightest hint of an upchuck.

Even better, for the first time in his life, Jackson found himself enjoying the taste of alcohol, especially the last three shots of the quintessential American drink, Jack Daniels.

"What happened to you, Jackson?" asked Norm, the barkeep. "Normally, you'd have made a beeline to the john by now."

"Guess I'm getting used to higher education," roared Jackson.

"Rock on. This one's on me." Norm poured a double

for each boy and himself. "Cheers," he said, raising his glass.

Jackson and Sonny lifted their glasses. "Cheers!"

A quick gulp with gritted faces and the drinks were gone.

Sonny leaned over and whispered into Jackson's ear. "I got something better than what you got. *Bingdu*. From North Korea."

Jackson's glassy eyes sparkled brighter. *Bingdu*. Crystal meth from North Korea. Normally, something he'd be afraid of taking but, already pumped full of liquid and pill courage, he was game for anything.

Jackson took a couple of pills from Sonny's covered hand, then swallowed. Ten seconds later, he announced, "Nothing's happening."

"Gotta wait half an hour," replied Sonny.

"Come on. That's too long."

Sonny squinted at his buddy, then nodded his head in agreement. "Well, then we better do something about that. Follow me."

Sonny snagged a couple of straws from the bar and motioned for Jackson to follow him into the men's john. Sonny locked the door, then went to the sink. He pulled a Ziploc bag from his pocket, produced an acorn-sized rock, and handed it to Jackson. Jackson lifted the translucent crystal to his eyes and rotated it.

"Kinda looks like a deformed mushroom," garbled Jackson, speech slurring. He blinked hard. It was getting hard to see and his heart started pulsing faster.

"Except it's got more kick than any magic mushroom you'll find anywhere. Gotta hand it to the Norks. One thing they know how to make right is ice. This is like a hundred percent pure." Sonny took the crystal back from Jackson and removed a few more from the bag. He ground them to a powder with a drinking glass on the counter.

Sonny then took one of the straws and handed it to Jackson. "You first. You're my guest."

"I... I never done this before."

Sonny shook his head. "I forgot. You're a wuss. Watch me." Sonny pushed one end of the straw deep into a nostril and placed the other into the small mountain of white powder. He snorted as much of the white powder as he could. Holding his breath, he pointed to Jackson to follow suit.

Jackson took his own straw and took one healthy sniff... then another.

"So what do you think?" asked Sonny.

Jackson stood still, holding his breath. For the first few seconds, there was nothing. He felt his heart quickening and was feeling hot. He began panting short little breaths.

Then, it hit—a lightness, an inner glow, a sense of elation...

"This is like the biggest head rush in the world," murmured Jackson as euphoria filled his being. "It is so totally awesome."

"I hear you. More?" asked Sonny. As if he really needed to ask.

"Yeah, man."

Sonny took out two glass pipes and filled their small bowls with more of the magic powder. He flicked a cigarette lighter, then rolled its blue flame under his pipe. With intent eyes fixed on the little basin at the end of the glass tube, he watched as the meth began liquefying and a sphere of smoke began forming. He then inhaled slowly and deeply.

Holding the smoke in, Sonny then put the lighter's flame under the bowl of Jackson's pipe. Grinning like the Cheshire cat, Jackson followed the example of his friend.

The two made idiotic faces at each other—sticking out their tongues, rolling their eyes, rocking their heads... then repeated the process.

The two had never felt such exhilaration in their lives before.

"Time for another drink," gurgled Jackson.

"Wanna try another way of nirvana first, or you done?"

Jackson's glassy eyes lit up brighter. "You got something else?"

"Yup." Sonny took a small blue-white rock, popped it into his mouth and chewed slowly. "Wanna try?"

Without waiting to answer, Jackson took Sonny's bag and snatched a couple of big rocks and popped them into his mouth. Walking to the door as he chewed, Jackson commented, "Remind me never to eat this stuff again. Too damn bitter."

Jackson's hand started twitching as he unlocked the bathroom door. As they stepped back into the bar, Jackson felt the light of the room sting his eyes, almost blinding him. "Whoa. Turn off the lights."

"You kidding, man? It's so dark," squinted Sonny.

"Whatever," said Jackson, squinting as they walked

toward the bar. He and Sonny hadn't taken three steps before Jackson's heart started pounding like a sledgehammer against his chest. He stopped and started gasping again, pressing his hand against his chest over the heart area.

"What's with you?" asked Sonny, wrinkling his face with annoyance.

"Screw you, asshole," shouted Jackson. He swung wildly at his friend, clipping him in the jaw.

"What the...?" As Jackson launched another roundhouse, Sonny ducked and butted his chest into Jackson's solar plexus.

As Jackson buckled, Sonny stood up. Holding Jackson's body at his waist level, Sonny reversed direction, pushing back and ramming Jackson's butt against the wall. Before Jackson collided with the floor, Sonny seized his hand and rotated hard.

The fumbling, stumbling Jackson had to follow Sonny's movement if he didn't want his arm yanked out of his shoulder socket.

With drug-fueled superhuman strength, Sonny lifted Jackson over his head and, running, carried him to the bar where he threw him on top of the counter. Jackson reached over to the half-empty bottle of Jack Daniels, picked it up, then bashed Sonny over the head. As the bottle shattered, Sonny fell semi-conscious to the floor.

As Jackson looked up, it appeared as if the individual drops of the amber liquid and fragments of glass were moving in ultra-slow motion. Almost like an out-of-body experience, he was feeling a mind/body disconnect as he watched himself say, "Wow," in a deep voice where every letter moved out of his mouth like thick molasses. Then he began shaking. A few short seconds passed and the quivering progressed to all-out convulsing. Jackson collapsed beside Sonny on the floor.

"We should do something, Norm," dribbled Lisa, the freaked waitress. "This looks real bad."

"Leave them alone. They'll snap out of it soon enough," replied Norm disinterestedly. Norm had been watching without concern at the far end of the bar. He'd seen so many drunken or stoned students over the years that he was inured to the violence and their outrageous and outlandish behavior. He "knew" that either sleeping it off or a couple of cups of very strong coffee could cure anything. He also knew that getting high somehow turned one into superman and there was no way he was going to get cocked by these wasted college kids.

Seeing them sprawled on the floor, Norm sighed. Clean-up time. He stepped from behind the bar to where Jackson and Sonny lay. As he leaned over to check the Chinese students, Jackson began screaming and thrashing his arms wildly.

Lisa ducked below the bar. "Norm! Do something!"

The irritated Norm pulled back to escape Jackson's wild vicious blows. "Okay, you've had your fun. Enough's enough. Call the cops!" Norm yelled to the hiding Lisa.

As Lisa's trembling hands fumbled with her cell phone, she heard Norm chortle a loud "AAH!"

"Shit," shrieked Lisa. She lifted herself to peer over the counter. Jackson had pulled out his car keys and jabbed them into Norm's chest. The barkeep was wobbling backward, keys sticking out from his T-shirt, blood gushing from the wound. She ducked to hide again.

Sonny had recovered partially and eyed what his friend had done. Not because of any iota of human kindness but because of fear of recrimination, he picked himself up and stumbled to Norm. He put a napkin on Norm's wound and applied pressure, hoping to stem the blood flow.

But the uncontrolled, deranged Jackson had another idea. He suddenly pulled a knife out of his pocket and drove it into Sonny's heart.

As Jackson repeatedly stabbed Sonny, Lisa steadied her twitching and punched a number into her cell phone.

"911. How can I help you?"

But Norm couldn't hold on any more. He fell to the old hardwood floor, dead. Lisa was so freaked that she could only pant in terror and mumble, "Um... ooh..."

"Hello? 911. Police, ambulance or fire?"

Jackson yanked the knife out of Sonny's body. He began roaring like a lion and stumbled toward the bar.

Lisa was in full panic mode. She had no idea whether Jackson was straight enough to have seen her or whether he heard her heavy breathing. Worse, if he chose to come behind the bar, maybe to get a drink, he would find her and who knew what would happen then. Summing up every last minute amount of courage she had, she stood up.

"Hey, Jackson. It's me. Lisa."

But when the waitress looked into Jackson's wild, glassy eyes, she knew that he hadn't heard her.

She bolted toward the door, but had taken only two

steps when she tripped over a barstool, sending her crashing to the floor. Ignoring the jolting pain, she tried to get up but couldn't—the fall had broken her leg.

Like a mad bull, Jackson waved his knife in the air and shuffled toward her like a wounded jackal.

"Please, Jackson. Don't. I've got a little girl at home—she's only three. Please, Jackson."

But Jackson was oblivious to anything Lisa said. Hovering over her, he raised his hand holding the knife, ready to come down on her.

"Die, bitch," giggled Jackson.

He plunged the knife toward her, but Lisa had formulated a plan. As Jackson's hand descended, she picked up the barstool she had tripped on and swung it horizontally. It hit Jackson on the side of his chest, knocking him over so that his head cracked on the floor.

He vomited, belching out a foul-smelling yellow puke. The young man began babbling as he writhed violently as if possessed by a thousand demons. Unable to make out distinct images, the off-balance Jackson clumsily threw his knife at an approaching blur before falling to the ground.

That blur was a policeman. When no one from the bar spoke after the 911 attendant took the emergency call, she sent police out immediately to investigate after she heard the calamitous noise in the background.

BANG! BANG! BANG! The cop squeezed off a succession of rounds. Bullets hissed by and splintered the wood wall.

PING! One bullet hit the knife, changing the trajectories of both knife and bullet. The tip of the blade deflected downward directly into Jackson's cranium. The bullet seared into his jugular. Blood began pouring out.

Lucky shot? Or great shot? Who knows? It was the first time a policeman had to fire a weapon in San Roca.

Jackson was beyond saving. Too many drugs and too much booze in too short a time.

One more casualty. Another young person. His first day of using drugs—legal and illegal. Some bought by himself, some by a good friend. Mix with copious amounts of booze.

The next tune in the bar jukebox started to play. It was the Eagles' "Peaceful Easy Feeling."

ELEVEN

MONSTER HOUSE

Extreme extravagance.

That was the basic design instruction that Ming Pang gave to his team of architects and designers when the Guangzhou billionaire construction mogul decided to build a new palatial home for himself, his wife and teenage daughter. Twenty miles outside of the city, the 50,000- square-foot Ming's Mansion sat in gorgeous rolling greenery nestled beside the Western Forest Park.

Of course, it would be nothing but showing off but hey—what's the point of having money if you can't flaunt it to your friends... and competitors. The Chinese philosophy of *feng shui,* the proper placement of design to produce proper harmony, was incorporated to ensure prosperity, long life and happiness.

And, of course, lucky numbers seven and eight figured prominently. There were seventy-eight rooms, including a dining room capable of seating eighty-eight, a private stage with seating for a hundred and thirty-eight, eighteen bedrooms, a wine cellar capable of holding eight thousand bottles, a luscious garden with eight hundred eighty-eight different exotic flora from around the world, and a garage capable of housing ninety-eight cars with room for another ninety-eight in the sweeping driveway.

Even though Ming neither swam nor played tennis, there was an Olympic-sized swimming pool and a tennis court with grass as immaculately groomed as the green courts at Wimbledon. Eschewing his Asian roots, crystal chandeliers and marble flooring were imported from Italy. Sprinkled through the residence were random fountains sculpted with BC Jade, grand rooms inspired by French castles, and handmade furniture from the finest Scandinavian artisans.

It took more than two years for construction, and then another six months to furnish it to his standards but, now that it was done, Ming was ready. All along the way, there were videographers documenting the progress. Ming had the three hundred hours of footage edited into a half-hour program.

The premiere showing for the film would be tomorrow evening at a gala housewarming party. Ming's family and most of the staff were in Guangzhou for the day, organizing last-minute refreshments, dinner menu, specialty imported wines and entertainment from Hong Kong and Taiwan.

Cost was not really a consideration. After all, Ming was a well-respected contractor for cement products. His clients included some of the most impressive skyscrapers and complexes in southern China, delivered with superior quality products at prices so low, many wondered how he was able to make money.

The answer was simple. These high-profile projects were loss leaders, designed to get him big contracts where he could take advantage of what he saw as a tremendous opportunity—taking advantage of what he felt was a false prediction by the government.

At the turn of the new millennium, the Chinese government targeted certain areas for industrial growth, funding them with massive resources. They built cities full of housing units, shopping malls, office buildings, entertainment complexes, sports stadia, bridges, high-ways... all that was needed was for people and industry to move in.

But the anticipated boom didn't materialize. While the mass exodus from the country to the city occurred, the "millions of jobs" that were promised did not, so no one could afford to live there. Millions of the planned urban units throughout China stood empty. They were nicknamed "Ghost towns." However, this was a misnomer—these complexes were never, ever alive. These were the white elephants that foolish bureaucrats from years past built as monuments to their own inept forecasts.

The prescient Ming thought that might happen. He gave lowball bids and was awarded almost one hundred lucrative contracts for supplying cement. Figuring that no one would ever find out because the ghost cities would never be inhabited, Ming substituted cheap sea sand into the cement mixtures while charging full prices. If there was ever a problem in the future, he would claim that it was lack of maintenance to the empty buildings, not the materials he provided. He made hundreds of millions of dollars or billions of the Chinese *yuan*.

However, Ming had a weak spot—greed. He didn't really need the money, but couldn't resist the offer when Wen approached him about cutting a deal with him for the contract to provide concrete for the building of two schools in Zongtian—it was money dropping from the sky. For Ming, it was pocket change, but it was easy pocket change.

When the earthquake hit in Zongtian, Ming was concerned only mildly. Like the rest of the corrupt officials and contractors, Ming wasn't worried about Wen speaking out. The bureaucrat loved his wife and son and knew one false word would mean their death—or worse. Prolonged, living torture.

While he was sure Wen would never betray him, Ming had an insurance policy. He would have Wen killed in prison. The only question was when.

LIKE MANY TOP-EARNERS around the world concerned for personal safety who hired ex- Special Forces operatives for protection, Ming employed a team of twenty, including former members of Russia's Spetsnaz, Britain's SAS, and America's Delta Force. Most of the time, six stayed with Ming and the rest rotated services between "disciplining" non-conforming employees or protecting Ming's new gated compound.

Back at Cencom, Julio had been mining every bit of

information he could from Wen's list. Finding out about Ming's housewarming, he discovered that songstress Anita Kwok, the temperamental Taiwanese superstar, would be the headline entertainment in the mansion's private theater. As soon as her private jet in Taipei lifted off, Julio sent a message to Ming's organizers that Anita wanted a full security detail of fifty when she landed in an hour and a half.

The staff was frantic, trying to find people that matched Anita's stringent requirements. Ex-special forces preferred, no local Chinese military acceptable. What was worse was that communication with anyone on Anita's jet was unavailable. There was no choice but to send all but two of Ming's security staff to the airport to attend to the diva and her entourage.

This left the home with minimal security staff.

BARRY AND CHUCK'S Imperial Suite at the Oceania had been christened "China HQ." Although they ignored the luxury of spectacular views, English sycamore paneling, and custom Japanese furnishings, the Fidelitas group found the important feature was the mid-size cherry table modified to have wires feed up from the floor through the center post. This allowed the four Fidelitas members ample room to sit comfortably and have three monitors set up without gangling wires in their way.

Julio, from one of the monitors, pronounced, "You've

only got two hours. After that, everyone will descend on the place for the final preparations."

"Sounds like we go without eating again," grumbled Chuck.

No one laughed. There was a job to do.

TWELVE
FLOWER POWER

A boring, small delivery truck rattled up to the gatehouse. A uniformed black security guard, obviously ex-military, asked the driver, an older middle-aged man, "What is your purpose here?"

Arthur, dressed in jeans and T-shirt, looked like thousands of other delivery drivers in the world. He cocked his head at the guard as if he were crazy. "Can't you read the side? I'm bringing flowers for the concert tomorrow."

"Your license plate is not on the list of vehicles expected."

"That's because we're not. We don't need to be," growled Rayna, sitting on the passenger side. "I'm Anita Kwok's *personal* florist. Who are you? She never, ever performs without me making the stage a garden wonderland first."

The guard gritted his teeth. "What's with this Anita, anyway? She's got all of us jumping over..." Before he could finish his sentence, someone crept out from behind the guardhouse and cracked an elbow into the man's head. Chuck hauled the body inside as Arthur ripped open the back of the truck.

Chuck gave the unconscious security officer's windpipe a quick stomp before stripping off his uniform and putting it on himself. "Sorry, bro, but you joined the dark side," muttered Chuck as Arthur and Rayna hid the corpse beneath the flowers in the truck.

Chuck casually took the guard's place in the gatehouse. "Good thing we all look the same. Right?"

It was a play on the expression that, "All Chinese look the same." A joke that neither Arthur nor Rayna found amusing, but hopefully it was still true.

Chuck snatched up the phone and punched in the number to the main house.

"What do you want?" asked a woman with a Filipino accent.

"There's a couple here with a truckload of flowers saying they're for Anita Kwok's concert."

"Wait while I check."

Five seconds later, there was a twenty-second tirade of cursing. After the expletives stopped, a Chinese man's grim voice grunted. "Bring the damned flowers in."

Arthur mouthed to Rayna and Chuck, "That must be Ming."

The truck glided down the fifty-yard gravel path and parked in front of the monolithic house. There was a lone guard outside the ten-foot tall solid oak doors. The dark suit could not hide the man's powerful physique—definitely ex-Special Ops. But of more acute interest was the AK47 he carried at the low ready and the bulky ballistic plate carrier barely hidden on his chest. Rayna and

Arthur brought no weapons, knowing they would not get through the metal detectors at the front gate if they did. Besides, if they needed one, there'd be plenty lying around.

"You stay in the truck," declared the armed guard to Arthur.

"But she needs help carrying the flowers in."

"I don't care. You just stay in the truck."

Rayna got out of the cab and strolled to the back with the guard stalking alongside her, his muzzle tracking her every motion.

As she popped the van doors open, Rayna took advantage of his drifting eyes and whipped one fist at his temple. With her other hand, she tried to grab the assault rifle, but the guard yanked it from her reach.

Which left his torso exposed. Rayna snapped off a swift kick right into his solar plexus.

The big man gasped, but didn't lurch over. Instead, he dropped the rifle, snagged her exposed foot and twisted.

Rayna let her body follow the curve of the guard's motion. She added an extra twist to free herself and send him to the ground.

He whipped out a Beretta with suppressor attached and fixed it on her. There was no way she was going to escape unless... Rayna squinted at some tattoo insignia on his neck. *Who dares, wins.* The motto of the British Special Air Service.

Rayna sat upright and smirked cockily. "You Limeys are wusses. Need a gun to beat a girl. Not man enough to do it yourself."

The guard snapped. "So you got a little kung fu in you. Big deal."

Rayna's eyes bored into her opponent. "A little kung fu? How about five black belts in different disciplines? How about a hundred kills in the Middle East? How about commander in JFT2? What about you? Water boy? Boot licker?"

The guard jerked his weapon to the side and fired at the truck's cab. Arthur saw the arm swinging in the rearview and ducked, for what little good it did. One round nicked his upper arm, spraying blood into his eyes. Blinded, he didn't see the second shot that hit somewhere in his chest.

Rayna didn't hesitate. The change in the gunman's angle gave her a brief opportunity. She threw her whole body weight against his knees, knocking him to the ground and sending the gun skittering across the driveway.

The muscles in her taut arms bulged as she pounded on his face. Right. Left. And again.

But the ex-serviceman deflected each of the blows with ease.

Rayna heard the truck door open. Out the corner of her eye, she caught sight of a bleeding Arthur tumbling to the ground.

In that split second of distraction, her assailant countered with a two-hundred-and-twenty pound thrust of his own. Rayna instinctively rolled her head to the side so that the man's steam-powered fist shot by her. Or at least mostly...

She howled through the pain and stars in her eyes.

With a quick twist, she locked his beefy arm in a tight hold and tried to break it, but the guy only laughed. There was no way Rayna was going to overcome someone who could bench press four hundred pounds. He jerked his arm out of Rayna's clutches and hit her on the side of the head.

She tumbled backward, but not too far. She leveled her swimming head just as the guard readied himself for another wallop.

Behind him Arthur, crawling on all fours, managed to flounder over to the Beretta. Just as the ex-SAS operative pile-drove his arm into Rayna's face, a bullet shattered his balled fist. Another muffled shot put a hole in his forehead.

Amazingly, Rayna didn't get a drop of blood on her. She crawled over and gave Arthur's wound a quick look.

"It's a through-and-through shot, Rayna," he told her. "No arteries or bones hit. Just bandage me tight and I'll be good to go."

There was no point arguing. She would never be able to complete the mission on her own. Chuck was too far away at the gatehouse. She and Arthur hastily loaded the dead guard onto the truck. Rayna ripped off the man's jacket and shirt while Arthur removed his blood-soaked shirt. Rayna tore off the lining from the jacket and used it to bind Arthur's wound tightly. They quickly hid the body beside the other guard.

They each picked up two large colorful plants, then closed the door. They rushed to the door and rang the bell, calming themselves immediately.

A young female voice answered the intercom. "Hello."

"Flowers for the stage set-up for Anita Kwok."

"I'll be right there."

Thirty seconds later, a uniformed maid opened the door to see Rayna and Arthur carrying the displays of exotic flowers. "I'll take you to the theater."

"No, no. These flowers are a special gift from Anita to Mr. Ming. She asked us to personally deliver them to him."

"That I cannot do. He will not take visitors unless he authorizes them."

Arthur angled his body with Rayna stepping beside him. Her position blocked the myriad video cameras in the hall from seeing Arthur's hand reaching into his pocket and slipping out the Beretta.

"Anita will be very disappointed. No one ever turns down her gifts. If she finds out about this insult, I wouldn't be surprised if she just stays on her plane and returns to Taipei."

"I don't know what to do. I don't know how to contact Mr. Ming," whimpered the trembling girl.

"Bring them to the Dragon room," boomed a male voice from some loudspeaker. "If Anita wants to give me a gift, I'll be happy to take it. The bitch charges me enough."

The maid led Arthur and Rayna down a long hallway, passing a labyrinth of rooms, each with its own decor motif: Japanese, Hollywood, Ming Dynasty, Cubist... Each room contained at least two million dollars' worth of artwork and artifacts. The Dragon

Room was at the far end of the hall. It was instantly recognizable because, in the center of the room, was a large jade dragon sculpture with intricate paintings of Chinese dragons on each wall.

"We are here," muttered the girl.

"Where is Mr. Ming?" asked Rayna.

"You can just leave the plants on the floor," announced the same male voice that boomed in the lobby. "Tell Anita I love them."

"Anita gave direct orders to give them to you personally," objected Rayna.

"Don't worry about it," retorted Arthur. "We got the rest of the truck to unload."

"This totally sucks," seethed Rayna. "It's idiotic. Stupid. Who the hell does Ming think he is? The arrogant prick. Does he know who Anita is? She's the biggest damned star in the universe, and he's some pipsqueak with a few bucks." Rayna picked up a small, multicolored dragon ceramic and threw it against the jade dragon sculpture. The ceramic shattered, sending fragments flying around the room, and leaving a big gouge in the jade piece. Rayna pulled a watercolor painting off the wall and tore it in half. "And this stupid house! You think for fifty million bucks you'd get something that was better than some tasteless piece of crap. Everybody that's coming is going to think he's just another rich bozo who has no idea what to do with his money."

"Who the hell do you think you are?" A large door hidden behind a painting swung open. Out stormed a very angry Chinese man, followed by yet another ex-military goon with an AK pointed at Rayna. "I am Ming, and you have just destroyed eight hundred thousand dollars' worth of Chinese history!"

Deceptively strong, Ming grabbed Rayna with both arms and tried to slam her to the floor, but she was alert enough to grasp Ming's ears and bring him down with her.

"You bitch! Shoot her!" screeched Ming.

The guard hefted the AK to his shoulder, but Rayna rolled over and used Ming to shield her. "Yes, please shoot so I don't have to kill him myself."

The enforcer searched for an opening, but Ming was much bigger than Rayna—it would take a crack shot far better than him to thread a bullet through the small opportunities available.

Rayna's hostage threw his head backward, hitting her nose. It bled profusely. With Rayna stunned for just a moment, it was exactly enough time for Ming to turn over and fling a wild swing at her head.

Rayna tilted her head at the last possible millisecond, causing Ming's hand to crash into the marble floor.

Now the guard had a clear shot from close distance. He squeezed off several rounds.

Rayna rolled behind the marble dragon. More shells struck the curvy dragon and ricocheted upward.

Rayna leapt high in the air. With one smooth lightning move, she plucked a shard of jade debris flying through the air and flung it back at the shooter, striking him in the head. The hit knocked him backward, stunned but not dead.

Ming's jaw dropped. He had seen moves like that in *Crouching Tiger, Hidden Dragon* and in Jackie Chan movies, but never in real life. Was this woman a martial arts grandmaster?

He wasn't going to wait to find out. He snatched up the AK and flipped to full auto mode. Ming was no marksman, but his spray-and-pray technique couldn't miss at such close quarters.

Then disaster—or a lucky break. Rayna tripped on a piece of broken jade just as Ming held the trigger down. She stuck out her hand at the last second to break the fall, slicing it open on a jagged ceramic shard. Her arm slid and her elbow smashed the floor, but at least she didn't have any new air holes. Her arm exploded with agony as she forced herself to stand while Ming reloaded.

On the far side of the room, it took every bit of concentration Arthur had to fight through the stabs of excruciating pain, but he broke off the stem from one of the hollow plants. He flicked out two poisoned darts camouflaged as stigma in the petals of the large flowers.

He put one of them into his makeshift blowgun and blew it at Ming. Arthur dropped to his knees as the tip embedded itself into a vein in Ming's neck. The toxins started spreading immediately. His body began to twitch, then spasm.

The strain of movement was too much for Arthur. Rayna hobbled to catch him before he crumpled to the floor. She pulled him up and he slid his arm around her shoulder to steady himself. Spotting the guard on the floor, Rayna plucked the other dart from Arthur and shoved it deep into his eye—he would soon meet the same fate as his boss.

Arthur's weight was too much for Rayna to support with her own body racked in pain.

"Just go, Rayna," quavered Arthur. "No point in two of us dying here."

Arthur was right. If they both stayed, it was only a matter of time before they were caught. A soft rustle in the doorway snapped Rayna's head around.

"I will help you," uttered the maid softly as she helped lift Arthur up. "Mr. Ming... He was a very bad man."

Between the maid and Rayna, they managed to keep Arthur upright as they slunk out the door and down the deserted hall.

Mumbling through his rapid, shallow breaths, Arthur uttered, "We got one of the bastards, but that's just a start."

Eyes flashing, Rayna sensed every nerve, cell and muscle tingling—she was in the zone. *You ain't seen nothin' yet.*

THIRTEEN

FIREWORKS

Once outside the door, the two girls helped Arthur into the flower truck. Once inside, Rayna began dressing her wound. No big deal. Done that a thousand times before.

"Will you take me, too? Please? I will do anything," pleaded the maid.

"Of course. Climb in," replied Arthur.

Rayna drove to the gate. Chuck was waiting there with Barry in a Range Rover. Barry poured gas over the truck as Rayna, the maid and Chuck carried Arthur into the new vehicle.

After the Range Rover drove fifty feet, Barry stopped the car long enough for Chuck to get out and hurl a lit flare at the truck. In three seconds, the entire truck was engulfed in flames, then KABOOM!

"Arthur, we're taking you to a doctor," announced Barry.

"It's only a surface wound," retorted Arthur. "Besides, we have to look pretty for our presentation tomorrow."

"You'll look better if you're not dead from blood loss."

"Please, spare me the melodramatics. You're patching me up and I'll rest tonight. Group, tomorrow, 5 a.m. Meeting."

The maid who had not uttered word since offering her help, squeaked out, "Can we eat first before sleeping? I haven't eaten all day."

Rayna turned to the girl. Instead of a maid, she discovered a frightened but brave young teen who had risked her life to save two complete strangers. "Let the men take Arthur to get fixed up. I'll take you for a bite. What's your name?"

"Ling."

Ling. Rayna's heart flew to her mouth. The hardass former Special Ops team leader melted. *Synchronicity.* Ling was the name of her birth mother.

Rayna made a call.

"Reverend Henry Tan. Can I help you?"

Rayna pushed her cell back, looking at it with a puzzled expression, then put it back to her ear. "Dad, I'll have to call you back. There's too much noise."

"No, no. It's the restaurant. It's huge and full of people. You wouldn't believe it, Rayna. They have five special rooms with just live seafood. A dozen kinds of fish, five different species of clams, freshwater shrimp, sea shrimp, river shrimp, lake shrimp, horse crabs, mitten crabs, hairy crabs and much more. It's amazing."

"That sounds fantastic. Dad, do you mind if I join you for dinner. I'm bringing a friend."

"Of course. That means we can order more. The reservation is in an hour and a half at the Guangzhou

Imperial Palace Restaurant. I just got here early to look."

"We'll see you then." Rayna turned to Ling in her maid's uniform. "Let's buy you some clothes first."

FOURTEEN

SHOPPING PARADISE

The Range Rover dropped Rayna and Ling two blocks away from the Guangzhou Imperial Restaurant at one of China's ubiquitous street markets. It had been awhile since Rayna had been to one, but the circus-like atmosphere of wondrous sights, boisterous sounds, and heady aromas always enthralled her. Hole-in-the-wall shops that were packed from floor to ceiling with all kinds of useful and useless items; small restaurants where you could see cooks working their culinary magic with woks over soaring flames; Chinese pastries being fried outside on open carts; an old man carrying his parakeet in his birdcage; an open air seafood restaurant with clams, oysters and fish on display; hawkers trying to sell fake iPhones or padded bras...

Rayna stepped into a tiny shoe store packed from floor to ceiling with loafers, pumps, high heels, flats, sandals... anything you could put on your feet at a fraction of the cost of department stores. No matter where you're from, no matter how much or how little money you have, women seem to have a universal desire to buy shoes.

Rayna and Ling picked out half a dozen pairs each for both of them to try, driving the frenzied, middle-aged female shop owner crazy.

"Why did you come to Guangzhou?" asked Rayna as she slipped on a pair of black pumps.

As Ling took off her brown sandals and pointed to a tan pair, she replied, "Our village is dying. All the young people left because there are no jobs for farmers anymore."

Rayna gave a quick affirmative nod as she stood up and looked at the shoes in the floor mirror. Ever since Chairman Mao's *Great Leap Forward*, there had been a push to transform China from an agrarian society to an urban one. "How long have you been here?"

"A year ago. I tried to get a *hukou*, but there was no chance so I started working for Mr. Ming. I make a thousand yuan a month."

"What?" gaped Rayna. "That's less than half the minimum wage."

Ling shrugged. "I don't know. The Mandarin got me the job. If I wanted to make more, I'd have to..."

The words hung in the air but Rayna understood. The world's oldest profession was not going to claim Ling. "Who's the Mandarin?"

"I don't know. I never met him, but he gets jobs for all of us."

"Stop looking! Start buying or get out!" squawked the shoe store owner. "I need the space for paying customers."

"We'll take this pair," decided Rayna, pointing to the shoes on Ling's feet.

"But only if you give us a ninety percent discount," glowered Ling.

"You robber! My children will starve to death if I give you that price. Ten percent discount."

Ling threw her arms in the air in disgust. "You're crazy. You think I'm rich? I'm going to go next door if you don't give me a better price."

"How much you want to pay?"

The back and forth bantering went on for another ten minutes. To someone like Rayna, who was not used to the intensity of Asian bargaining, the insults and gnashing of teeth over pennies was crazy. However, Ling knew her stuff. In the end, Rayna had bought all six pairs of shoes for a sixty percent discount.

"You did pretty well in there," admired Rayna as they carried Ling's bags of loot.

"I'm going to do better in here," asserted Ling resolutely as they entered the clothing shop next door. "And, this time, let me do all the talking. I'll get a better deal that way."

"Yes, ma'am."

BY THE TIME, the hour was up, Rayna's and Ling's arms were full of bags of clothes, shoes and purses. What really astounded Rayna was that everything they bought had a designer label. When Rayna pressed the clerks about the authenticity of their product, they all vigorously defended the genuineness of their goods. Rayna couldn't argue. She frequented high end boutiques and the goods she and Ling bought had the same quality and feel as items that she would have gladly paid ten times the price she bought them for.

Outside the restaurant, Rayna called Tex, who promised to come right away. She then cautioned Ling, "Whatever you say, do not tell my father about what went on today at Ming's home. When he asks, and I know he will ask, tell him that your boss just died and the family couldn't keep you any longer."

"That's not a lie," exclaimed Ling. "It's the truth."

"Yes, but not the whole truth. Got it?"

Ling nodded knowingly.

FIFTEEN

HEARTBREAK INNOCENCE

The restaurant hostess led Rayna, Tex and Ling through the cavernous eating establishment. Typical Chinese restaurant, people were shouting loudly, laughing raucously and enjoying their meals while drinking copious amounts of the famous Chinese alcohol—*Bai Jiu* (white alcohol).

"Here you are," said the hostess as they arrived at a private room and opened the door.

"Welcome, welcome, welcome," greeted Henry, rising as Ling entered the room. "I'm Henry Tan. Please sit."

As the three newcomers seated themselves, Ling introduced herself. "Thank you, Uncle. I'm Ling. Thank you for inviting me to dinner." (In keeping with Chinese custom, "uncle" or "auntie" are normal titles when addressing someone older who is more than a business associate but not a family member.)

The attentive waitress poured Jasmine tea into small Chinese porcelain cups for the group. "Ling?"

Henry shot a glance at his smiling daughter. "That's a very nice name. Quite meaningful. How did you meet Rayna?"

"Rayna is most kind. She saw me crying. I was a maid for the last few months. It was my first job. My boss just died and the family could not keep me any longer."

"Oh, that's too bad. Do you have any plans yet?"

"I... I'm not quite sure yet, but I will have to get a job."

"A young girl like you should be in school. How old are you?"

"I'm fifteen, but I cannot go to school. No school will take me. I don't have *hukou* for Guangzhou."

Henry nodded his head. His pastor's mind was churning but he wasn't ready to say anything yet. "Well, you're a young girl with your whole life ahead of you. Are you going to get another job?"

"I guess so. I think the Mandarin can find me another job." Ling's eyes brightened. "But, if I could, I want to be a singer or movie star or doctor."

"That's a strange combination. Singer or movie star I understand, but doctor? Why's that?"

"Because my grandfather can't afford one. And I think he will die soon if he doesn't see one."

"How about your parents? Don't they have any money saved up?"

"They died. They came to work here a few years ago but got sick and nobody would treat them. No papers and no money."

A waitress brought in a large bowl of soup and ladled it out in individual bowls. Ling's last comment silenced all until after the server finished placing the bowls onto each person's plate and left.

"Where are you from, Ling?" Henry asked.

"Our village is a twelve-hour bus ride away. It's called *Tiansahn* (Heaven's Mountain.)"

"Rayna has meetings tomorrow." Henry smiled. "Maybe Tex can drive us there to visit your grandparents."

"Could you, Uncle?" cried Ling in a voice filled with I-can't-believe-this-is-true. "I haven't seen them since I came here."

"I'm at your disposal," quipped Tex as he checked his smart phone for directions. "If I drive, we should be able to get there in seven hours."

"Sounds good to me. Rayna?"

"That's great, Dad. Ling can stay with us tonight then."

The meal suddenly tasted a whole lot better and the din created in the private room was about as cacophonous as the main restaurant.

ABSOLUTELY STUFFED AND EXHAUSTED, the three returned to the Oceania. Their two-bedroom suite featured beds lined with thousand thread Egyptian cotton sheets, Italian marble bathroom floors and original pieces of Asian fusion art on the walls.

Ling studied the room critically, noting the wide-trimmed crown moldings, soft understated hues of paint, Scandinavian custom-designed lighting and the hand-knotted Tibetan rug covering the mahogany hardwood floor.

"Mr. Ming's place is nicer than this. It's a lot more colorful. This is kind of boring," said Ling. "But I'd rather be with you here."

Rayna grinned. To a teenager, gaudy indulgence trumped understated elegance every time.

"Thanks, Ling. Get some rest. We have a long day tomorrow," yawned Henry. He went directly to his room. A few minutes later, Rayna put her ear to the door and heard the gentle snores of her father.

Fifteen minutes later, Ling crawled into bed and snuggled beside Rayna. The young girl leaned over and kissed her on the cheek. "Thank you, Rayna, for caring."

"You're welcome."

"Can I ask you a question?" Ling asked.

"Sure, why not?"

"How come you're not married?"

Rayna sat up. "Did my father tell you to ask me that?"

Ling shook her head. "No, I'm just wondering... You know, I want to meet a nice, good man and fall in love. He'll love me even though I did some bad things. We'll walk in the park, sing karaoke and he'll cook for me."

"Anything else?"

Ling's schoolgirl eyes lit up. "He must be the handsomest man in the world."

Was I like that at her age? Yeah, for sure. Rayna raised knowing eyebrows as she turned off the light beside the bed. "Good night, Ling. I hope you meet your prince someday."

"I hope you do too, Rayna."

SIXTEEN
ROCK MY WORLD

Her moans grew louder, her breaths more rapid as exquisite, painful passion overcame her. Shivering and quivering, her nineteen-year-old body had never experienced anything like this from any of the college boys that she did for free or any of the obese American tourists who willingly gave her five hundred dollars for an hour of her time.

Annalee pulled the man tight to her tender breasts, never wanting the waves of ecstasy rocking her body to end. Her fingernails clawed at his shoulders as his tongue drove down her throat.

He had been with her for five years, pulling her out of the shanty town and giving her this place to stay. She didn't call him her "pimp." He was much more than that. But he never cared who else she bedded. Every visit, she made sure that she gave him two-thirds of her earnings. He never asked for it but she had heard what happened to those that "forgot" a payment.

But that meant little to her... she was his.

And then the phone began to ring. The man froze for a moment, then stopped.

"NO! Not now!" she screamed, but he ignored her and pushed her off his body.

"Stupid bitch. Don't you ever tell me what to do again."

The tone of his voice spoke louder than words. "I'm sorry. Of course. It's just that you are…"

The special ring tone was given to only one person—his son, and no matter the circumstance, he would always take his call.

Especially since the boy had not called for almost a week.

Finally. He tapped the answer button on cell. "Jackson. Good of you to call. What's happening? How's school?"

The voice at the other end responded. It had the accent and resonance of a middle-aged American black man. "No, sorry, sir. I'm not Jackson. Are you his father?"

The man sat upright in the bed, pushing the girl who was trying to paw him onto the floor. Darkness covered an evil face as he mouthed at her to f*** off before answering. "Yes, I am Jackson's father, the Mandarin. What's going on?"

Idiot name. "Mr. Mandarin, I'm Sheriff Ron Clemens from the San Roca Police Department in California. I'm very sorry to inform you that your son Jackson is dead. I found your number by going through the names list on his cell phone."

The man was stunned and couldn't speak, he was

shaking so hard. After seven seconds, the policeman came back on. "Mr. Mandarin? Are you still there?"

"Y... yes, I am. Are you sure it's him? What happened?"

"It's a positive identification, Mr. Mandarin. Lisa Henderson, the waitress at the bar where your son was a regular, confirmed it."

"Bar?"

"Yessir. Jackson was a combination of both drunk and high when he attacked his friend, the bartender and the waitress in the bar. He then tried to assault a police officer by hurling a knife at him. In self-defense, the policeman shot back. Unfortunately, the knife deflected into your son."

The man tried to control an erupting volcanic anger. "My son doesn't drink nor does he use drugs."

"I'm sorry for your loss and I understand how you feel. Would you like me to text you a photo?"

"Yes. Please do."

The girl watched the man. It was impossible to know what he was thinking. But definitely, something was very wrong.

It didn't take long for her suspicions to be confirmed.

A few seconds later, a photo of a very dead Jackson arrived on the man's phone.

The man was struck dumb. With one small image, his carefully constructed world had shattered. "I will be in San Roca tomorrow and make all arrangements then."

"Thank you, sir. And my condolences for your loss," said the law officer on the other end of the phone with phony solicitousness.

The man clicked off the phone and glared at the girl on the floor. He latched onto her and yanked her onto the bed. For the next hour, he savaged and brutalized her, expending every bit of energy and hurt he could on her. She tried to satisfy him, but he was in no mood for her feeble attempts. His blazing eyes burned into hers as his body punished her with his anger.

At the end of an hour, he pulled himself off her. He threw a thousand dollars at her, and then went to the washroom where he took a shower and freshened up. After he was finished, he went back into the bedroom and started putting on his clothes. He had not spoken a word since he got off the phone with the policeman.

This is what Annalee had dreamed of. She thought the only reason the Mandarin didn't want to marry her and make her his own was because of his son.

And now that impediment was gone.

"Did I make you happy?" she asked, rubbing her body against his. It was an act, the last remnant of hope.

The Mandarin yanked her off him and threw her body against the wall with such force that he broke a few of her ribs.

"Happy?" gnashed the Mandarin. "You are a whore. Whores are good for only one thing. But I will never see you again."

With that, the Mandarin walked out.

Annalee started bawling as she tried to pull herself off the floor.

An hour later, all the tears had been vanquished. Her eyes were crimson, her arms were blue from being crushed, her loins were raw from his unrelenting savagery, her scalp was tender because he had almost ripped her hair out, her breasts showed the purplish bite marks and drops of blood where his teeth had broken through her skin and her broken ribs ached...

She never again wanted to spend another second in bed with a man again.

The truth was, she probably couldn't. Without using any whips, ropes, rods or any other items that her deviant partners inflicted upon her, the Mandarin, with just his body, had so severely devastated her that it would be months before she healed, let alone earn some money for her tuition and living expenses—she wasn't much of a saver.

She had been poor before but she would not be poor again. There was no point in trying to complain to the authorities... the man owned many of them.

There was only one solution.

She stepped through the open glass door of the apartment, then climbed onto the balcony's concrete railing.

Eyes welling full of tears, she whispered, "Goodbye, Mandarin."

The young mistress took a step forward... then plummeted thirty stories to her death.

PART TWO

THE MANDARIN'S VENDETTA

SEVENTEEN

INTENTIONS

It was 9 a.m. Henry and Ling had left with Tex three hours ago to travel to Ling's village.

At China HQ, Barry, Arthur, Chuck and Rayna were conferencing with Julio via video telephony as they worked on their third cups of coffee.

"Including yesterday, we've taken out half a dozen of the people on Wen's list. Now it gets hard," stated Arthur, flinching slightly from the lingering pain in his shot arm. "From last count, there will be at least a dozen and a half reps from the different companies at lunch today."

"Eighteen? That's damned good. We can take them all out and go home after lunch," said Chuck.

Arthur shook his head. "Not that easy, Chuck. All of them will likely bring bodyguards or muscle. High level killers and, with maybe twenty of them and four of us, I don't like our chances."

"A dozen is pretty damned good," responded Barry. "You did a good job in spreading the word, Julio."

Julio nodded slightly at the acknowledgement of more than a decade of contrivance, creation and obfuscation. For years, Fidelitas had been investing money on behalf of a number of fictitious criminals that were supposedly clients—arms dealers, drug dealers, stock manipulators. These mythical malefactors were quiet legends. Everyone knew who they were but no one could actually trace their dealings.

Chappa del Fuega was head of a medium-sized Mexican drug cartel that distributed product from San Francisco to New York. Lin Bo Fan headed a Taiwanese financial management company that manipulated three stocks in the Shanghai stock market like a yoyo, making millions whether stocks went up or down.

In the pitch to the invitees to the lunch, Fidelitas' connection was mentioned as reference. This raised the eyebrows and interest of all the invitees, helping gain a much higher rate of acceptance than if it were just another lunch.

"Anybody in particular we should watch out for?" asked Rayna as she scanned the guest list.

"All of them contributed to the Zongtian disaster," said Arthur. "But there was one that Wen didn't give a name but called, 'bigfish.' Haven't been able to get a name or talked to him personally but he did say he'll come... That's about all we can hope for."

"So, what's your pitch, Rayna?" asked Barry. There was no need to ask Arthur—he was a veteran. But Rayna? She was a newbie.

"Deeds, not words." The motto of JTF2, the Canadian Special Forces unit that Rayna had been part of for three years.

"That's not much of a plan," muttered Chuck.

"It's good enough. Or did you forget this from your Navy SEAL days? *No plan survives first contact with the enemy...* I'm going to read the room and go from there."

EIGHTEEN
INCOGNITO

The Mandarin sent a text to Mary, telling her he was unavailable but did not specify a timeframe. Mary was used to that. Whenever there was a deal that required his full attention, the Mandarin went incognito. It did strike her as unusual that this time he had not given her any notice but she knew that he always had several items cooking, any of them which might have blossomed to the stage of needing his undivided attention.

She texted back, "What do you want to do about your lunch meeting?" He didn't respond and Mary didn't expect him to. When she saw that the lunch was going to be at the Oceania and the picture of a bikinied Rayna brandishing an assault weapon, she decided that she would go to represent her employer. She had never eaten at a six-star hotel and the intriguing picture of Rayna? Well, there was a reason she never married.

IN AN UNUSUAL MOVE FOR HIM, the Mandarin took a taxi to the airport rather than using his own limo driver. That was because he wanted privacy and didn't want to explain to anyone what he was doing, even Mary. As soon as he finished his conversation with her, he turned off his cell phone. It was the first time in years the Mandarin had done so.

While normally the Mandarin was content with business class air travel, the extra privacy availed in traveling first class was important, especially on this trip to Los Angeles—he was not in the mood to engage in idle chit chat with anyone.

He instructed the flight stewardess not to interrupt him and that he would neither eat nor drink for the duration of the flight. While the attendant smiled attentively and said, "Of course," inwardly she was wondering why he would spend fifteen thousand dollars on a flight and not take advantage of any of the airline's amenities for VIP travelers.

With only three others traveling first class, he had as much privacy as the Boeing 777 would allow and donned the airline-provided top quality noise-canceling headphones. However, he did not choose any music or podcasts to listen to. The silence gave him lots of mental and physical space as he grasped for meaning in this bombshell that rocked his world to its core.

The minutes and hours hung like eternity as he stared at a photo on his phone of Jackson wearing his Pacifica University sweatshirt, leaning on his pristine gold Ferrari fresh from the car detailer. The kid looked like many college students. Hair a trifle long, a little undernourished and world-conquerer cockiness on his face.

NINETEEN

FABULOUS

The thousand-square-foot President's Room at the Oceania Hotel with its capacity of fifty was "the place" for all major events or meals where security was paramount. In addition to hotel surveillance, guests were allowed to bring their own protection should they wish— and most did. Elegant, intimate, functional and safe, the President's Room had hosted more top international dignitaries, heads of state and billionaires over the years than any other facility in Asia. While many of the affairs were public occasions with signings and celebrations, others were ultra-exclusive closed-door events.

This included the luncheon that Arthur arranged for today. Most of this high level group of crooked industrialists and government officials had a connection with the Zongtian schools' disaster. They were used to being pampered and it was going to take more than just a boring speech by Arthur and a picture of Rayna in a bikini to bring them out. They were all jaded professionals and could buy almost any woman they wanted.

But one thing not for sale was uniqueness, especially when it came to food. These guests had had so many five-hundred-dollars-per-person meals that a meal had to be really special to attract their attendance.

It was. The meal would be prepared by a Japanese chef whose credentials included not only preparing meals for the Japanese emperor but also the leader of Japan's largest Yakuza group. They had all heard about Hirito. The legendary master had owned a five-star Michelin restaurant in Tokyo but then suddenly disappeared. They were all intrigued to discover that Hirito now worked for Arthur exclusively.

That made Arthur special.

All the guests were male, save Mary. These men included the brawny bodyguards who stood by the walls of the room. While possession of firearms by private citizens was illegal in China, the telltale bulges under many of their suit jackets showed that the law was clearly being disobeyed.

As Arthur pulled out a chair for Rayna, he whispered in her ear. "Bigfish didn't show. But his secretary did. Reel her in."

Rayna turned and kissed Arthur on the cheek. "Of course, darling."

IT HAD BEEN A FABULOUS MEAL. Hirito and his team of assistants performed magic that none of the guests had ever experienced. Oohs and aahs, lip smacking and finger licking accompanied every course at the long rectangular table. No one cared about table manners when the food was this good. The only thing that could have made it better would be if alcohol were served. But that was a minor quibble. They knew that the price of admission meant their full attention on the presentation that would follow.

Arthur took the podium.

"Thank you so much for joining us for lunch. Undoubtedly you have all done your research and know of our spectacular successes, a level of secrecy surpassing any government or intelligence operation in the world, and a fanatical dedication to serving our clients of all backgrounds. And, naturally, how we charge more than anyone else trying to provide similar services."

There were small grunts of agreement. Arthur's prices were exorbitant. He could see the skepticism on his audience's faces. Some looked at their guards, indicating that they would leave in short order.

Arthur was undeterred. "We have two items to present to you today. I will present the first one and my colleague will follow with the next. But, before I do that, I want to show you what our team did less than an hour ago, while you were enjoying your meal."

On the two screens flanking Arthur, a video began playing. All the guests froze when they saw a man in a prison uniform appear. It was someone they worried about, someone who had the capacity to do them serious harm if not destroy them completely.

It was Wen.

All sat fixated on the screen as the camera followed him. A meager portion of boiled vegetables and rice were put on his plate. It would be barely enough for a child, let alone a grown man. One of Wen's fellow inmates tried to grab Wen's plate. When Wen tried to protect his lunch, another convict jammed a chopstick in Wen's neck, piercing right through his interior and exterior jugular veins. Blood began gushing out and Wen was dead within a minute.

The video stopped. The unstated subtext of what they had just seen was: *I know who you are. I know what you have done. I know where to hunt you down should you cross me.*

Arthur resumed his delivery.

"That's who I am and that's what we do. We solve problems that no one else can solve. And I know you have special problems, particularly in getting your money out of China."

There were knowing nods of heads. With the Chinese government continually cracking down, it was getting increasingly harder to funnel their funds, legal or illegal, out of China. Every one of them had lost a substantial amount when trying to get their money out. Sometimes, it was a crooked bank official, sometimes a "mule" carrying the cash was caught, sometimes it was a dishonest broker or realtor in North America. And, recently, confiscation of funds was the least of one's worries. Death was a bigger risk.

"You've all done it the old way for small amounts. Get some of the endless supply of paupers to make deposits into friendly banks, then do bank transfers...

Yada, yada, yada. It's supremely inefficient and highly suspicious for a peasant to be making a deposit of $50,000 or even $500—not to mention the possibility of theft. So what's my solution?"

Arthur took a sip of water, not because he was thirsty, but because he wanted the tension to mount.

"For clients like you, 'return on investment' is not important. What is important is 'return OF investment.' If you are willing to invest the money, I will guarantee its safety. Upfront, this will cost you twenty percent of your investment. But, after fifteen years, you will have recovered your initial capital."

The expressions at the table indicated that this was a lousy deal. Arthur's eyes pierced his audience as he continued. "But, most importantly, and this is something no other organization can provide, we will guarantee that, within six months of your investment, your entire immediate family will get American green cards or landed immigrant status in Canada. We have gained entrance even for those who do not meet the minimum threshold for admittance and... those of you who have criminal records."

Arthur paused to allow this to sink in. "So how do we do it? The answer is that every situation is unique. I will discuss details with interested parties privately but, to start with, you must have the equivalent of fifty million U.S. dollars to invest. Before you say that's too expensive, I will say that my offer is a bargain... Every one of you needs me. You are all a hairsbreadth away from joining Wen."

Arthur touched a sensitive nerve. He could see worry

in the eyes of his guests. His job was done. Time to move on. "Now, I'd like to introduce my associate Rayna Tan to make our next presentation."

TWENTY
THEN AND NOW

The Mandarin stayed pretty well in the same position during the entire fourteen-hour flight from Guangzhou to Los Angeles. In his solitude, he had time to reflect—something he had never done before—but death had a way of changing one's perspective on life.

The Mandarin's empire was vast. Drugs, construction and manufacturing were the mainstays of his operation.

How did a poor rural kid catch the brass ring when millions of other undocumented workers never got past groveling for pennies as part of the morass of perpetual underpaid labor?

It wasn't easy. Back then, he was not called the Mandarin but Deng Xiaoping, named after the paramount Chinese leader who led China through visionary market-economy reforms. His parents hoped for great things out of their only son, but never had a chance to see their vain hopes dashed. Typhoid attacked their village, wiping out half the residents, including Deng's parents when he was twelve years old.

It was time to become a man. He left for Guangzhou, planning to work hard and make his fortune. What the youngster didn't know was that, without the proper *hukou*, he had few options. He wound up in a squalid shanty town, sharing a crowded room, sleeping in the same bed as strangers, putting up with mold on the walls.

But Deng refused to be a victim. Unknowingly, or just by dumb luck or a genetic accident, he had several attributes of people who manage to get ahead: he needed much less sleep than the average person; he had no interest in socializing or gossiping; he preferred fresh vegetables as opposed to fast food junk; he possessed an uncommon natural strength; and he was a self-starter who plunged himself into learning whenever he had spare time.

But his most important trait was his drive to succeed —he did anything and everything. His first job was as a human camel, delivering jugs of water to offices. By working harder, longer and stronger, he distributed three times as many jugs per day as the average laborer.

Later, on a construction site, he did everything from excavation to mixing and pouring concrete. After work, instead of joining his fellow shanty town mates in gambling and drinking, he made extra cash by putting in hours at any of the sweat shops that needed temporary labor—making shoes, T-shirts... anything.

A turning point in Deng's life occurred when he was a railway laborer in the employ of *Yao*, a "4 percent man." (Corrupt railway officials were given this nickname because four percent of every contract they awarded went to their personal coffers.) A fellow worker cheated Deng during one of his rare times of gambling. Incensed, the now-fifteen-year-old used his bare hands to break his compadre's neck. Yao heard about this and ordered Deng be brought before him. Rather than chastising him or turning him in, Yao hired him for "personal services."

Deng was impressed with Yao's wealth: the official could afford to buy three houses and send his children to American private schools. Yao had two mistresses and could easily have had a dozen more had he wanted.

Deng's job was to keep people honest. Anyone that did not pony up Yao's fees felt the wrath of Deng's strong arms or his sharp small knife. By the time he was twenty, Deng had sent three men to their final destinations. Not a huge number, but there was a practical reason: dead men make no money. A vicious beating almost always reformed anyone stupid enough to renege on his debts to the railway man.

Deng could now afford to leave the shanty town and move into a regular apartment. He would happily have worked for Yao forever had there not been a disastrous set of events that set his life on a different course.

Deng was tasked to pick up Yao's daughter at the airport when she came back for summer break. She hid this from her parents but her first term in Portland was miserable. One of the few overseas Chinese in her school, she was unable to make friends or communicate properly. Even worse for the teenage girl, a severe case of acne developed and she didn't know how to get proper treatment. As he drove her home, Deng made the mistake of telling her that she needed to "stop eating greasy American food so her skin wouldn't be so bad."

He thought it a helpful comment but it devastated the girl. She told her father that Deng tried to rape her and showed him her bruised breasts.

Unaware that the injury was self-inflicted, Yao went berserk and Deng was lucky to escape with his life. No longer in Yao's employ and wanting to hide, he moved back into the shadowy shanty town with the illegal migrants.

There, he had an epiphany—this hellhole would be his gold mine. He knew the people, their strengths, flaws and habits. They all wanted to work but didn't have access to the jobs. Deng had connections and he had smarts. While there were many other employment brokers, they didn't screen the migrants well enough or weren't able to keep them in line.

Shaving his head gave him a more commanding presence. He started calling himself "The Mandarin."

The Mandarin brazenly returned to Yao and told him that he could provide him with workers that were two-thirds of the cost he was currently paying. While Yao was still angry because of his daughter's accusation, greed surpassed his family loyalty.

Within two weeks, the Mandarin had recruited three hundred workers for Yao. He made money on both ends. The Mandarin charged Yao a fee for getting cheap quality labor and he also charged the workers a commission for getting them work. No one complained, though. For Yao, productivity increased because the Mandarin's workers had a low turnover ratio and were hard workers —no one wanted to get the Mandarin upset.

After a few months, Yao felt the Mandarin was making too much money off him and called him in to renegotiate the deal. That night was Yao's last night on earth, or at least it was rumored to have been. Not a peep from the railway boss was heard ever again. There was no digital footprint, no sightings nor did anyone touch any of Yao's holdings or bank accounts.

Word spread about the Mandarin's ability to get good, cheap labor. He became a first-call recruiter for workers for China's huge construction boom. Especially when head contractors discovered the Mandarin's willingness to cut corners and give generous kickbacks.

Remembering his own time in sweat shops, the Mandarin expanded into counterfeiting. Not money; that was dangerous. But clothes, DVDs and women's handbags—getting into this biz was a gift from heaven. He supplied factories with thousands of workers. When free Internet downloads killed the pirated DVD market, the Mandarin decided to open his own handbag manufacturing factory, using his "art of persuasion" to get some of the workers he had recruited for international designers to work for him instead.

While he himself never used or dealt in drugs, he couldn't help but notice how many users there were in the shanty town, including his own workers. The Mandarin decided to capitalize on this built-in market. He focused on crystal meth and chose to get his product from North Korea. While it wasn't the cheapest source, their ice was a hundred percent pure. It was reliable, the price was guaranteed, and profits easily calculated.

While it would have been easy to expand into heroin, he saw the devastation that smack caused. The Mandarin didn't care about the human toll. What he was concerned about was that if his own workers started using the white stuff, there would be a corresponding lack of productivity or an increase in death. He remembered Yao's admonition, "Dead men make no money."

The Mandarin knew his limitations. While there were huge profits if he could be the kingpin distributor for either his factory-made goods or the drugs that he got from North Korea, he didn't like the fact that he couldn't control it and needed others to help. Yes, he was sorely tempted, but his English was virtually non-existent and he really didn't trust white people.

But then, Danny from the China Red gang approached him. The younger, brash hipster persuaded the Mandarin to go in with him on a small American shipment of synthetic drugs as an experiment. It was overwhelmingly successful and it was all the Mandarin could do to restrain himself from negotiating a further buy when he met with the North Korean general.

And then, a haunting thought. Was it possible that the drugs that killed his son were from the shipment that he helped put together? There was no way to know and that ate at him all the more.

TWENTY-ONE

MORE THAN A HOT BABE

Rayna got up from her seat and stepped to the front. Her eyes made a quick circuit of the room, scrutinizing the group with a mischievous, almost taunting look. All of them were men, ages fifty and up except Mary, but Rayna could see from her ogling that Mary's mind was in the same gutter as the male guests.

Rayna winked coyly at her gaping audience as her dress dropped to the floor—she stood tall in an even skimpier bikini than the one that was sent over in the invitation. She jumped onto the table and slowly rotated. Sexuality oozed from every pore of her perfect body. Without saying a word, her message was perfectly clear. *I can get into the room of any man with a heartbeat.*

She looked upward and inhaled, then jumped to the floor. Her eyes lasered on the group. "You don't hire me to do the things that you can get from your girlfriends, wives, mistresses or hookers. You hire me because of the things I can do that they can't... I have more than a hundred kills to my credit. But you don't hire me for that. You can get anyone..."

Rayna pointed to the bodyguards at the side of the room, "...or even do it yourself. You hire me because I can get into places or people that others can't. I can kill in ways that others can't. And I have the ingenuity, experience and smarts that others don't. But, most importantly, I am a leader and there is no task I'm not capable of."

Rayna picked up her dress and slipped it back on. "I'm former Special Forces. Canadian JTF2, to be exact. Similar to the US Navy SEALs or British SAS. Have you ever heard of Operation Big Box?"

None had.

"Good. Because, if you said 'yes' you'd be lying. Afghanistan. Hundred degree heat for months on end. Never knowing if the bulge in the pocket of a kid was a pomegranate or a grenade... never knowing if you were coming back from bringing powdered milk to a starving village... I was stationed at FOB Sunshine. I was always on 'thirty minutes notice' to move. Had to snag a few winks whenever I could because, once a mission started, you never knew when or how it would end. It was the end of the poppy growing season, which meant a ton of fighting-age males were going to become available to the Taliban. Also, things were heating up in Kandahar, and I'm not talking about the weather. Insurgents were making their presence felt; too much unrest among the natives who were ready to turn; random unexpected gunfire and explosions from normally peaceful parts of the city; more Taliban dressing like cops and soldiers... Kandahar was a powder keg waiting to explode."

This was all completely new to the audience. Very little was known about operations in Afghanistan, especially in China where news was often censored.

"Part of our job was to mentor the Afghan National Police (ANP) and the Afghan Provincial Response Company (APRC), a hundred-and-thirty-five illiterate amateurs divided into three platoons. There were times when it was more dangerous to be with them than to fight the Taliban because you could never, ever count on them to deliver. The only ones who really had your back were the other members of your team, or other coalition forces. Like when we got a thirty-second alert to go while we were having lunch. Officially, because it went through the ANP, they were supposed to take charge, but there was no way in hell that would happen. The Taliban attacked on multiple fronts: a police substation, the mayor's office, a couple of schools. Pistols, machine guns, RPGs and, of course, plenty of suicide vehicles crammed with explosives. They wanted Kandahar to swim in blood... and the bastards sure came close."

Rayna's tone became deadly serious. "That was May 9—a pivotal day in my life and the beginning of the reason why I am here today—when I became the first female to lead a special forces unit in combat from any country from anywhere in the world."

No one uttered a sound, but the expressions on their faces spoke it all. *Omigod.*

"We were part of a Special Operations Task Force (SOTF) led by Captain Kevin Browning. There were twenty of us in SOTF-99, plus twice that number of APRC. I had almost half under my wing and Browning had the rest. I was pretty stoked for all of three seconds until the responsibility hit me. Especially when I realized that, despite my feelings about the Afghanis, I was responsible for them, too... just as the shit hit the fan. Ten suicide bombers blew themselves up at the governor's palace compound. We loaded up, jumped in our vehicles and were on the go to Kandahar's biggest commercial shopping complex just outside the palace. The insurgents had barricaded themselves inside, using it as a central firebase to rain hell on the palace and other buildings in the area."

Rayna paused a beat. Every eye was riveted on her, even as she took a sip of water.

"Browning coordinated with the Americans for us to assault the building. When we got to our target, there wasn't much left. I don't mind telling you I was freaked. I had shopped there before and it was so vibrant, huge and crammed. People selling fruits, rugs, clothes... but now, just debris and body parts everywhere. We dismounted from our light armored vehicles, established a casualty collection point and gingerly made our way to the huge building. Much as we wanted to hurry, we knew that an IED was likely to blow us to bits if we weren't careful."

Eyes flashing, Rayna balled her fists tightly and gritted her teeth. "Adding to the problems was that we had lost radio contact with the Americans. What if there had been a change of plans? That happened so often, but we had no way of knowing, so we just continued. We were all shocked when we got there. This mega-mall shopping center was a ghost town. Now that it was empty, it seemed bigger than ever. We all had the same thought. *How the hell is our little group going to manage?* Thank God for Browning— he's either the stupidest or bravest guy I ever met. By now the radio started working again and he just called everyone. 'We're going in.' And we all just said, 'Sure.'"

Rayna stared at the ground, then turned her head back up. "While the Afghans and Americans exchanged fire from outside, we were the only coalition forces inside the building. Browning decided that our best chance was to breach the basement. My team would clear the rooms, while Browning's secured the entrance and stairwells. Easier said than done, though. Inside every room might be a hidden insurgent waiting to take your life. Or maybe in any of those random bags was a bomb just waiting to be detonated. We were just about to begin when things got a whole lot more complicated—people dressed in ordinary clothes appeared from nowhere. You could read the fear in the faces of the APRC. *Do we really have to do this?*"

Rayna shook her head. "Was that kid a young insurgent or someone whose family were peddlers in the complex? Was that woman wearing a suicide vest underneath her loose-fitting clothing? Who knew? We sure didn't, but we still had a job to do. It took what seemed like forever to sweep the basement in our search for insurgents. We had to be thorough and careful as we went through each unlocked door and poked every large pile of debris. In that hour in the hellhole, we must have found over a hundred million bucks worth of heroin and opium. Right then, I realized that I should quit and become a drug dealer."

TWENTY-TWO

SUCKERED

The guests laughed as Rayna grinned. "So we finished the basement and didn't find anyone. Browning's group took the first floor, but that's when we all felt an unseen danger. You know how, in a multi-level mall, you can look down from an upper floor and see the floors and shops below you because there's all that open space in the middle?"

Spellbound faces throughout the group nodded. There were malls like that everywhere.

"Except this one was a whole lot bigger. The basement was a self-contained floor but from the ground floor on up, there were these huge open areas that you could look down on and spy on anything that might be coming. While Browning's group was searching for the enemy, mine had their weapons sighted on the upper floors to see if anyone was waiting to take a shot. Was there? No and, because nothing happened to us in the basement, the APRC let down their guard."

Rayna wagged her head in disgust. "They opened

doors without ducking or stepping to the side. Idiots. If there were Taliban there, they never would have stood a chance. The morons wandered freely and quickly through the floor, poking piles of rubble or debris without paying proper attention. We tried to get them to be more careful but they wouldn't listen. And it only got worse, since we didn't find any insurgents or explosives on the main concourse or the next floor above it... they grew even more complacent and confident. Stupid. Stupid. Stupid. All of us had just made it to the third floor and were about to begin our search when an RPG roared. Machine guns opened fire simultaneously. Bullets whizzed by, rifle fire bursting all around... We were pelted by an onslaught from all sides."

Rayna pantomimed the sputtering sounds of machine guns firing and the detonation of grenades. "Within a dozen seconds, ten of the locals were dead or injured. Browning got hit trying to pull one of the APRC to safety. The others ducked or sprinted for cover as streams of lead found their targets. 'Come back,' I screamed as I shot one of the charging insurgents in the head with my pistol, hoping that would stop them, but those a-holes kept going. It took the rest of SOTF-99 to keep them there. There was one APRC, Ghazi, who was decent. He and I snaked on our bellies to get to Browning. He was bleeding like crazy and was going to go into shock if we didn't get him out of there fast. We managed to drag him to the stairwell and some of the guys got ready to take him down to the CCP. But, before that happened, Browning rasped, 'Wait,' and pointed to me. 'Rayna's in charge now.' I had never heard such foul obscenities in all my life except from our so-called allies. A woman was in charge. And she was young. And she was Chinese."

Rayna breathed in deeply—the memory of her abrupt promotion was indelibly written into her soul.

"With that, Browning blacked out and a couple of his teammates took him downstairs. Others gathered more casualties while I hugged a wall trying to assess the situation, my first and foremost job as commander. The insurgents had barricaded themselves in a large shop about twenty yards from us. Like many stores around the world that are worried about theft, the shops the enemy chose had metal shutters and iron bars. This made breaching them difficult, but also gave them strong protection while they pumped lead into us. The smartest thing would have been to flush them out with tear gas and then gun them down, but we had no gas masks so this was unfeasible."

The group was transfixed. All of them were used to causing death, but this was a woman and these were battle-hardened terrorists she was fighting, not the country bumpkins, cheap thugs or corrupt officials that had spines of jellyfish.

"It was getting dark and electricity went out in the complex. While we had night vision goggles, the APRC preferred flashlights. The idiots... Anyway, we hugged the wall to get close so those in the shop couldn't get an angle on us with good vision. I threw a couple of grenades in front of the store and tried to maneuver us for a better firing angle. But then the APRC idiots turned on their damned flashlights and the Taliban hurled a deluge of automatic fire at us. Rounds whistled by. Grenades exploded. One of our guys got shot right through the eyeball. Instant death. He dropped to the ground, mouth agape, staring wild-eyed with his good eye at the ceiling."

Rayna's face darkened at the memory. "You never forget stuff like that."

Her fists balled with anger. "The cowards took off without firing a shot, forcing us to retreat as well. The Taliban must have been as surprised as we were, since they couldn't react fast enough to cut us down. I gave Browning a call and thankfully he was coherent. He told us we needed to quit with the subtlety and get more fire-power. Five minutes later, we got help—a pair of m240 machine guns. Two guys laid down a base fire against the door of the shop, while me and another sniper hoped upon hope that we would get a chance for a shot. No luck. But the tracers and grenades did at least start a fire, which only riled up the bad guys. Return fire ripped through the broken window panes from the shop toward us. Then someone tossed a grenade through the holes in the window."

She threw up her hands to accentuate the blast. "BOOM! Confusion, yelling, gunfire ripped the air again. Screams told us that another man was down and we returned a long, heavy burst of fire in the direction of the shop, but I had no idea if we hit anybody or not. Thick, black smoke choked us, which gave me another idea... If we couldn't see the insurgents' shop, that also meant they couldn't see us. I got half a dozen of us to grab a bunch of grenades and told the remaining APRC to go in the opposite direction and keep firing and pitching grenades —they were going to be our distraction. This was a move that had to be done fast because it would be easy to get caught. We raced through the black smoke and into a shop two stores away from where the insurgents were holed up... I chucked a grenade at the front door and we raced in before the shrapnel stopped zinging. Then another grenade. BOOM! We raced into the store next to the shop and just tossed grenades through the damaged wall like we were paid per blast. The grenades gave the whole area a weird reddish glow, like something out of hell. I managed to sneak a look inside the shop after a few minutes. They had an arsenal capable of taking down a small town. Rifles, grenade launchers, flame throwers and something I definitely didn't think I was going to see— bayonets. These guys were ready for everything. With the APRC's racket, the insurgents must not have noticed our initial grenades in the other shops. By the time we were on them... it was too late. It took hours to pick through the wreckage and bag all the body parts, but at least we didn't have to deal with any prisoners."

Arthur. Rayna. These guys are for real.

The same thoughts echoed through the room from all the guests.

Except for one.

"You're full of crap," piped up the sole white face in the attendance. "You look more like a two-bit hooker than a Navy SEAL. And there's no way anyone's gonna trust you with a boatload of smack."

With lightning speed, Rayna reached into the folds of her dress and pulled out a martial arts flying star. She jettisoned the pentangle missile at a huge, scarred black hulk who stood behind the white guest, hitting him in the chest with such force that the sharp edges slashed through his shirt and jacket—blood gushed out of the wound.

Rayna then leapt onto the long table, tore down a few steps and did a handspring, spreading her legs. As she descended, she wrapped her legs around the white man's neck and twisted. By the time he hit the ground, he was motionless. From another fold, Rayna pulled out a hypodermic needle and moved it toward his temple as Arthur stepped toward her.

"No, no," simpered the fallen attendee.

Arthur took Rayna's hand and pulled it away. He pointed to the white man. "Go."

The Caucasian and his black bodyguard got up and headed to the door. Just before he exited, the white man turned and gave Arthur and Rayna the finger. "We should have killed you people when we had the chance." With that, the duo huffed out.

Arthur exhaled and addressed the remaining group. "I hate white people. I'll take their money but never, ever be their friend."

Arthur's racist comment broke through the uneasiness that had descended upon the room. Every person of color, no matter their wealth, professional or social status, had been the victim of racism at some point.

Arthur held up his hands to stop the clapping. "But money is money. And I will work with whoever and whatever to make it. And, if you want to make inroads in America, be prepared to do a deal with the devil."

The door opened and the Caucasian and black man re-entered.

"Meet my associates from America, Barry and

Chuck. Barry works with me on the deal making and Chuck is involved in our operations. Thank you for coming to lunch. Please feel free to stay behind as we are happy to answer any of your individual questions."

THERE WAS no doubt in any of the lunch guests' minds that there was an opportunity somewhere. Male chauvinists that most of them were, their discussions were focused with Arthur, Barry and Chuck.

This gave Mary a chance to approach Rayna. "I'm Mary. You are very impressive, Rayna."

Rayna sized the executive assistant up. Even though Mary was a substitute for her boss, that she was there meant she had some connection to the Zongtian affair. Rayna had already noted Mary's sexual interest. This info might or might not be used. One thing that was out of place was Mary's outfit. What she was wearing could easily have cost five thousand dollars or more. Maybe she had a sugar daddy—or sugar mama—somewhere. But wouldn't someone like that prefer a younger plaything?

"You're so kind to say that. What brings you here?"

"This and that..." answered Mary evasively. "Do you have any specialties?"

"What I thrive on is challenges. Making the impossible happen when no one else can pull it off. Life's too short to be satisfied with the ordinary."

A sigh escaped Mary's lips. "I wish I could say that for myself. I look after the details of running my boss's operations. You know, a little bit of this, a little bit of that."

That's twice she didn't answer. Rayna tried a new tactic. "I know how you feel. There are many things I do as well or better than Arthur but he has me running around doing the things he doesn't want to do."

Mary nodded with complete empathy. "That's me, too. We manufacture women's clothing and accessories. It is extremely profitable and I'm the one handling all the work. Do you know I can make a fake Salvatore handbag that can fool the Italians at ten percent of the cost? Not only Italian, but French and New York, too."

Gotcha! "You're kidding. I've got to get to know you better. I spend a fortune on purses and handbags. Five hundred here. Two thousand there. All genuine designer labels. Costs me a fortune." Rayna pointed at Mary's handbag. "Like I'd love to have a Bartolini but no way I'm going to pay thirty-five hundred for one."

"You want it?" Mary sensed an opening. "I'll give it to you."

"What? No way."

Mary took a napkin from the table and began placing the contents of her handbag on it. "I can get another from our factory."

Rayna's lips pursed in a silent whistle, then uttered quietly. "I've got fifteen thousand in cash upstairs. You think I could do a little shopping? I mean, if that's okay and everything."

"It's... not exactly nice."

"I've got fifty girlfriends and nieces back home. I

would be a star if I brought them all a designer bag. They wouldn't be able to tell the difference, right?"

"There is no difference. A lot of our staff worked at the big shops before we convinced them to join us."

Convinced? Right. "So it's okay? I'll buy as many as you'll let me take for the money."

"I won't sell any of them for your friends, but I'll give you six for yourself." Mary's eyebrows raised in amusement as Rayna's face lit up. *Girls will be girls.*

"Omigod. That's like twenty thousand. When can we go?"

"Now," said Mary. "But there are some trade secrets that I have to guard."

"Guard away."

As Mary and Rayna walked to the door, one of the bodyguards joined them at the door. Rayna noted that he was lithe, muscular and had the aura of a martial arts grandmaster. A quick glance indicated that Jun had seen Rayna's demonstration and would be more than willing to take her on.

"This is Jun," introduced Mary simply. "I don't advise you cross him."

"Nice to meet you, Jun," greeted Rayna cheerfully as they stepped through the door.

After they exited, the men all looked at each other. Some smiled knowingly; others snickered; a few out and out guffawed.

Arthur summed up their feelings perfectly. "Women, they are all the same. Shopping. Shopping and more shopping."

TWENTY-THREE

HIDDEN

A valet brought a beat-up, made-in-China Great Wall Motors SUV to the front of the Oceania.

Mary was apologetic. "This will be nothing like the vehicles you're used to riding around in, but when we get to our destination, you'll understand."

"Mary, a car is a car as long as it gets you from one place to another and you don't get shot at like what happened all the time I was in the Middle East."

As the valet opened the doors, Jun took out a sleeping mask and handed it to Rayna.

Mary gave Rayna an apologetic look. "Precautionary measure. Until we know that we are going to do business, the Mandarin doesn't like anyone to know the exact location of our factory."

The Mandarin! That's who Ling said got her the job for Ming. She wished she could send this info to Barry and the boys but she couldn't risk being caught. "I understand. My boss has crazy ideas, too."

Rayna put the sleeping mask over her eyes, then

allowed Jun to tie an additional blindfold around her head.

Let the games begin.

IN CHINA HQ, Barry, Arthur and Chuck were wrapping up the post mortem of the luncheon presentation.

"I've got everything I need right now," said Julio. "I'll dig up more about the potential targets. It's too bad the "big fish" didn't come."

"Rayna's working on it," said Barry.

"Yeah, well, she better be careful. Just a cursory look at what you've given me shows that some of them are bad dudes and, if Wen says someone is a 'big fish...'"

WHILE RAYNA COULDN'T SEE anything, she and Mary maintained an almost constant conversation. However, little of what was discussed was of any substance—neither wanted to or could share business or personal details. Music they liked, hobbies, places they'd been to, the kind of men they found interesting.

Both of them were lying about almost everything. They both knew it but kept up the pretense. There was a possibility that they would do business at some point and the relationship had to start somewhere.

After what Rayna guesstimated to be about three-quarters of an hour, the car slowed down considerably. There were a lot of stops, starts and turns for the next fifteen minutes until the SUV stopped and Jun announced, "We are here."

Rayna was let out of the car. The blindfold and sleeping mask were removed.

She opened her eyes and was in complete shock. Instead of the prosperous metropolis with an eclectic political, economic, scientific, educational and cultural center, she was in the center of poverty. Housing and buildings were old and in disrepair. The "houses" were made out of plywood and scrap metal, patched tin houses and dirty cloth tents. The tenement buildings weren't much better. The sinks by the front doors indicated that many didn't have running water and that no air conditioners hung out of most windows showed that electricity was non-existent.

While she had never visited one before, she knew she was in a "migrant city," an area those from rural areas, farms and villages inhabited when they first came to the city. Without proper working papers, they worked for substandard wages and lived in places that should be condemned.

The place was brimming with people. Young people. No one in sight over forty. With no place to bathe and sleeping in flea-infested beds, no wonder the inhabitants were chronically ill, unwashed, unkempt and wearing raggedy, filthy clothes.

And sadly, there were plenty of the lowest tier of prostitutes. "Women who live in a shed." Not attractive or young enough to work in a bar or hotel, these women sold themselves for a bowl of noodles or a fried bun to end the loneliness of the male migrant workers who lived in this shanty town.

The denizens of this poverty-stricken ghetto looked with curiosity at this trio wearing clothes that were clean, pressed and new—in contrast to their own T-shirts and jeans that hadn't been washed in weeks, maybe never.

Mary pointed to an old, dilapidated six-story property halfway down the block. "That's our building." Blending right in with its neighbors, Mary commented as they waded through the inhabitants, "The whole building is ours. The main floor is for packing and shipping. Our customers come here to pick their orders up."

Unlike its neighbors, the Mandarin's building had extreme security. In front of the double doors were iron bars that gave a prison-like feeling. Behind the bars was a protective metal door. Jun reached his fist through the bars and banged loudly on the metal door, shouting. "Hey, you. It's us."

A six-inch window in the metal door slid open and Rayna saw a young man with a cigarette hanging out of his mouth checking them out.

"Okay." The heavy door opened and the young man unlocked the "prison bars" with one hand. He had an assault rifle poised to fire with the other.

Rayna furrowed her brow as she looked over the surroundings. "Looks like you have a huge theft problem. Or at least you believe you have a theft problem. You should let us handle that for you."

Mary pushed the weapon away, nodding in the affirmative. "Once every few months, we have to clean up a hell of a mess. Someone always thinks they can out-tough us, out-gun us." She glanced at Jun. "Not a chance. Right, Jun?"

The muscle grunted in agreement.

There was no elevator so the trio began trekking up the stairs.

"Six flights," said Mary, not missing a beat.

"This your way of getting cardio?" teased Rayna.

Mary's response was matter of fact. "No, but it's harder to steal stuff the higher you go."

On each floor was another bolted door with another armed guard. While Mary and Jun were immune, the filth and stench of stale sweat, cigarette smoke, urine and feces were almost unbearable, even to battle-hardened Rayna.

Arriving at the top floor, Mary declared, "The top floor is one of the safest places possible for an operation like this. Thieves, police and inspectors are reluctant to do the climb."

The sixth floor guard took out a set of keys and opened the bolted metal door.

TWENTY-FOUR
OMIGOD

Inside was a sight of mammoth exploitation and abuse. There were almost two hundred young women and children, some not even ten years old. So focused were these inmates that none bothered to look up as Jun, Mary and Rayna entered. Each sat at a sewing machine, with a huge mound of cloth or leather beside them. Each piece in the pile was pre-cut to exactly the same dimensions as every other piece. For daily wages of less than a double non-fat latte with caramel drizzle, all were industriously sewing luxury handbags that would sell for hundreds, even thousands of times what the women and children earned.

There were ten rows of twenty drenched-in-sweat workers with hands moving expertly and with incredible speed at the sewing machines. So as not to waste any time, children with wheelbarrows continuously made the rounds, picking up the bags as the sewers completed them. That way, no one had to take a break to move them to the packing area themselves. At the head of each row was the name of a well-known Italian designer. Venezia. Bertolucci. Caravaggio. Puccini...

Mary stopped one of the children with a wheelbarrow. "Check the quality of these out, Rayna. Give me your honest opinion."

Rayna reached in and pulled out several bags and examined them closely. The stitching was perfectly even with no loose threads. The seams all matched. The leather was top grade. The hardware was solid—not hollow like cheap fakes. Most importantly, all the bags had the feel of quality. "These are beautiful."

Rayna saw another wheelbarrow emerge from the row called *Salvatore*.

She walked over and took out one of the handbags. She carefully ran her finger over the stitching and rubbed the leather to check its quality—again, both top grade. She then took the metal frame, clasps and buckle, running her fingernail along them. Solid and with heft. She looked inside the bag to see engraved on the leather *Handmade in Florence at the Salvatore Design Studio*.

Rayna looked at Mary. "I have one exactly like this. It cost me eight hundred and fifty dollars and that's with thirty percent off."

"That cost less than twenty dollars for us to make."

"That's impossible. I swear it's the same one I bought in the store."

Mary grinned. "It may be; it may not. When the ladies see them and touch them, they will pay. You'd have to be an expert to tell the difference. But, even then, that might not be good enough. I had a buyer from Rome come last week. When he saw what I had, he tripled the order right away. Didn't even ask for a bigger discount."

"You're getting Italians to buy fake Italian bags?"

"Of course. If no one can tell the difference, why should they pay more? I wouldn't be surprised if half the stores in Rome bought their bags from places just like mine."

"How do you do it?"

"So easy. I get the foremen from three of the "real" designers to sell me their secrets. I use the same methods and patterns they use in their factories, only fifty miles away. And a lot of our workers come from the designer factories."

"What are you selling your bags for?"

"About forty-five dollars each for bulk orders."

"That's too little!"

Mary exhaled. It was a losing discussion she'd had many times with the Mandarin. "We know what we're good at and we focus here only on manufacturing. We just sell to customers at our factory. They look after the shipping and distribution... And my boss hates working with white people."

Rayna put the bag back in the wheelbarrow. "You need to work with us. We can make you at least three times as much money without doing anything more than you are already doing. And tell your boss, he never ever would have to look at a round eye. I'll do it."

As Mary gave a slight shake to her head, Rayna saw something that disturbed her more than seeing the worker abuse—Jun emerging from the aisle at the side of the room, buckling his belt. Two seconds later, a naked, crying young girl ran out from the same aisle, carrying a ripped T-shirt and shorts. It took every iota of self-control for Rayna to not pulverize Jun's penis when she saw the red splotches on the child's body.

Rayna noted something almost as awful—no one in the room paid any attention to the girl. She realized her initial impression that the workers were focused on their tasks was wrong. Theirs was not an expression of concentration. It was avoidance... and fear.

As Jun walked toward Rayna and Mary, Mary asked him, "You done now?"

"I'll wait for you," replied the big man.

"No, take Rayna back first. I'll be a while." Mary turned to Rayna. "Jun will give you a ride back to the hotel. Hope you like what you saw. It gives you an idea of our operation."

"It certainly does. Gives me some good ideas..."

Mary gave Rayna a large plastic bag. "There's six of them. Enjoy."

Rayna beamed. "Thank you so much. I hope we get to do real business!"

TWENTY-FIVE

INVESTIGATION

After clearing United States customs, the Mandarin spent a few minutes searching on his smart phone for a Chinese-speaking Uber driver who could also act as his translator. Morgan Xi fit the bill. He was a graduate student in Chinese studies from Shanghai and drove a nondescript three-year-old Ford Fusion, a perfect vehicle to hide in plain sight with. Including fighting the traffic, it took three hours to get to San Roca. It was a friendly chat as the Mandarin asked Morgan about his background, his family and aspirations in America.

The first stop was the town's police station.

"Come with me. Tell them I am Jackson's father," ordered the Mandarin. Morgan reluctantly obliged. Like many immigrants, he was reluctant to have any dealings with the law, even when he had done nothing wrong.

When Morgan explained the Mandarin was Jackson's father, the two were admitted immediately to speak with the sheriff who had used Jackson's cell phone to call the Mandarin. In person, Sheriff Clemens was an imposing figure, bigger and blacker than the Mandarin imagined. Only a few sentences of translation were needed for the Mandarin to assess that Sheriff Clemens had a complete lack of investigative expertise. Two minutes of conversation later, he concluded that Jackson's death was inevitable in the small town. Without a hospital or even a paramedic available, there was little chance for survival for anyone suffering more than a cold.

"You know your son had problems. Spending money like it was going out of style. He was dealing prescription drugs. I don't want to say your son had it coming but, the way he was living, sooner or later something bad was going to happen."

As Morgan translated, he was amazed at how calm the Mandarin was. If it had been his son that Clemens had so callously discussed, he would have gone ballistic.

Speaking through Morgan, the Mandarin said, "Thank you, Sheriff Clemens. I know you are a busy man, but would you mind if I took a look at the crime scene?"

Clemens nodded at Morgan. "Tell your boss, 'Sure.' I got to go there anyway to clean up the details," was his insensitive response.

THE HUSKY BLACK sheriff unlocked the door to Bangers. "We sent blood samples to LA to get an analysis. Final report will take a while, but preliminary results are that there was a whole lot of shit in his system. Coke, Ritalin, Adderall and some more stuff they've yet to identify. You combine that with a blood alcohol content of over two percent, and you knew bad things were going to happen. Funny thing, though. Jackson's buddy, Sonny, was just as messed up, but managed to survive."

That was really funny.

The sheriff, Morgan and the Mandarin entered to see the empty bar room in disarray with broken chairs, upturned tables and glass fragments all over the place. The Mandarin noted that there was only one chalk outline of a body and walked up to it.

"Where is everybody?"

"Well, we don't actually have enough money to get a proper CSI in but your son was the only fatality. The others managed to get stitched up in the hospital half an hour away and they've been released."

"Thank you." The Mandarin bowed deeply, his head almost touching the floor.

As he straightened himself, the Mandarin launched an uppercut into Sheriff Clemens' jaw. There was so much force that the officer's body lifted two inches off the ground.

On Clemens' descent, the Mandarin delivered a vicious right hook to his jaw. There were two distinct cracking sounds. One was of the sheriff's jaw breaking. The other softer sound was of his neck snapping.

As Clemens buckled over, the Mandarin delivered a powerful chop to the base of his cerebellum.

The mortified Morgan was too paralyzed with fear to move. As Clemens' body hit the hardwood floor, the Uber driver and the Mandarin watched the last few quivers of life seep out of the law enforcement officer.

The Mandarin fixed his eyes on Morgan. "Did you see anything?"

"No. No. Nothing," stammered Morgan.

"Good boy. I like you."

The Mandarin took the sheriff's revolver and the two left.

———————

BECAUSE SAN ROCA was too small to have a morgue, Morgan took the Mandarin to the town's sole funeral home where Jackson's body was being kept. The Mandarin tolerated the inane condolences of Richard Jones, the director of the funeral home, delivered before taking him to Jackson's body.

The Mandarin took a full stoic-faced minute to examine Jackson's face. Then he asked the director to remove Jackson's clothes. It was an unusual request until the Mandarin explained that the police had told him his son's death was due to a drug overdose.

"I just want to check," said the Mandarin, firmly quiet.

"Of course," replied Jones, suddenly feeling uneasy with his strange new client. He couldn't put his finger on what it was, but there seemed to be something that reminded the funeral home worker of the iconic sociopath, Hannibal Lecter.

The Mandarin examined Jackson's body fastidiously, noting that there was not a single needle mark anywhere. None in the obvious places like the veins in the arms;

none in the less obvious places like the underside of the feet or chest or between the toes.

Jones' stomach knotted. "Addicts can be pretty creative as to where they shoot up. I even saw a corpse where he'd stuck the needle in the veins in his bag."

When the Mandarin glared, measuring him up for a cheap coffin, the director pointed to his scrotum, "You know, like the bag?"

"My son was not an addict. He was not even a user."

The Mandarin's calm assertion freaked Jones even more. "My bad. Sorry about that."

"Put his clothes back on," ordered the Mandarin.

Jones meekly obeyed.

"Can we cremate him now?"

The funeral director was taken aback. "We weren't told about this. I've got to pull someone in... maybe tomorrow?"

"We will begin in half an hour."

Hannibal Lecter. There was something so sinister in the Mandarin's quiet understated tone that Jones knew the cremation was going to begin in half an hour—even if he had to do it himself, which he had never done.

AFTER THREE HOURS, Jones put a portion of Jackson's pasty white remains into a small flask the Mandarin had brought along. Although this was something he had done thousands of times, his hands twitched as he was trying to turn the cap tightly on the urn. Finally, success.

"There you go. I must admit this is most highly unusual. I wouldn't normally..."

The funeral operator didn't have a chance to finish his sentence. The Mandarin had stepped behind him, cupping his hands. With a thunderous motion, the Mandarin clapped hard on both of Jones' ears. The violent vibrations burst the eardrums, causing internal bleeding in the brain.

Jones was dead within seconds. Morgan helped the Mandarin lift the body into the cremation chamber. The Mandarin locked it and turned it on.

"Are you sure you're doing that right?" asked Morgan.

"It doesn't matter. I am never coming back."

FOUR HOURS LATER, the car was back on the road. Instead to going directly to LAX, there was a side trip to visit the Port of Los Angeles at San Pedro Bay, twenty miles south of Los Angeles. The busiest container port in the United States, the shipment the Mandarin had sent to America arrived at this port. Not as big as Shanghai, Hong Kong or his home city of Guangzhou, but big enough.

As Morgan pulled the handbrake in the quiet parking lot, the Mandarin reached over from the back seat and throttled him. Morgan gurgled and flailed, but he was no match in strength for the Mandarin. Within three minutes of intense pressure on the carotid artery and no new air getting into his lungs, Morgan was dead.

There were no witnesses around so the Mandarin got out. He opened the front door and put Morgan's jacket over his head—it wasn't unusual for someone to grab a few winks, so it might be days before the kill was discovered.

Walking to the offices further down the terminal, it wasn't too hard for the Mandarin to get an impromptu tour from a Chinese company that operated one of the terminals. The official pointed out the extensive railroad system of enormous capacity that led to more than a dozen major destinations throughout the United States and Mexico. When the Mandarin mentioned he was more interested in a local customer base, he was told that there were almost twenty million people living within a two-hour drive of the port and that San Francisco was just a couple of hours more.

The Mandarin made silent note of this. He also had a chance to see a few thousand of the almost twenty thousand employees that worked there. He asked his guide what the policy was for hiring people from prisons or with less than stellar records.

The shipping guide shook his head in disgust. "Americans give everyone a chance and second and third chances. They are so stupid."

WHEN THE SHIPPING official discovered that the Mandarin's Uber driver had abandoned him, he gladly gave the Mandarin a ride to the airport.

"I will not forget your kindness in giving me the ride," thanked the Mandarin.

"I'm glad to show a countryman around, especially one we will do business with soon!" grinned the driver.

"For sure. Goodbye."

"Goodbye."

The Mandarin took out the sheriff's gun and shot his host through the temple.

TWENTY-SIX

INTEL

Rayna walked into China HQ to find her fellow team-mates enjoying a glass of single malt while Julio proferred the latest intel.

"Hey, you should have waited for me," she sniped.

"No, Rayna, we need you to concentrate on the big fish. Any news there?" asked Barry.

"Yes, no given name, but Mary called him "The Mandarin," which is what Ling called the person who got her the job with Ming. Can't be a coincidence that there might be two people with the pretentious moniker of the Mandarin who are in the people recruitment business."

Julio's fingers flew across the keyboard. "Nothing that I can guarantee for sure just yet, but we may have just found the motherlode. There are at least a thousand workers that worked on the Zongtian schools that came from one as yet unidentified source."

Barry poured Rayna a healthy shot of the amber liquid. "Anything else?"

"Yeah, he runs a sweat shop in the old shanty town. I only saw the top floor where they make killer knock-off designer handbags, but the whole six floors must be making basketball shoes, women's clothing..."

Arthur took a sip of his scotch before offering, "Julio got enough on three of the lunchtime guests to make 'personal visits' worthwhile."

"Shouldn't I be going, too?"

Before Arthur could answer, there was a loud knock on the door. Chuck, the closest to the door, went to open it.

"Can I crash the party?" asked Henry as he stepped in.

"Have a seat. Want a drink?" asked Chuck.

"Not today, thanks."

"Good day, Dad?"

Henry let out a thoughtful breath of air. "It was a long ride to Ling's family's village and back but totally worth it. Ling's grandparents are salt-of-the-earth people."

"Yeah?"

"Yeah. The grandfather was happy and suspicious. Happy because Ling was back and suspicious that I wanted to take her to be my sex toy."

"Why would he think that?" Like a lot of kids, Rayna found it impossible to think of her parents having sex.

"Because I told him I was going to try to find a way to bring her back to Canada with me."

"You what? Why?"

Henry bounced his head up and down, a habit he had

when he was thinking about something that he really didn't have the answers to. "I had to, Rayna. 'Whatever you did for the least of these, you did for me.' I might need your help to pull this off."

Rayna had nothing to say. Her parents had always acted this way... it was why they adopted her. It's why Henry gave up a successful business career to become a pastor.

"I'll be glad to see what we can do," offered Barry. "Arthur and I know a person or two."

Relief shone on Henry's face. "That would be so kind of you if you did... How did your presentation go?"

Rayna hated to lie but the truth wasn't going to set her free. "Straightforward introduction to the firm. For the investors that Fidelitas wants to attract, they want to know who they're dealing with is successful. Look the part, act the part, be the part. You know that. You dealt with them all your working life."

"Sounds boring, but I guess this job is a lot safer than dealing with terrorists in the Middle East."

If you only knew. "Yeah, it sure is."

"Yeah, I am so glad you gave that up," Henry said with no small amount of relief in his voice. "Maybe you can concentrate on finding someone who will make me some grandchildren? Who knows? Maybe back in your home village."

"Speaking of which, why don't you take tomorrow as your personal day to visit your home village?" Arthur asked. "Just keep your cell phone on in case we need you."

"What are you guys going to do?"

"I'm sure Julio will find us something to do. Right, Julio?"

Julio's face beamed. "Most definitely."

TWENTY-SEVEN
NEW FAMILY

Flashback - Twenty-six Years Ago

It was an exciting time for newlyweds Henry and Vivian Tan. They had known each other for six years since the time they were both international students at the University of Washington in Seattle where Henry, from China, was studying commerce and Vivian, from Hong Kong, was studying to be a teacher. Sparks didn't exactly fly then but, after they graduated and Vivian moved back to Asia and Henry stayed to work in Seattle, they realized something was missing in their lives. That something was each other. An intense year-and-a-half long-distance relationship ensued with the culmination of a happy wedding day in Hong Kong. It was a dream wedding with over five hundred guests attending the wedding and reception at the luxurious Harborside Peninsula Hotel.

Though they were exhausted the next day, there was one duty to perform before they embarked on their European honeymoon—they had to visit the graves of

Henry's grandparents in a rural village in the Guangdong Province. They took a train from Hong Kong to the bustling metropolis of Guangzhou, and then hired a private taxi to the rural farming region of the Pearl River Delta to the village where Henry's grandparents were born: Golden Corner.

In this town of a couple hundred or so, everybody knew everybody and all claimed to remember Henry's grandparents. Grandfather Tan left the village in his teens as a newly married man to make his fortune in Beijing. Hard-working and clever, within two years he was able to bring his bride to live with him in the big city. He was always progressive—especially when he gave his three children Western names. His two sons were Benjamin and Tony, and his daughter was named Grace.

Tony married Lily and the two of them had Henry. While they would have liked more kids, China's "one child" policy was in full force and precluded that possibility. That was okay with Tony. A small family meant he could spend more time at work at his two bookstores. Although he was by no means wealthy, after Henry finished high school, Tony sent his son to Seattle to study at the University of Washington. There was one sad event that Henry had no control over. In the midst of his final exams, his beloved grandparents and father died in one of Beijing's frequent car accidents. His mother did not tell Henry until after exams were over.

Henry regretted missing the funeral services but promised his father and his grandfather's souls that he would pay his final respects and introduce his new bride when he got married.

Which is why today this newly married couple stood over a slightly elevated hump of grass in a knoll. There were no markers, plaques or tombstones—not even a piece of wood with someone's name on it. No, all there was, was a slight mound that indicated that something might be buried underneath it. It followed the customs of what people in this village had done for centuries: buried people in this quiet grassy field on the town's outskirts. One of the village elders led Henry here, assuring him this was definitely where his grandparents and father were buried. Henry bowed thankfully and gave the elder a lucky red bag of money. The elder left the young couple to pay their respects to their ancestors by themselves.

Henry lit eight incense sticks and held them with both hands. With fragrant smoke rising in the air, he raised the sticks above his head, then lowered them to belly-button level. He and Vivian bowed three times in front of the ancestors. Henry then planted the smoking shafts into the anonymous dirt mound.

"Grandpa, Papa, Grandma, I want you to meet Vivian. I met her when I was in school and we got married. I hope you will love her as much as I do."

Then it was Vivian's turn. She bowed deeply and respectfully.

"Mr. and Mrs. Tan, thanks so much for letting me marry your Henry. We will do our best to honor you."

The two bowed another three times, then started the walk back to the village.

Their ears perked up as they heard the sound of a female voice crying in the distance.

Henry pointed in the direction of the woods. "It's coming from over there."

The two quickly dashed in the direction of the sound and into the small forest.

"It's behind that tree," broke in Vivian.

The two quickly stepped to a gnarled pine tree and saw why there was so much yelling—a young girl was giving birth. The baby was almost out.

"Oh! Oh!" screamed the shaking, sweating girl.

Neither Henry nor Vivian had any experience at all in midwifery but, with no one else around, there wasn't a lot of choice. About the only thing that either of them knew about delivering babies was learned from watching the occasional hospital television drama.

THREE HOURS LATER, success. Ling, the new mother, slept as Henry and Vivian looked on.

Vivian rocked the baby in her arms. "She's so beautiful. Like a doll."

"More like a shriveled prune if you ask me," whispered Henry with a man's tact as he touched the baby girl's face.

Ling woke up, shuddering. Fear covered her face.

"It's okay. The baby's fine. You're going to be fine." Vivian offered the infant to the mother.

"I don't want her," cried Ling. "I never wanted her."

"She's beautiful. You must be so happy to have her."

"No! No!"

Post-partum syndrome set in fast.

"Don't press it, Viv," whispered Henry. "I've been thinking there is something wrong. Why else did she have the baby here in the middle of nowhere?"

Vivian shrugged her shoulders in ignorance.

"The baby must have been born out of wedlock. Otherwise, where's the father? Where's the family?" asked Henry seriously. "And maybe the issues are deeper."

He touched the girl. "Don't worry. Someone will take care of her. We can find someone in the village."

"NO! NO! Not there! You cannot stay. You must leave now! Take her with you!"

Ling struggled to get up. As fast as her tired body allowed, she sprinted away from the tree and into the field.

Henry dashed after her and took hold of the crying teenager.

"I cannot keep her. Please take her. You must. Please."

With typical male right-brain analysis, Henry thought he knew what the problem was. "Don't worry about the one-child policy. I will help you pay the fine and you can have another."

"It's not that. Not that at all. I don't want to bring another child into the world like me." Ling rolled up the sleeve on her arm to reveal a series of needle marks. Opium? Heroin? Who knew? Whatever it was, Ling felt that she was unfit to raise the child.

"Who is the father? Maybe he will take her," said Henry.

"He is the last person I want to raise her." She unbuttoned her blouse, revealing dark fresh bruises. "If he did this to me, what do you think he will do to her? You must take her. Please."

With that, she took off. This time, Henry did not follow her.

Vivian edged up to him, cradling the child. It was obvious to Henry that the bonding process had already begun.

To bring the baby back to America was not too difficult. Vivian told the airline and government officials that she was further advanced in her pregnancy than she thought.

Examining her documents, one official noted the baby as well as the date of their marriage. She gave a knowing wink. "Shotgun wedding?"

"Something like that."

THREE YEARS LATER, the reason that Rayna became part of the family was revealed to the devout Christian couple. They were unable to have natural children of their own.

TWENTY-EIGHT

FAIRY TALES COMING TRUE

Even though an awesome buffet breakfast was included in the price of the room at the Oceania, a pot of room service coffee was enough for Rayna and Henry this morning.

As they booted out the door, Rayna tried hard not to show her excitement.

"Rayna," called out Henry.

"Yes?"

"It's okay to be happy and excited."

Rayna grabbed her dad and gave him a big kiss.

FIFTEEN MINUTES LATER, they were riding with Tex in the limo, witnessing the Guangzhou sunrise.

"Now I don't want to disappoint you," explained Tex, "but the first thing to know is that it is no longer called 'Golden Corner.' It is all grown up now and called 'Golden City.'"

"Whatever."

Henry had not been back to the home village since he and Vivian arrived as newlyweds and left as young parents. As Tex drove, Rayna's father was both fascinated and dismayed by what he saw. Fascinated to see the changes from the bleak Communist country to a vibrant and thriving nation. Dismayed because urbanization, industrialization and commercialization had destroyed the quaint rural landscape.

"Look at China now. We're no longer just rice and chicken farmers," stated Tex proudly. "Chinese are now world leaders in everything. I will be, too, someday. I'm not going to be the driver of a car like this. I am going to own one! I have a plan."

"Okay, I'll bite," said the bemused Rayna. "The real reason I'm in China is to find investments. Tell me in thirty seconds what your idea is and, if I like it, I'll invest twenty-five thousand American dollars."

"Let's make a deal!" shouted Tex. The young wannabe cowboy couldn't believe his good fortune. A quick glance in the rearview mirror showed Tex that Rayna was serious.

"I want to turn my passion into a business. I want to start a chain of Texas-style barbecue restaurants, the "Texas Rangers." When you walk in, it's going be like walking into a saloon from the Wild Wild West. We start with food. Chili, of course, and all kinds of ribs—cooked over mesquite, marinated and barbecued over hickory, rubbed with spices then cooked over indirect heat. Then we're gonna have the clothes, hats, jeans, boots, lassoes.

We'll have big screen TVs to watch the Cowboys, the Oilers, the baseball teams..."

Rayna paused briefly, then announced, "It's so crazy it might work. I'll do it. And you're gonna need a lot more than twenty-five thousand. Even in China, I think it will cost at least a hundred thousand dollars per restaurant to get going. We will start off with six restaurants in Beijing. If it works the way I think it can, who knows how far it can go?"

Tex asked timidly, "Um, what's in it for me?"

"You get a straight ten percent of the profits."

"But it's my idea," protested Tex. "You have nothing without an idea. Ten percent is nothing."

"No, Tex. You are wrong. You have nothing without money and my group will finance everything. You are going to be the face of the restaurant. You will be everywhere."

"Can we make it twenty percent?"

"Fifteen and we have a deal."

"We have a deal!" yelled Tex. "I have so many great ideas. Do you think we can get John Wayne to come? He's amazing!"

"Tex, John Wayne's been dead for years."

"I know that. I'm talking about a lookalike. We get a look-a-like John Wayne and Jesse James. Maybe the real Clint Eastwood and Chuck Norris will come!"

Rayna loved Tex's enthusiasm. She had no doubt the Texas Rangers would be a colossal hit. Tex connected his Bluetooth to the ultra-smooth car stereo speakers. Greatest cowboy hits started blaring: Elvis with "Love Me Tender" and "Lonesome Cowboy." Hank Williams crooning, "I'm so Lonesome I could Cry," and "Ghost Riders in the Sky," sung by Johnny Cash.

For the next hour, Rayna, Henry and Tex sang along to these moldy oldies, ignoring almost everything as Tex sped along. After an hour, Tex made a turnoff and flicked off the music. He announced, "We'll be at Golden City in five minutes. What do you want to do first?"

"Let's just cruise the town and see what's happening."

"Your wish is my command."

Rayna winked at Tex. It's funny how you get a lot of cooperation when you've just agreed to invest over half a million dollars into someone's pipe dream.

TWENTY-NINE
BROTHERS

The three brothers—Ponytail, Sting and Johnny—were second generation gangsters. Their father, Big Mouth, had led the Destroyers, a small but ferocious gang in Guangzhou that trafficked drugs, girls, organ parts, luxury cars and antiques.

From an early age, Big Mouth had his sons doing target practice, martial arts, boxing and pumping one hell of a lot of iron. By the time they finished their teenage years, they were key lieutenants in his organization. Big Mouth trusted them with everything from punishing anyone stupid enough to try to skip out on a debt to making sure that heroin shipments reached their overseas destinations.

But what the brothers really loved were the cars. Big Mouth had a big garage in an industrial park and he imported luxury cars from abroad or stole them from rich local Chinese, modifying them so that new buyers never knew they were not legit. The boys spent hundreds of hours learning the finer points of paint jobs, changing or erasing VIN numbers, and how to sell the vehicles for big bucks without being caught.

While the fine attributes of culture were foreign to them, the huge easy money availed of dealing in rare antiques was not. When Big Mouth got the boys to raid museums, temples and collections for Chinese artifacts, they were initially dumfounded. Yes, they could understand how someone would pay half a million plus for a Ferrari or Bentley, but to shell out dough for an old vase or small carving? That was insane... and highly profitable.

However, it was an easy adjunct to the car biz. There was lots of storage space in the garage. And besides, many home owners who bought cars that the boys stole had crazy artifacts in the gardens or the entrances to their homes that were irresistibly easy pickings.

When their father was gunned down in a hail of bullets during a gang turf war over drugs, the boys realized that, as macho as they were, they were no match for the big boys and were lucky not to get killed themselves. They approached their father's rivals and made a deal—they would get out of all their family's operations except for the car and artifact businesses.

It was a no-brainer deal. Modifying cars was difficult and their father's enemies knew nothing about the art market. It took less than five minutes for the agreement to be struck.

STING, the youngest brother, was the "chauffeur" who spotted the brand new Mercedes Maybach at the airport.

He had been monitoring the vehicle, but the German car spent most of its time in busy parts of Guangzhou—not a good place to steal a car. The next day would have been perfect. The quiet powerful beast went on a long, largely rural road trip. It would have been ideal to snag the car then, but the brothers had to accompany their mother to their father's graveside in their home village to honor his memory. Criminal or not, this was an obligation that all Chinese fulfilled if they could on the anniversary of a loved one's death.

BIG MOUTH'S family stayed overnight in the father's village where they were treated like royalty. While they didn't have to pay for any meals or lodging, money gifts totaling ten thousand dollars were distributed.

They left early the next morning for the three-hour ride home, then dropped their mother off at her suburban home.

Now out on the open road, the China-manufactured Great Wall Motors SUV was crawling toward Guangzhou through the sea of motor vehicles. As Ponytail and Johnny dozed, Sting was fuming at yet another early morning traffic jam.

Suddenly, a loud honking sound emanated from Sting's phone. "Yes! That's the alarm telling us the Mercedes Maybach that I tagged at the airport has left the city."

"Cool," nodded Ponytail, the oldest brother and leader of the trio.

"Well, what are we waiting for? Let's go."

Ponytail shook his head. "Not quite so fast. Let's drop off our stuff at the warehouse first. Then we can bring everything."

"Do we really need to?" asked Johnny.

"Did you forget Dad? He was so excited about the huge score, he didn't realize he was walking into a trap. For a car like this, I want to have enough firepower to get the job done and then some."

No one argued with that logic.

THIRTY
DECISIVE

The Mandarin sat by himself staring at nothing in particular in his First Class pod on his return flight to China. He had spent less than sixteen hours in the United States, sixteen valuable hours he could not delegate to anyone.

Of course, he was almost overwhelmed by pain when he first heard about Jackson's death. Pain transformed to fury as he heard the sheriff describe the events. His initial reaction was to liquidate his assets, hire as many thugs as he could and go ballistic on America. However, he knew that decisions made strictly in the heat of passion almost always backfired. He needed time to chill before evaluating and, ultimately, acting. There was no one he trusted except himself to do it.

And now that he had completed his investigation, he could formulate a plan.

The Mandarin would not grieve. Grieving was a sign of weakness—but anger was not.

And the Mandarin was very angry. Righteously angry.

The Mandarin was not going to forgive. Nor was he going to forget.

First, the facts:

1. His only son Jackson was dead. Victim of a combination of prescription drugs, illegal drugs and alcohol in California. Sure, he had two daughters from a prior mistress, but they didn't count. Women, to the Mandarin, served one main purpose and that definitely was not running a multi-million dollar enterprise of the scope and complexity the Mandarin had built. He had counted on Jackson to do that.

2. The only person who died was Jackson. Sonny should have died, too. As should the bar staff that served the underage drinkers.

3. The town of San Roca was complicit in his son's death by not providing adequate emergency services. As a small town, much of its funding for services came from the state. Therefore, by this connective tissue, the state of California was guilty as well. But it went even beyond the state level. With over a trillion dollars that the United States had spent on the war on drugs, it was still as easy to get a hit of smack as a bag of potato chips.

The sheriff's death was at least a start.

The undertaker? His cavalier attitude was unforgivable. No one talked to the Mandarin like that.

The Uber driver and shipping clerk. Unfortunate collateral damage.

These were the facts as the Mandarin saw them.

And now it was time to determine the retribution. Who should be on the list?

Who else should be on the list?

Sonny. All the staff at Bangers. The president of Oceania College.

This small group would be easy. He would ask Mary to take care of it. He doubted that it would cost more than fifty thousand dollars to hire an assassin for two days' work at most.

But was this enough? Of course not. Nothing would ever be enough. But something...

And then the clouds of his mind departed and the cold light of clarity shone brightly.

America, you took away my son. You will repay with the deaths of one million of your own children. One million. One million. ONE MILLION.

What the punishment should be was now established. The next question was *How?*

TIMEFRAME, costs, method and personnel needed to be determined.

The Mandarin decided that the timeline was ASAP. Rationally, that meant at least a month for coordination. But that was too long. Punishment needed to be inflicted immediately.

The next questions were "how" and "how much?"

The "how much" question was fairly easy to answer. The Mandarin was worth over two hundred and fifty million dollars. About half of this was in cash or squirreled away in bank accounts around the world. Without Jackson, all this was meaningless. Not just for his late son, but also for himself, he needed to spend big—he would allocate up to half of his net worth to achieve his goal—half of two hundred and fifty million was one hundred and twenty five million.

Which meant the Mandarin was willing to spend up to a hundred and twenty-five dollars per death. Not that he expected to, but answering the question of "how much" would help answer "how?"

Hiring trained assassins with assault weapons and millions of rounds of ammo, and sending them into schools, theaters and malls, was not practical. He loved the idea but he just didn't have the connections or American infrastructure to pull it off.

Of course, dropping bombs on LA, San Francisco, Chicago and New York would produce the desired result in the shortest period of time but that wasn't going to happen either. Chances were that the planes would be blasted out of the sky long before they came close to an urban center. It was impractical but it gave him pleasure thinking of the havoc it would wreak.

As he pondered more, a cruel sneer formed across his face as a realistic plan began to form. His new partner in the American venture, Danny, could pull it off in a week. He had proven himself to the Mandarin and, while poisoning people with product was not what the gangster had in mind, the Mandarin figured that a ten million dollar payday plus expenses would be more than enticing.

The Mandarin had chosen the weapon. It was ironic

because he would use the same instrument of death that killed Jackson. Drugs.

He could hardly wait until the plane landed.

THIRTY-ONE

GOLDEN CITY

No longer a small village, the renamed Golden City was now a mid-sized industrial town. As the Mercedes drove up and down the streets, there was no sign of the old rural village that Henry's family was once part of.

"This isn't what I call a 'quaint, idyllic village,'" commented Rayna, citing a description she found on TripAdvisor.

In fact, there was not the slightest evidence of remotely quaint, idyllic or village-like in sight. It was more like a sterile junior metropolis. During the past quarter century, Golden Corner's population had mushroomed from a few hundred to a few hundred thousand. Shopping malls, busy streets and a spate of factories spewing smoke announced its arrival as part of the new China. There were zero older buildings and only slightly more people with gray hair in sight.

After the twentieth cookie-cutter street of characterless modernity, Tex asked, "What exactly are you looking for?"

An excellent question. Henry squinted, gritted his teeth and muttered, "Pull to the side and let me get my bearings."

Tex obediently pulled to the side of the road.

"Let's get out, Rayna, and go for a walk."

Tex shook his head, "You'll find every street is going to be the same. When the new companies take over, they bulldoze everything old and put up new buildings."

Rayna didn't know and Henry couldn't argue—he had seen this movie before. The three got out of the car and looked down a long street that seemed to be just like the others.

"This is nothing like I remember. So big, nobody, nothing I recognize. Where did they all come from?" murmured Henry with a twinge of nostalgia that longed for yesteryear.

Tex shrugged. "It's like Beijing or Shanghai or Guangzhou. Everyone goes there but no one is from there. Everyone comes for the jobs."

"There used to be woods and rice paddies and less than a hundred homes," Henry reminisced wistfully.

Rayna had been standing quietly, trying to get a handle on the tangle of feelings bombarding her. She had never been that interested in finding out about her birth parents. She always knew Henry was "Dad" and the late Vivian was "Mom." That was all that was important. She also knew that her birth mother gave her up because she knew she was unable to look after a baby for whatever reason, so Rayna had peace about that.

However, when she was at CenCom and watching Julio and Helena and their entourage of adopted kids from difficult circumstances adopted from around the world, that sparked something in Rayna. She wanted answers, too. What were her birth parents up to? Were they part of the new Golden Corner or had they left? Were they even alive?

For sure, her romantic vision of coming back to a small rural village had been shot down. What other surprises lay in store? Looking at this industrial complex, it seemed probably the answers were not here.

"I guess we can go then, Dad. Not much here to see," said Rayna nonchalantly.

Rayna's seeming indifference might fool some but Henry knew his daughter too well. "We're not going until we find something, Rayna. There has to be somebody who remembers something."

Rayna hid a grateful look as they hopped back in the limo. "Drive until you see some old buildings, Tex."

"No one wants to see that junk," sniffed the thoroughly modern Asian young man.

"Shut up, Tex," snapped Rayna.

Rayna's brusqueness jolted Tex. "Sorry. Sorry... My family was around during the Cultural Revolution and anything that hints of that terrible ancient time... I just don't want anything to do with it."

It was another reminder of the contorted, complex and confusing history of China's not-too-distant past, when Chairman Mao crushed a burgeoning capitalist and democratic growth. It resulted in families breaking apart with children accusing their parents of "bourgeois" activities. Books were burned, museums and artifacts destroyed. Students were ripped from schools to work in factories and farms. While it was ultimately unsuccessful, some felt the end of the Cultural Revolution began China's one hundred eighty degree turn toward "communistic capitalism."

The limo spent another fifteen minutes trolling the streets. All the buildings seemed to be variations of the same interchangeable mold—bleak, grey and spewing enough pollution to wreak havoc on the health of any living organism unfortunate enough to breathe its toxic smoke.

Then, a surprise.

Henry pointed to the end of a long street where an old, small concrete building stood by itself. "Let's check that out."

They drove up to it and parked. Getting out to take a better look, they discovered it was an old, ramshackle church. The only throwback to yesteryear in the village-turned-city, this church was definitely not an argument for "maintaining cultural heritage." With no upkeep, the exterior was deteriorating with ruts and cracks in the walls.

"In the rush to modernity and materialism, spirituality is often abandoned... China has forgotten its soul."

"You're preaching again, Dad."

"Sorry."

"Do you really want to see it?" asked Tex apprehensively. "It looks like it has ghosts in it."

"I thought the new Chinese didn't believe in ghosts," said Rayna.

"Of course, there are ghosts. We just can't talk about

it and I don't want to see one, either," replied Tex. "But whatever you do, I am not going in."

"You're a wuss." On the spur of a crazy moment, Rayna raised her hands and yelled, "Boo!"

"AAH! What the hell are you doing?" screamed Tex in genuine fear. "I'm going to sit in the car."

As Tex stepped back into the car and locked the doors, Henry turned to Rayna as they walked the few steps to the church.

Hanging on one of the double wooden doors at the church entrance was an information plaque. *This church was built by the London Missionary Society in 1888 by Dr. and Mrs. James Monroe. For current information, please contact Pastor Martin.*

The church obviously wasn't expecting a lot of inquiries because there was no contact information for the man of cloth.

Father and daughter stepped inside the battered place of worship.

THIRTY-TWO
MEMORIES COME ALIVE

Inside, there was no electricity and, despite the open windows airing the building out, there was a strong rancid smell. Clearly, this was not a church full of vibrant life.

Looking to the front, Rayna and Henry saw the back of a grey-haired woman of maybe seventy, by herself, kneeling in front of a large, rough-hewn wooden cross. Dressed in fashionless dark, drab clothing, she was the oldest person they had seen in this former village.

Henry whispered, "Let's wait for her to finish."

Rayna and Henry noiselessly and respectfully slipped into the back pew. As the moments passed, despite the physical signs of neglect and desolation, Rayna felt an inexplicable warmth coming over her. She tried to dismiss it, saying to herself that she was just being sentimental, but the truth was she couldn't deny this rich feeling of... waves of love engulfing her.

HENRY AND RAYNA gazed around the church while they waited for the old woman to finish praying. Looking at the walls, it was clear that, once upon a time, someone had bashed them with something hard—the patch job was spotty at best with obvious cracks and fissures. There were a dozen rows of old wooden pews that had burn marks on them. In all probability, this old building and its contents were victims of the youthful Red Guards during the Cultural Revolution.

Half an hour later, the old woman finished her intense praying. She forced her arthritic body to stand up from the floor and turned around, surprised to see others in the room. She glanced at Henry, then she and Rayna caught each other's eyes.

A shattered world suddenly found itself whole again. The old woman saw herself in Rayna and Rayna saw herself in the old woman.

They gingerly stepped toward each other. Rayna allowed the old woman to touch her cheeks, then to stroke her arms.

"Are you the one I have been praying for?" the old woman asked, voice barely rising above a whisper. "The one I thought I would never see...?"

This was just the beginning of a long conversation but, for now, these few words were all the communication needed.

Rayna and the old woman burst into tears.

"What is your name? I'm your grandmother, your *Popo*."

Rayna, former Special Forces operative, hardened veteran of innumerable enemy kills, current investment advisor handling millions, couldn't move or say anything to this frail, elderly Chinese woman.

Henry stepped in. "This is the baby girl I helped deliver more than twenty-five years ago, the last time I was here in Golden Corner. Ling gave her to us and what a wonderful gift she has been! Her English name is 'Rayna.'"

Popo's face beamed. "Such a wonderful name." She looked at Henry. "Where is the woman who helped you deliver Rayna?"

"Vivian passed away a couple of years ago," said Henry quietly.

Daring to hope, Rayna uttered quietly, "My mother? Where is she? Can I see her, Popo?"

Popo fought back a tear. "She went to hide from that man... your father. She has not come back. Maybe she doesn't know he is dead."

Rayna swallowed, stifling the outburst of emotion welling in her that screamed to release itself. "My father is dead?"

The old woman's eyes caressed her granddaughter, trying to soothe her inner turmoil. "I never liked him. Ling didn't like him... but he just forced himself on her... God is just."

Twenty-seven Years Ago

Jimmy, a strong, powerful man of twenty-five, chased after Chew, a man more than twice his age, through the dirt streets of Golden Corner.

"Where is that bitch daughter of yours? Where is my wife?"

The local gangster thug, brandishing a gun in each hand, fired at Chew but the would-be victim was nimble and, with random side-stepping, he avoided each zinging bullet.

"She is not your wife. My daughter would never marry an animal like you," shouted Chew as he hit the end of the block and turned around the corner of the church.

However, Chew was not fast enough to escape all the hot wads of lead. Three of them found their target: one in his arm, one in his back, the other in his leg.

"AA!" screamed Chew as he tripped, bleeding. On all fours, he painfully crawled past the church and rounded the corner.

Jimmy slowed down—no need to rush any more. He strode confidently, squeezing each gun and ready to fire. Lips curling, he sneered, "You will die, old man."

As Jimmy turned onto the street that Chew bled down, a hundred-and-fifty pound piece of timber came bashing down on his skull before he could unleash his small, deadly missiles. Chew had summoned every bit of strength he had to lift the log that weighed even more than he did.

Jimmy's body started to spasm as he hit the ground, but not before he saw a hole in the front of Chew's shirt— one of his bullets that whistled into Chew's back went right through his body and exited through the front.

Summoning strength from who-knew-where, the profusely bleeding Chew lifted the log one final time. His final act of life was to flatten Jimmy's skull, preventing him from ever hurting anyone again.

. . .

POPO POINTED to the wooden cross that hung on the wall at the front of the church. "That was made from the log that killed your father... "

"Chew was my *Gong Gong* (grandfather)... your husband?"

A longing look filled Popo's face. It had been a long time since she had bottled up her feelings. "Yes, Gong Gong was a good man, a farmer," she said, whispering hoarsely. "He always made sure that Ling and I had enough to eat before he ate himself... Those were hard years."

"My birth father, Jimmy, he was a farmer, too?"

"No. His family was all bullies—rich people in the village. They just took whatever they wanted. The only reason Ling married him was that he threatened to kill all of us if she wouldn't. But she could take it for only a few months before she couldn't take it anymore and ran away."

"Even though she was carrying... me? His baby?"

"Especially because of you, Rayna. Ling knew that Jimmy could never be a proper father." She turned to Henry. "You saved her."

"But where did Ling say she was going, Popo? Where is she?" asked Henry.

Popo sighed, clearly disturbed. "To hide in 'Heaven's Gate Monastery.'"

"Where is that?" asked Henry.

The old woman shook her head, balling her fists tightly. "I don't know. I looked everywhere. There is nothing with that name anywhere."

Nobody had noticed but, during the time Popo,

Henry and Rayna were talking, a thin bearded man in his forties dressed in clerical garb entered the church. "Hello, Popo."

Grandmother looked to him and cried out, *"Mook see! Mook see!* (Minister! Minister!) This is my granddaughter, Rayna! She has come to visit from America!"

The minister looked guardedly at Rayna, then bowed. "Very pleased to meet you."

Trained in psychology and having to judge people instantly as a soldier, Rayna detected telltale signs of anxiety in the shepherd. Slight compression of lips, a bit of blinking before settling down, a tense bending of fingers... *He's hiding something.* "Nice to meet you, too. Pastor...?"

Rayna's careful attitude was obvious and the man gently responded. "Long ago I was Lau but now everyone calls me Martin."

Henry and Rayna were dumfounded. "You're Pastor Martin?"

Martin nodded. "After Martin Luther." Looking at Henry, he asked, "And you are?"

"I am Henry. I'm Rayna's father."

"You are very blessed, Henry."

That's a strange comment. "Yes, I guess so." Henry's eyes penetrated Martin's for answers. Henry sensed Rayna's unease and yes, there was something about Martin's attitude that didn't jive.

"Martin is so good to us," praised Popo, oblivious to the tension. "He is the only person who did not take a job with the factories. He just makes sure that all of us are well, teaches about Jesus on Sunday and makes sure we all get to Heaven when we die!"

"Popo, I am nothing special." Eyes inhaling her, Martin turned to Rayna. "What brings you to China?"

"I work in investments and there are some opportunities in China. I'm here for meetings. While I'm here, I wanted to see if I could find out something about my birth parents."

Martin gave Henry a wary look. "I see. Have you found out anything?"

"Yes, my birth father was a brute who drove my mother away." She glanced at Popo. "If my grandfather hadn't killed him, who knows where I'd be... If my father..." Rayna glanced at Henry, "...hadn't helped Ling give birth and been willing to take me in, I don't know what would have happened to me."

"Well, Ling, Rayna's birth mother, didn't give us much of a choice," said Henry remorsefully as he ruminated on the young girl in the field. "Rayna was my one and only opportunity to be a midwife. Thank God I didn't screw that up. You know, it's funny how God works. Only He would have known that Vivian and I wouldn't be able to have kids and He gave us Rayna on our honeymoon... Rayna asked me to join her here so she could find out something about where she came from, but I don't think I can help—everything here has changed... Even my grandfather's grave site—I think there's a factory sitting on it now."

"No, no," disagreed Popo. "The cemetery was a little way out of town in the other direction. It's still there. Why don't you take them there, Martin? I want to make a special meal for my granddaughter and celebrate."

As Rayna shifted uncomfortably, Henry asked,

"Would you mind, Martin? We would be so grateful if you did."

Martin bowed deeply. "I would be honored to do so."

"Excellent. Excellent," exclaimed Popo. "This will be the best meal you have ever eaten."

Rayna flashed a smile that could melt an iceberg. "I'm sure it will be," said the newfound granddaughter, eyes glowing as she threw a gaze back at her grandmother.

As Martin, Henry and Rayna walked toward the church exit, Popo called out, "Don't be too long!"

"Yes, Popo! We'll be quick," exclaimed Rayna, steps tingling in a way they never had before.

Popo. It has such a nice ring to it. The old woman turned and knelt before the cross again. "Thank you, God, for letting me see what I thought I would never ever see..."

THIRTY-THREE

TRUTH BE TOLD

As Rayna, Henry and Martin closed the door to the church, Martin confided, "Popo's getting a little old. There is no cemetery and yes, there is a factory on the hill where our ancestors rest."

Rayna abruptly stopped. Sharp eyes turned to Martin. "What is really going on, Martin? You haven't stopped undressing me with your eyes since we met."

"Rayna, stop it," chided Henry. "Any man with a pulse would give a second and third look at you."

"Dad, I work in intelligence. I know when something's not right and this has nothing to do with sex." She glared at Martin. "You cringed when Popo told you I was her granddaughter. I saw you clench your fist when Henry introduced himself as my dad and I saw the trembling in your hands." Rayna reached into her purse and pulled out a revolver. "I'm not taking any chances. Now, what is it? Who sent you?"

Henry was stunned to see Rayna so confidently ready to shoot someone, but Martin provided the greater surprise. His face softened as he exhaled a small groan of relief. He forced a whisper. "Yes, I have been looking at you, but not for the reasons you think. Can you wait here for a few minutes while I go back to the church? I live there and need to do something."

"Go with him, Dad." She handed Henry her gun. "And use it if you need to."

"Okay," exhaled Henry nervously.

Henry reluctantly followed Martin into the church. Popo was still on her knees. Martin opened a door and led Henry into a small room that housed a bed and sink. Martin fished a pair of scissors out of a box from under the bed and then stood in front of the wash basin.

Martin began snipping off his beard.

"What are you doing?" quizzed a flabbergasted Henry.

"I have had this beard for twenty-six years trying to disguise who I am, but there is no need for me to hide anymore. Especially with Rayna here."

"You are confusing me, Martin. Why are you concerned with what she thinks?"

"You will see," replied Martin enigmatically.

For the next five minutes, while Henry pointed the gun at him, Martin cut off the straggly hairs of his beard. He then reached under the sink and pulled out a rusty razor. After splashing some water on his face, he began shaving off the stubble. With the gun aimed unwaveringly, Henry watched Martin carefully, studying his every move. As the hair on Martin's face disappeared, Henry's impatience turned to *Oh, my God.*

Henry put the weapon into his pocket—he didn't need it.

When Martin was almost done, Rayna, without warning, barged in the door. "What the hell is taking you so long?"

Martin, now clean-shaven, turned around. There was a hint of melancholy on his face as he looked at her.

"It's okay, Rayna." Henry held Rayna's hand.

Pain and joy welled in Martin's eyes. "Rayna, I would never hurt you... I am your father, too. I am the one responsible for giving you life on earth."

Rayna had survived launches of grenades, stab wounds, shots in the leg, had an arm broken by vicious insurgents but nothing had ever hit her as hard as Martin's last few words. "You? My birth father?"

Henry looked at the two of them and there seemed to be no resemblance at all—unlike the obvious similarities between Rayna and her grandmother. "It's true, Rayna," whispered Henry.

"But how can you know?"

"Look at your faces," ordered Henry.

Martin and Rayna complied.

"Notice anything unusual?"

Both shook their heads.

Henry's voice sharpened and his eyes focused on the pair. "That's because both of you have exactly two identical unique physical traits. You are so used to them you don't think they are out of the ordinary."

"What's that?" asked Martin.

"Both of you have earlobes attached directly to your

head. That's a hereditary trait caused by a recessive gene."

"That's not enough, Dad," responded Rayna.

"No, but now smile at each other."

The two grinned—each of them had a prominent dimple on the right cheek in exactly the same spot. Rayna stared at Martin, heart pounding. "But I thought Popo said my birth father was killed by my grandfather for beating her." In the past half hour, Rayna's world had turned upside down.

Martin shook his head. "That's what everybody thought. I never told anybody the truth... Ling and I loved each other... she got pregnant. We were both scared. Jimmy didn't know about it when he forced her to marry him. But she couldn't hide it from him. They had only been married a short time and she was already getting big. That's why he beat her. To find out who the father was... That's why she ran away... to protect you. And me."

"Didn't Jimmy or anybody suspect the two of you were together?"

"Your mother, Rayna, was the sweetest and most beautiful girl. Guys not only in Golden Corner but from all the surrounding villages were interested in her. They gave her pastries, bags of rice, vegetables, fresh fish, wood for the fire..."

"So how did she choose you?" queried Rayna, full of curiosity.

"I was different. I didn't give her anything but I... I read to her. She loved poetry and so did I. I read to her for hours and hours. Then one day, when we were alone in the woods... the place where you were born... she kissed me. Half an hour later, well, I guess that was your beginning."

Martin turned to Henry. "Months later, when you found her, she had been hiding in those same woods for three days, sick with fear Jimmy would find her and kill her... I'm glad you took care of her. You did a better job than I could ever have done."

"What happened to her after she left?" asked Henry. "Vivian and I always wondered."

Little rivers rolled down Martin's cheeks. "She came back late at night to say goodbye to me. She was extremely weak from childbirth. I stole a car and we were going to run away together. But I had never driven and was terrified of driving and I... I got into an accident. I survived but Ling didn't... I am still haunted by the memory of causing her death."

Rayna and Henry exchanged glances. Up until she joined Fidelitas, Rayna had hated driving and avoided it whenever she could. Most people thought that was just a quirk or oddity in her personality, but hearing Martin shed a different light... Could there possibly be some kind of psychic connection? Another inherited quirk?

"What about my mother? Where is she then? Popo said she's in Heaven's Gate but she didn't know where that was and I couldn't find anything on the internet either."

A warm and impish expression came across Martin's face. "I didn't want to lie to your Popo but I couldn't exactly tell her the truth, either. Yes, she is at a monastery. When I took Ling, she was on one side of

Heaven's Gate... then she crossed over to the other... I will take you there."

The three stepped out of Henry's room and looked at the wooden cross on the wall. Because it was a Protestant church, there was no body of Jesus hanging on the cross, but it wasn't hard to imagine the bleeding Christ with nails pounded through his hands. A few moments of contemplation and the meaning of sacrificial death took on a whole new meaning.

Then another coincidence or a miracle, or was it synchronicity, struck Rayna. She stopped to look at her two fathers. "Both of you are pastors. Now what is that all about?"

"Probably nothing," said Henry. "Or maybe everything."

Martin smiled. "Let's go."

THIRTY-FOUR

THE BEST LAID PLANS

"Where the hell is he?" Mandarin was in a quiet spot in the Guangzhou airport where he had been trying to get hold of Danny for the past half hour. He had called three different numbers and sent multiple texts, but there had been no response. Normally, he would give up and move on, but the Mandarin didn't trust or know anyone else he could use.

Fed up, he called someone else he knew would always answer.

"Hello, Mandarin. I hope you are well."

The Mandarin hid his anger but not his impatience. Normally, he put up with the inanities of "How are you?" or "Glad to hear from you," but not today.

"My health is of little consequence. I need you to contact Danny. I want to step up our North American drug distribution. See when he's free. The sooner, the better. I tried but can't get through."

"I'll set something up."

"Good. I'll call you back in a few hours."

The Mandarin clicked off, then punched in another number.

"Mandarin, so soon?" answered a surprised General Park. He didn't expect to hear from the Mandarin for another three weeks. "Good to hear from you, my friend."

"Can we meet? I've decided to do something in America."

The Mandarin could hear the smile in the general's voice. "I knew you would come around. Shall we meet next Monday in Pyongyang? I will arrange for some extra special delights."

"How about Linfu? Today. In three hours. At the airport."

"I will be there."

"Good." Again, the Mandarin ended the call without pleasantries.

General Park recognized the undertone of urgency. Normally, the Mandarin would be delighted to indulge in the deviant pleasures that he arranged in the North Korean capital. The fact that the Mandarin wanted to meet in Linfu, on the China side of the North/Korean border meant this would be a quick, no-nonsense trip.

Park beamed. That meant fast money was coming. The only question was, "How much?"

MARY WAS INTRIGUED. From the time she started working for him, the Mandarin had been resolute that he didn't want to do business in America—until just recently when he finally relented to Danny's badgering.

She had monitored the experiment and knew that it was wildly successful. If the Mandarin insisted on talking to him, this was going to be big. For her, it meant that she might travel sometimes to Los Angeles, San Francisco, New York. All those places where she... she could allow herself to be who she was.

She looked up Danny's number on her Rolodex and called. There was no answer and no voicemail. That meant nothing. In this business, you wanted to leave as little traceable footprint as possible. She would call back until she finally connected.

THIRTY-FIVE

HUNDRED HANDS

The-two hour drive north on the main highway in the Mercedes passed by quickly as the re-united family approached the Jade Mountains. They had a lifetime of catching up to do. Martin never married. He figured he'd done enough damage for one lifetime. Rayna told him about being in the military while Henry told of his family roots in Golden Corner and subsequent journeys to Beijing, Seattle, Hong Kong and Vancouver.

"You should visit sometime, Martin," invited Henry.

"Maybe someday," answered Martin, not wanting to share that was something he could never afford.

Henry read through the reluctance instantly. "I'm serious. Our church will sponsor you to talk about Christianity in China The problems, the promises, the possibilities."

Martin's eyes glistened. "I would need at least a week to talk about that."

"Exactly. You could stay with me."

It was amazing how quickly bonding occurred

between the two fathers. While Henry and Martin engaged in a discussion about abstract matters of Christianity and China, Rayna looked outside, studying the transformation in scenery. In the distance, stone peaks towered above white clouds. At the sides of the road, they noticed young, flowering Phoenix trees and jade-colored lakes.

Martin's eyes perked up when he saw a side dirt road that led up a mountain. The Chinese pastor pointed. "Go there."

"That's going to wreck the car," objected Tex. "Can't you just walk?"

"It's steep and five miles."

"Okay, okay."

The bumpy, slow crawl up was fascinating. They passed little stone bridges built perhaps a thousand years ago when monks first came here. Interspersed among the richly-hued flora, eons of nature had shaped red sandstone rocks into unusual formations—one looked vaguely human, another like a bird, others like animals.

And suddenly, a dirt clearing. Tex gently braked to a halt.

"We are here," announced Martin. "The Hundred Hands Temple or, as I told Popo, the 'Heaven's Gate.'"

The temple was not nearly as big as those found in the cities, but that did not stop it from being spiritually and visually impressive. Behind an ornately colorful front mountain gate guarded by two ferocious stone lions stood a red pillared gate with no doors. A slate sign hung on the Chinese-style curved roof with gold Chinese characters.

Tex inched the limousine farther into the dirt clearing by the temple entrance.

"Not a lot of cars come here, I guess. No parking lot," stated Tex as he hopped out and opened the doors for his passengers.

"More than you think," corrected Martin, stepping out and heading toward the temple grounds. "I come here every year to say hello to Ling."

"Right. I'm going to stay and guard the car. Don't want anybody to steal it," declared Tex with false bravado, trying to hide his anxiety.

"You mean you don't want the spirits in the temple getting mad at you for a thousand lifetimes of your sins," replied a poker-faced Rayna.

"Don't talk like that. The spirits can hear," croaked the alarmed chauffeur. "And, if something happens to me, who's going to run 'The Texas Rangers?'"

"George Bush?" asked Rayna.

"Never heard of him," said the Chinese limo driver. "Is he a cowboy, too?"

"A lot of people think so."

MARTIN, Henry and Rayna walked through the gate and stopped to savor the sight of a functioning thousand-year-old Buddhist monastery. There was a long courtyard flanked by ancient stone buildings. Orange-robed monks with shaved heads were sweeping the walks, chanting, and entering or leaving any of the dozen buildings.

Immediately in front of them was a circular bronze brazier filled with lit coals.

Further down a hundred feet from the entrance were twin two-story pagoda-like buildings: the Drum Tower and the Bell Tower. Throughout the courtyard were upright wooden or stone columns, inscribed with Chinese writing

"The cemetery is through the back. Follow me." As Martin led, none of the monks paid any attention to them. "Don't worry about it. They're not tour guides."

The monastery was a treasure trove of antiquity that Henry and Rayna marveled at. There was a wall with nine huge dragons carved into its stone that guarded the complex from invading evil spirits. Rayna noted the care of detail put into the small complex of ancient concrete buildings, statues of Buddha and grimacing temple guardians, intricate wooden and stone carvings and religious artifacts. In the center of the temple courtyard, a one-storied pagoda stood, with a sharp steeple pointing to the heavens. As they passed the Great Hall of Heavenly Kings, they looked inside to see a giant, laughing bronze fat Buddha-like figure sitting cross-legged with one hundred arms and hands uplifted to the skies.

As they continued, Martin stopped in front of the largest building. "This is the Main Chamber. Take a look."

Henry and Rayna were in awe. Three serene Buddhas in meditation pose sat on Lions' Thrones. Beside them, half a dozen monks sang, accompanied by temple musicians playing a Chinese zither, oboe, bamboo flute and percussion.

It took them to another time, another place, preparing them...

Finishing their passage through the courtyard, they entered the temple gardens. At the far end, they could see the cemetery flanked by two Chinese swamp cedar trees and a larger forested area behind

"Over there," pointed Martin. "Those trees are over five hundred years old."

As the trio walked over a stone bridge that covered a babbling brook of crystal waters, Rayna asked Martin, "If you're a Christian pastor, how did you come to bury your wife at a Buddhist monastery?"

"Back then, I hadn't seen the light. I didn't know any better. Jesus, Buddha... everybody was all the same. I had no idea where to take Ling's body but had heard about the Goddess with a hundred hands of mercy. Ling needed mercy and I thought that a hundred hands were a lot better than my two. I brought her here."

When they arrived at the ancient trees, a number of small pagodas were revealed. These more elaborate structures were for senior members of the monastery who had passed away. There were many more little shrines and plaques for monks who had not achieved the necessary level of enlightenment.

"Where is she?" asked Rayna.

"Not yet," said Martin. They walked past the graveyard to the base of a taller tree—a hundred-foot-tall camphor tree. Looking upward to its glossy, waxy leaves, Martin recalled, "When I buried her, this tree was not even up to my waist. Seeing its growth is like the love I still feel. Growing upward and always."

Martin knelt and brushed off a small plaque at the camphor's base. The plaque had two words engraved on it: *Love* and *Ling*.

He got up and the three stood reverently beside each other.

"Hi, Mom," said Rayna. Words eked out slowly as her emotions took over. "I haven't seen you for a long time but I just wanted to thank you for giving me the chance for the life you never had... I'm here with my dad right now. Actually, I'm here with both of my fathers." A small gasp of air emanated from Rayna's mouth. "My mom, well, she's... I guess she's with you up there somewhere... I guess that sounds kind of stupid. You're my mom, too..."

Henry squeezed his overwrought daughter's hand and took over. "Hello, Ling. It's good to see you again. This is your baby that Vivian and I helped deliver. She's all grown up now. Thank you for entrusting us with this precious gift." Eyes full of grateful tears, he turned to Martin. "And thank you, too, Martin."

"I'm glad you were there at just the right time. But, then again, we know it wasn't a coincidence, don't we?" Martin lifted his hands in prayer. "Almighty God, only You could have ordained this time where what was lost is found. What was hurt is reconciled. Thank You for giving Ling and me the chance to see Rayna. Bless her always. In Jesus' name. Amen."

Martin stooped down and dug some dirt out from the base of the plaque. After a few minutes, he had dug down about six inches and pulled out a small metal box. He opened it. Inside was a gold ring. "Ling would want you to have it... I want you to have it."

Rayna took the ring. She tried fitting it onto a number of her fingers. The only finger that it properly fit was her right hand pinkie. She held it up to the sun and beamed as the sunlight glinted on the minuscule diamond.

"It was all the money I had," an embarrassed Martin explained. "I'm not sure the gold is pure, either."

"I love it," beamed Rayna. "It's perfect."

Martin's face glowed.

THIRTY-SIX

GETTIN' READY

"Are you sure the tracking unit is reading right? Who would drive a half million dollar car on a road like this?" snapped Ponytail as their SUV began the dirt trek up the mountain.

Johnny checked the coordinates on the tracking device. "No, it's good." He did a quick internet search on his smart phone. "Can you believe it? There's a temple up here in about five miles." He read off his phone's small screen. "Hundred Hand Buddhist Temple was established in AD 500 in a remote rural area, a hundred and fifty miles northwest of Guangzhou City. An unheralded gem, the temple and monastery is home to a hundred monks."

Sting shouted, "Now I know there is a God and He loves us!"

THIRTY-SEVEN
EUPHORIA

Linfu was a pretty city by the Yalu River on the Chinese side of the North Korea/China border. Its two million people were largely Chinese, but there were also close to sixty thousand ethnic Koreans. The Linfu Airport was remarkably small for a city of Linfu's size. There was only one terminal but, even with that, traffic wasn't a whole lot—maybe two incoming or outgoing flights per hour. However, despite its limited use, those that did travel were important in terms of the economy of Northern China and North Korea. Linfu was a major portal for the Hermit Kingdom to China and the world at large for goods, money and intelligence, legal and illegal. Because of this, Linfu crawled with spies and informants from both the Chinese and North Korean regimes.

The Mandarin's Air Beijing flight landed five minutes early and it was easy for General Park to spot the Mandarin as he entered—there was only one entrance from the landing strip to the terminal.

"Welcome, my friend. What would you like to eat,

Mandarin?" asked the friendly general. Out of the hundred times that the two had met over the years, ninety-seven percent of the time involved a meal or some other kind of hospitality when business was conducted. "Chinese or Korean?"

The Mandarin said quietly, "I've been sitting on planes for more than thirty hours in the last couple of days. I think I need to stretch out my legs. Do you mind going for a walk on the Yalu River?"

Decoded, this meant, "I want a private conversation without risk of anyone knowing what we are talking about." In any dealings with North Koreans, caution was mandatory at all levels of the military, government and general public.

"Splendid idea." General Park patted his rotund tummy. "Maybe it'll go away."

PARK UTILIZED simple strategies for survival in the tumultuous and unpredictable North Korean regime. While overpaying bribes was key, it was also important to draw as little attention to himself as possible. This included his choice of cars. While he could have been one of the few North Koreans to afford a luxury European sedan, he chose instead to drive a modest North Korean-made sedan. After a few minutes of mindless chit chat about the weather and their perennial discussion of the best cognacs, the general parked his car close to the river-bank where the two got out for their private stroll.

"So what are you interested in, my friend?" asked the general.

"The new synthetic drug you told me about at our last meeting. I want to eliminate some people."

"You're not going to hire a hundred gangbangers to do your dirty work?" snickered the North Korean military leader, reminding the Mandarin of their recent conversation.

"Ten thousand are not enough to do what I want to do."

Park stopped. This had suddenly become very interesting. "What are you talking about?"

The Mandarin looked his comrade directly in the eye. "One million people. I want to kill one million Americans."

Park's eyes bulged and his mouth opened wide. One million of the people that North Koreans hated more than anyone else. One million of the animals that had killed twenty percent of their population during the Korean War, that tore off the limbs of their children and cut off their noses and lips. If he, the General, could be part of their destruction, his place in the halls of history would be made forever... not to mention the potential profits.

"I am completely on your side but this is not an inexpensive proposition."

"Of course not. Working with you has never been the cheapest way to do things. I want to make you some money."

"Which means you want to make some money, too.

You didn't need to make a special trip just to tell me that, Mandarin."

"Park, there is no money for me at all in this. But this must be done."

"Of course I will do whatever you require."

"I want to use N115 as my weapon. How soon can you deliver it?"

"It's still experimental. I don't know if I can..."

Before he finished speaking, the Mandarin threw his hands around Park's neck. His congenial veneer vanished as he started squeezing. "Don't play games with me. Are you ready to talk?"

"Yes," gurgled the hapless general.

"Good." The Mandarin released his hold on Park's thick neck.

The general wiped the sweat off his brow with his sleeve. "Are you crazy, Mandarin?"

"You are wasting my time and I want to get started. Tell me more about it."

Park looked at the Mandarin. There was something definitely different today about the Mandarin—it was all business. *Good.* "N115, like other synthetic drugs, gives this incredible high."

"You told me that. How about after you decompress? Hypertension? Loss of appetite? Fatigue like the others?"

"None of our test cases have gotten that far. They're dead within three hours."

"What's the success rate?"

"We've tried it on twenty prisoners. Every one of them died. There is no antidote."

"So what is the downside?"

"It's extremely toxic. Just don't be stupid enough to try it yourself."

The Mandarin did some mental arithmetic. If it were one hundred percent effective and there was zero wastage, it would take maybe five kilograms. That, of course, would never happen. There was bound to be some wastage. The Mandarin budgeted for ten kilograms.

"What's the cost? I don't want to haggle. Just give me your best price to start with. Ten kilograms."

Park's adrenaline began pumping. "That's enough to kill everyone in a mid-sized city."

"Exactly. Now what is your price? I want delivery ASAP."

"Two million dollars per kilogram and it will be delivered in ten days."

"I'm not going to bargain but I will only agree to the price if you can deliver in a week."

The North Korean started breathing hard. What the Mandarin wanted was an enormous amount, a hundred times more than presently existed on earth. But the money was irresistible. Normal prices of high quality crystal meth was up to a hundred grand per kilo, a lot more if it were sold to Aussies, the country with the world's highest addiction rates. But N115 wasn't a recreational drug in that sense...

"You have a deal."

"Agreed. We will be in touch about delivery details. I will arrange for a five million dollar deposit."

"Ten," said the general firmly. "I'll have to pay a premium to get such quick delivery."

"Done."

Park sucked in a huge gulp of air. All his life, he had waited for a break but he never expected one of this magnitude nor that it would come from a Chinese. "Why are you doing this, Mandarin?"

The Mandarin took a deep breath, then spoke solemnly. "The Americans killed my only son and they blamed him for what happened. That is unforgivable... and I will not forgive. I will take one million of their children in return. They killed my son with their lax laws on drugs. I want to teach them a lesson."

All crystallized for the military officer. "You want justice. I understand. This is *the Mandarin's Vendetta*."

"Exactly." The Mandarin tilted back his head and looked upward. "General Park... I want to see for myself that N115 works."

"In that case, you've got to come back to Pyongyang with me."

PART THREE
SQUEEZED

THIRTY-EIGHT

CHANGE OF PLANS

The Mandarin would go berserk when he found out. Mary was so paralyzed that she couldn't leave her desk even though her work had been done two hours ago.

But she wouldn't leave until she talked to her boss.

RING. Finally, an answer.

"Hello, Mandarin."

"What did Danny say? Is he free tonight? I need him to join me."

"Mandarin, Danny's dead."

The Mandarin hadn't asked what happened but Mary was so nervous that words sped out of her mouth. "He was pushed off the balcony by his anorexic ninety-five-pound sixteen-year-old singer mistress. And he was forty-three! She was angry because he let her precious Persian cat fall over the balcony ledge. She was so mad, she flew at him and the two tumbled over the rail. Only the stupid white cat survived."

Mary could feel the fumes steaming out of the Mandarin's head over the phone.

"What an idiot. Killed by a whore? What kind of man is that?" snarled the Mandarin. "I've got to find someone else like Danny. Someone who knows shipping and distribution of drugs in the United States." The Mandarin grunted out loud, like an exasperated ape.

Mary bit her tongue. This was uncharacteristic behavior for the Mandarin. It was a bit of a concern that she, who usually knew everything about what went on with the Mandarin's operations, was kept completely in the dark.

There was an uncomfortable silence for what seemed like an eternity to Mary although, in reality, it probably wasn't more than fifteen seconds.

Then, the Mandarin spoke. Quietly, firmly and with a knife edge in his voice. "I have the biggest project I have ever done ahead of us," began the Mandarin. "We are going to kill one million Americans."

Mary gasped. While she was just an employee expected to carry out orders and not question her boss, in this case, the magnitude of what her boss just said was... spectacular... and insane. She blurted out, "Why?"

She immediately regretted asking and was shocked when the Mandarin answered. "Jackson died from American incompetence. They let him die from a drug overdose. I'm going to make them pay. They will weep and wail for years."

So that's the reason. Mary felt a slight remorse. While she didn't love Jackson, with the Mandarin so busy at work, it was left up to the forty-five-year-old single woman to look after the details in Jackson's life, about the closest she would ever come to being a mother.

She knew the Mandarin better than to offer support or condolences. *Keep it business. Don't ask 'how?'* "Is there anyone else you want me to contact?" ventured Mary carefully.

"There isn't anyone I trust but I definitely need someone... Can you think of anyone?"

Mary was flabbergasted. The Mandarin had never asked for her opinion before.

"There is someone. When you said you couldn't go to the lunch yesterday, I took the liberty of taking your place at this one."

"I have no idea what you're talking about. What lunch was that?"

"The one that had the invitation of the girl with the gun and the bikini. They were very professional... and they knew about Zongtian. And one more thing."

"What?"

"We watched live as Wen was killed in prison. Chopstick to the throat at lunch... it was something neither we nor anyone else was able to arrange."

Time hung in the air. Mary had no idea of knowing whether she would be fired with the next sentence or praised. With the Mandarin staying quiet, she continued. "They have worked on some big names. Cartels. Casinos. Drug runners. Arms dealers. Their Hong Kong office is a satellite. Their head office is in San Francisco... They moved a billion dollars from China to North America last year from all sources. I got the impression that what they don't do, they can easily pull off."

"Call them now. Let's find out how real they are."

While the Mandarin had given her the go ahead to

contact someone else, she was nervous. Was she really that impressed with what Fidelitas had to offer... or was it... Mary punched a number into her phone.

"Fidelitas Enterprises, may I help you?" greeted the friendly but businesslike female receptionist at the CenCom in California in Mandarin.

"I'd like to speak to Mr. Arthur Yang. I met him at a lunch he hosted the other day," said Mary.

"You must be Mary Wu. I hope your boss is feeling better."

"Much better, thank you... How did you know it was me?"

"You were the only female guest at the luncheon. I will patch you through to Mr. Yang. It'll take a few moments if you don't mind holding."

"Please take your time."

Mary was impressed. Fidelitas had an actual person answering the phone. That meant that the company didn't get so many calls that her call would be routed through a series of automated responses. The secretary also knew who she was and the circumstances under which she was invited to the luncheon—she had made an excuse that the Mandarin was feeling ill, hence her filling in for him. She might have been even more impressed, and worried, had she known that her exact location in the Sunrise Tower had been tracked as well.

But, at least, Fidelitas didn't know the Mandarin was listening in, too.

THIRTY-NINE
HARDBALL

Arthur and Barry were in their hotel suite conducting an in-depth post mortem of yesterday's presentation when Arthur's cell phone began vibrating with a text message from Gillian, the multi-lingual receptionist at CenCom. *Mary from your luncheon with Rayna on the line. Do you want to take the call?*

Arthur typed *Yes.* "Julio, track the call and see what else you can find out."

"Roger that. Ever and always."

Arthur gave Barry the thumbs up as the call was transferred. "Hello, Mary. Arthur here. How can I be of assistance?"

"Mr. Yang, I was hoping we might have a chance to speak about distribution possibilities in America."

"Call me Arthur. I'm sure we could arrange that. Can you give me some details?"

"I'd prefer to do so in person. Would you and your female associate Rayna be available to come in now?"

Yeah, right. Arthur waved his phone in the air. "I'm sorry. There are some pressing matters I need to attend to first. Can we meet early next week?" While there was nothing on his schedule, Arthur knew that to let any potential client know that he was doing nothing and could meet on a moment's notice would not be seen as a good sign.

Strained silence flooded the room. Neither the Mandarin nor Mary were used to not getting their way. The Mandarin texted her: *Offer twenty thousand to come in today.*

Mary awkwardly responded. "If I gave you twenty thousand dollars, could you make it today?"

"Mary," said Arthur with the voice of someone who was doing her a tremendous favor, "I am working on a deal that is more than two thousand times that size. It requires huge sensitivity with the State Administration for Trade and Commerce and Deputy Minister Zhong Li. It demands my full attention... But Rayna and I can be at your office next Monday at 8:00 am. Is that acceptable?"

Mary and the Mandarin were taken aback. They both had the same thoughts. *Were they really that busy?* The Mandarin texted *Try two days at 8 a.m.*

Mary munched on her lower lip, contemplating. "Is there any chance that you can make it earlier? Maybe in two days' time at eight in the morning?"

Arthur paused before responding. "Can we make it at 4:45 a.m.?"

"Yes, of course. My office is at..."

Arthur cut her off. "I know where it is—you're in the Sunrise Tower. And we will see you then."

He hung up and made another call.

"Hello, Arthur."

"Hi, Rayna. A heads up. We have a meeting at quarter to five in the morning in two days."

The Fidelitas board member heard a chuckle. "What's so funny?"

"I just met my grandmother and birth father in a small old church in Golden Corner, discovered both my birth father and father who raised me are pastors, and just saw my birth mother's resting place and now you call to remind me of why I'm really here."

"Sorry to do that. Enjoy the moment."

Arthur hung up and turned to Barry. "Did you hear that? Unbelievable. Was that synchronicity? Coincidence? God?"

Barry smiled at his colleague. "To everything there is a reason."

MARY ASKED THE MANDARIN, "Did you catch that? Can you be there?"

"You take the meeting. I'll listen in. Also, why don't you see if he's really doing something with Trade and Commerce's Zhong Li. Rumor has it he's corrupt to the bone. If it's true, then maybe he'll be okay." The Mandarin ended the call.

Mary didn't have any religious beliefs at all but, like

many Chinese, she had some belief that there was something "out there." Was it possible that the fates had determined that she sit in for the Mandarin at lunch with Arthur and Rayna for a time such as this?

FORTY

DEATH OF A DREAM

Sitting inside the Mercedes limo in the quasi-parking lot in front of the monastery, Tex was totally focused on his cell phone conversation. "We are going to be rich, babe! I'll buy you a ten carat diamond ring, a house on the hill and we'll have our own private jet."

"Tex, how real is this money, though? She might be just another American trying to get money from the Chinese," answered the lilting young woman's voice.

"We don't have any so she's not going to get any from us. Don't worry, Mei."

Tex heard sniffles. "What's the matter? What's wrong?" he asked.

"I think she just wants to steal you away from me," wailed Mei.

"You're crazy, Mei. I'm going to be Roy Rogers and you're going to be my Dale Evans!"

"Who are they? You're the only one I ever loved and now some rich American is taking you away."

"Mei! Stop it!" yelled Tex but Mei had already hung up.

Before Tex could call Mei back, the car door was yanked open. Ponytail's strong hands pulled hard on the bandana around Tex's neck. It happened so fast that the cowboy chauffeur had no chance to defend himself as burly arms dragged him out of the car. While he thrashed about trying to free himself, Johnny socked a hard right fist into Tex's stomach.

Tex tried to yell but nothing other than muffled gurgling came out of his mouth. A ferocious roundhouse fist knocked Tex out cold.

"Nice work, Ponytail," nodded Sting.

"Well, we can't have his blood anywhere in the car. You watch those American cop shows? If he leaked even just a bit, it would be a bitch. They always find traces of blood, no matter how well the crooks clean up."

"Where do you want him to go?"

"Let's stash him behind those bushes," growled Ponytail, motioning toward a hedge by the monastery's wall. "But first..." Ponytail released the bandana and put his two hands directly around Tex's throat and squeezed as hard as he could. There was a crack as Tex's neck snapped. Ponytail stared intently at Tex's body. Satisfied that there was not a hint of movement, he reached into Tex's pocket and pulled out the keys. Then he, Johnny and Sting carried the body and hid it behind the thicket.

Ponytail took a look at the curved pointed roof with the gold Chinese characters. "We're gonna make a ton of money here," he cooed softly. He turned to his brothers. "Let's get ready."

FORTY-ONE

PARADISE LOST

It was time to leave if they were going to have a meal with Popo. As Henry, Martin and Rayna strolled back to the monastery, clouds overhead started to darken.

"Our timing was perfect. Fifteen minutes more and we would be drenched."

The courtyard bell began to toll.

Martin grinned. "The monks are being called to prayer. By the time we get there, the monastery grounds will be empty, since they'll all be in one of the halls."

As they retraced their earlier steps, a whistling wind made them fold their arms over their chests to shelter themselves.

Martin was only partially right. As they entered the monastery grounds, the courtyard was empty of the physical presence of the monks, but full of their monotone, rhythmic chanting.

Walking contemplatively toward the front of the monastery, Rayna breathed out slowly as the Kafkaesque experience unfolded. *Here I am with two men, both of*

whom are my fathers, both of them who wound up being
pastors. My biological father was not there at my birth, but
my adoptive father was. How weird can that be?

Her meditative musings were interrupted by the
sound of three soda-sized black cans bouncing in front of
them. One container spewed orange smoke, the other two
spat out a black shroud.

Rayna knew exactly what they were and what was
likely to come next.

She grabbed the hands of Henry and Martin. "Turn
back. Run!"

Too late. Thick smoke permeated the air, impairing
the trio's vision. Martin collided with Henry. Both men
fell to the ground, coughing.

"Crawl," commanded Rayna. "And follow me."

On their hands and knees, Rayna led them to the area
where she remembered a statue stood. It was a case of the
blind leading the blind, only discovered when Rayna's
head collided with the statue's base and Henry and
Martin bumped into Rayna. She put her finger to her
mouth to keep her fathers quiet as she barked in a low
voice. "Move to the back of the statue for protection and
stay put."

"What are you going to do?" asked Martin, alarmed.

"Got no time to explain. You tell him, Dad."

Rayna, still on her hands and knees, galloped like a
horse until she reached open air.

She stood up to assess the situation. There were three
men. One had a long ponytail. He wore a bandolier and
carried an assault rifle. Rayna recognized it as an old
Chinese version of the M16.

The other two men had savage-looking crew cuts. One of them sported a tactical vest with at least two dozen grenades. The third one had a flame thrower.

"No!" Rayna yelled as monks poured out of the halls to see what the commotion was all about.

Pacifist monks or not, invaders had swarmed their domain and they had to do something.

"Go back!" Rayna screamed, but it was too late—a grenade landed in front of the first group of monks. A second later, an explosion rocked the courtyard compound and the unsuspecting monks closest to the explosion's epicenter were blown to bits, while those behind them were thrown back hard.

Another grenade came in. The ground erupted and a statue of a serene Buddha toppled, crushing an innocent fleeing acolyte.

BOOM! BOOM! The impacts hurled monks haphazardly in all directions.

Now, a new problem. The flame thrower unleashed its orange-red hell on the bleeding and injured monks.

The world was afire and black smoke furled throughout the complex. Nirvana was displaced with the hellish sight of dead and dying monks. Those that could picked themselves off the ground and turned to escape, but an unseen hand tossed another grenade at the fleeing clerics, detonating in front of them before they could shift direction. Terror-filled moans and cries for help filled the air. Others crawled away without legs, bleeding out, dazed, unaware and praying at the sky for help that would never come.

Then a reprieve. No grenades, no more flames.

FORTY-TWO

PILLAGED

As the smoke began to subside, Rayna scanned the monastery grounds for clues, then saw the three armed masked men lugging rucksacks and backpacks. They were doing the unthinkable. Relaxed and calm in the midst of the devastation, these worse-than-Satans guffawed insane laughter.

Rayna kicked herself. She was so wrapped up in her personal thoughts of meeting her birth parents that she had let down the guard of suspicion that had been ingrained into her psyche as a soldier. *Be prepared at all times. The world is a dangerous place.*

And then there was a bigger concern. Not only had she been unprepared mentally, she had neglected to bring any kind of weapons with her. Not a gun, nor even a pocket knife. *No point in worrying about what I don't have. Is there anything I can use?*

Rayna's face tightened with tension as she pondered the possibilities, observed the masked predators, searching for weaknesses. Worry transformed to fear as their steady confident pace indicated they were used to danger and death. They paid no attention to the monks and their focus was constantly shifting. That indicated they were looking for something. Or someone. The psychopaths stopped outside the Great Hall and peered inside.

"In here," decided Ponytail. He pulled a couple of smoke grenades and tossed them ahead.

BOOM. BOOM. Monks that hid in the hall streamed out with their hands up—they were easily gunned down.

The attackers quickly donned gas masks and entered.

Rayna got up and scampered to the front of the building. She noticed the grenades they used now weren't frags, but simple flashbangs. That would limit the damage done to anything inside, but would disorient the senses of anyone in the vicinity of the detonations.

A light went on! Of course! These men were after the monastery's historical relics. This isolated Buddhist monastery had treasures that antique collectors around the world would love to have.

And would pay any price for.

INSIDE THE GREAT HALL, Ponytail, Johnny and Sting were in awe of their windfall as they scooped up the treasures. Small and intricate vases, ornate jade Buddhas, hand-carved miniature pagodas, golden vessels. This place had it all.

"We're gonna retire after we sell these," said Ponytail.

"I'll put them up for sale one piece at a time and, within a year, we should get more than two million dollars. Easy."

Sting added, "And that's giving the suckers a bargain. Can you imagine anyone paying even fifty bucks for something as useless as a fat Buddha or these little chunks of stone?" He held up his hand, which was full of little bits of what appeared to be colored stone.

"Get more of those. Those aren't rocks. They're *sarira,* the jewels and pearls left after monks were created. Don't insult the customers, Sting. Bad karma."

"Hey, Ponytail, speaking about customers, what about the tourists we saw out there? The ones that came in the Mercedes. Did you notice them?" asked Johnny.

"What about 'em? We scared them to death and they took off," shrugged Ponytail. "Vanished. Poof!"

"Yeah, but what if they weren't tourists? How do you know they aren't like ninjas or some other gang?"

"Gimme a break. This place has never been cased in a thousand years and you're trying to tell me that they'll get hit twice in an hour?" laughed Sting. "I don't think so."

"Just the same, we should be careful. I mean, hell. Guns and grenades are cheap."

"Did you check out the girl? She was hot, man!"

Ponytail snickered. "I guess that's why she was able to get two sugar daddies. I wonder if she's looking for another?"

FORTY-THREE

FATHERS' LOVE

As Rayna waited by the hall's door, three smoke bombs flew outside. She dropped as the ominous black carbon particles filled the air.

The cracking sound of a semi-auto burst shattered the silence. Then another and another. A couple of random bullets flew over Rayna's head.

She slithered away from the hall's entrance, desperate to find any bit of safety from the lead storm.

"Get out of the way, Rayna!" shrilled Martin. Of course, he had disobeyed Rayna's order to stay put. He had left her once before and he was not going to do it again. Martin saw Johnny pull a grenade from his vest and yank out the pin.

When Rayna glanced at Martin, he realized she couldn't hear the pop and whistle. She was unaware of the pineapple-shaped grenade coming right in her direction.

He dashed toward her without a second thought. Only then did Rayna see the hissing de-pinned grenade flying at her. The small bomb fell at Rayna's feet. She tried to back away, but another explosion on her other side knocked her down. She glanced up to see the live grenade not even four feet from her nose.

"No!" screamed the racing Martin as he leapt on top of the deadly baseball.

The force of the blast blew Rayna back. Body parts of the man who gave her life—and then saved it—fell from the sky. Martin's severed hand knocked Rayna's head.

Rayna's mouth gaped open as she saw Martin's dismembered thigh lying on the ground in front of her and the two halves of his bleeding head and torso at the landing point of the grenade.

The monastery was alive with death, a field of slaughter.

By now, visibility was virtually non-existent because of all the smoke. The air would soon clear but, meanwhile, the clouds of smoke had one virtue—if Rayna couldn't see, neither could her enemy. She took off toward a blurry mass. Rayna hoped that was the small, steepled pagoda she remembered from earlier.

The bandits opened up as she shot past. With tracers cracking around her, Rayna threw her hands out in front of her, bouncing up in a front grand handspring to the top of the blur.

Lucky guess or karma? Didn't matter. Rayna found herself with two feet precariously balancing on the roof of the pagoda. The vantage point gave a clearer picture of the sources of destruction.

Rayna saw the toughs charging to the entrance with their fully-packed rucksacks. Obviously, the weight of one of the bags was considerably more—or maybe one of them sustained an injury. In any event, one thug lagged behind the others. He shrugged the bag off and looked around.

Rayna growled as the thief caught Henry making his way toward the trio. She couldn't draw attention to him by shouting. She just watched helplessly as he dashed to a statue, then hid behind it. His next step was to move stealthily to the giant copper bell. He dropped to his belly, then slunk toward the bandit.

The thug took a grenade out of his pocket and drew back his arm.

There was no time for Rayna to get off the pagoda, run to the assaulter and disarm him. *What to do?*

An instant later, Rayna bent down and broke the pointed tip off the steeple. Stretching her arm back like a baseball pitcher, she hurled it at the thief just as he released the pineapple.

Despite the adrenaline, Rayna's throw was pinpoint accurate—the steeple's tip hit the grenade, exploding two feet away from the assailant. The explosive detonated immediately, killing the thug instantly—exactly how Rayna fantasied it would happen.

One down, two to go.

The explosion drew the attention of the dead man's colleagues. They spotted Henry roaring toward them. Ponytail yanked out a handgun and aimed at Henry.

"No, Dad, no!" yelled Rayna as she sprang off the pagoda.

She rocketed toward her father, but the gunman had already fired. Rayna screamed as one... two... three bullets plowed through Henry's chest. Even a lousy shot would have a hard time missing when the target was less than twenty feet away... and this enemy was no lousy shot. Henry faltered.

With a sudden swivel of his body, the marksman turned his attention to Rayna and aimed.

Rayna scooped up the torso of a headless dead monk en passant, and used it as a human shield against the fresh barrage of bullets storming at her. Blocking the deadly missiles with the holy man's corpse, Rayna approached the gunman, then hurled the body just in time to absorb a hail of bullets.

The forward thrust of the monk's body pushed the thug downward. Rayna was about to leap onto him when he rolled over, jumped up and reached into his pants with both hands.

As he pulled a knife from each pocket, Rayna threw a straight jab at his nose. There was a sickening crunch, but the man stayed on his feet. Enraged, he charged. He waved his arms like a windmill, slashing at Rayna.

Rayna avoided the whirling blades, then stooped to a crouch and kicked at her attacker's legs, tripping him.

As he fell, he drove one of the knives at Rayna's head.

She quickly rotated to the side, and the blade sliced through her hair rather than her scalp.

She leapt up and paced in a circle around him. She smirked while he spit out blood. "Big man trying to beat up a little girl. And then the little girl beats you like a pussy. Not so tough, are you, asshole?"

The thug twirled to his feet, directed his remaining knife at Rayna's heart and charged. She held her ground and caught his wrist as he closed, yanking the blade away with a sharp twist. "Oh, little boy, now you got nothing."

He swung his free hand hard and wild. Every curled knuckle had knockout written on it, but he swung too wide. And way too slow.

"You know, I like real men. Real men would know what to do with me, but you? Go away, little boy. Play with your dolls."

The bully unleashed another wild right hook at Rayna's temple.

With lightning reflexes, she grabbed his wrist as it arrived. Twisting with his momentum to carry the two of them, she fell sideways, using him as a cushion.

With one hand holding his wrist and the other holding his elbow, she lifted his forearm and broke it over a piece of rubble.

He squealed in pain. "Bitch! Bitch!"

Rayna pulled him by the hair to her face. "Now, who the hell are you and what are you doing here?"

BANG! BANG! BANG! Rayna released the thug and dropped to the ground. She looked up to see the third assaulter holding a rifle in the distance. Ponytail had shot his brother before he could answer. The bullets ripped right through his body and into Rayna's chest and abdomen.

Rayna was bleeding out. She picked up a rock, reared back and prepared to heave it.

Ponytail, seeing the damage Rayna had already inflicted, bolted like an escapee from hell with his remaining loot out of the courtyard.

With her last bit of strength, Rayna reared back and

slung the piece of rubble. She had no idea what happened. By the time she finished the throwing motion, she blacked out.

Henry screamed as he forced his arms to pull his body toward his unconscious daughter. She was only another thirty feet away now, but it might just as well be a thousand miles.

Goodbye, Rayna. I love you... No, damn it. No. No. I can't go. I can't go!

With strength from an unknown place, Henry forced himself to stand. An unexpected chill overcame him as he stumbled the last yards to his daughter, collapsing on top of her, crying for the baby he had helped bring to life twenty-six years ago.

The screams of the dying monks were louder than the gunfire and explosions. The air was heavy with gritty, stinging smoke. The flames of Hell were consuming Heaven, growing more intense, more vivid, as the powerful heat purified the sinners.

FORTY-FOUR

ONE TOUGH SOB

Outside in the dirt clearing, Ponytail loaded the Mercedes with his bag of relics. He was smokin' mad because a woman had done what some of the toughest toughs in China had been unable to do—take out two of his brothers.

"I am going to get you, bitch," he muttered under his breath.

He glanced toward the monastery entrance and saw something unbelievable—Johnny was stumbling out. Ponytail rushed to his brother and supported him as they walked to the car.

"You are one tough son of a gun, bro," complimented Ponytail. "Get in the car. I've got to get you to a hospital."

"No!" shouted Johnny, trying to control his pain. "I'll take the SUV. The shot went through and through. Bandage me up tight and I'm good to go."

"You're crazy, man."

"Ponytail, if I bleed all over this babe, we might not

get the blood out and we lose half a million or more. Bandage me tight so I don't lose more blood. I'll drive."

Ponytail stared at his kid brother with a new respect.

FORTY-FIVE

HOLY CRAP

On one of China HQ's monitors, Julio was laughing. "Arthur, when was the last time you had a meeting at 4:45 in the morning?"

"Never one I purposely scheduled. It's gonna kill me to do it then," quipped Arthur as he lifted his eyes to the ceiling in mock exasperation. "The things we do for this company."

"Yeah, and the pay is great, too!"

Another joke. Julio, Barry and Arthur never took a salary, not that any of them needed to. Independently wealthy, they each contributed millions every year to help fund Fidelitas' operations.

"Let me call Rayna. She'll be thrilled to know about tomorrow." Arthur punched in her cell number.

"Thank you for contacting me. I am currently unavailable but if you leave me a message, I will contact you as quickly as is convenient."

"Rayna, it's Arthur. Call as soon as you get this message."

"What's that about?" asked Barry. "She knows she has to answer our calls."

When a call to a Fidelitas operative came from one of the board members, Barry Rogers, Arthur Yang or Paulina Rossini, it was to be answered immediately... unless there were dire circumstances.

"Maybe she's caught up in the moment of being where she was born."

"I don't think so but, if she is, we can't have her as part of us anymore," stated Barry, none too pleased.

While Barry called Rayna, Arthur made another call to Tex, the limo driver. Again, straight to voicemail.

"What's up, man? You want a driver, that's me. Let me know. And be on the watch for our new restaurant, the 'Texas Rangers,' opening soon."

Concern swept the faces of Arthur and Barry.

Barry made a third call to Henry. Same canned result. "Hello, you have reached the direct and private voicemail of Reverend Henry Tan. Your message is important and will be responded to as soon as I am able to."

Not good suddenly became *holy crap*.

"Julio, can you see if you can get the locations of Tex, Rayna or Henry through their phones? Or crack their voicemails so we know if there are any clues?"

"Roger that. Let me check first with their phones, make sure there's no problem with reception."

Fidelitas' phones had been modified so Central Command could track and monitor their activities virtually anywhere in the world.

Barry and Arthur could hear Julio's fingers clacking

away on a keyboard. "All three phones are stationary, as in not moving at all."

Not a good sign. Wrinkles furrowed the foreheads of all three. Several seconds later, Julio blurted out, "There's a voicemail on Tex's phone. Here it comes."

A young Chinese woman's voice was heard. "Hello, my wonderful, handsome, fantastic Tex. I'm so sorry I was jealous. Of course I will be Dale Evans. I love, love, love you!"

"Who's Dale Evans?" asked Julio. "Never mind. I've got a feed coming in from Rayna's camera."

On the monitor in Cencom and in the room at the Oceania, the three could see the Buddhist monastery in smoldering ruins. While the buildings were intact, there was debris everywhere. Mixed in with the rubble were dead bodies, severed heads, arms and other body parts.

Concern filled Arthur's voice. "There's no sign of Rayna, Henry or Tex."

"It might be the position of the phone. If any of them are behind it, we wouldn't be able to pick it up. I've got the location—about a hundred and fifty miles north of Guangzhou."

"Hang on, Julio." Arthur quickly dialed a different number on his cell phone.

After two rings, Deputy Minister Zhong Li, a senior bureaucrat in the State Administration for Trade and Commerce, picked up the phone.

"Arthur, good to hear from you. Are there any final details that you wanted to go over before the treaty signing?"

"None at all, Deputy Minister Zhong, but there's an

emergency I'm hoping you can help with. The Hundred Hands Monastery north of Guangzhou has been under attack. We see rubble and smoke but are unable to see anyone alive. Three of my group are dead or unconscious and we're eager to find out their status."

"I will find an Air Emergency Response Team and get it there. Where are you?"

"At the Oceania."

"Does the hotel have a helipad?"

Barry took a quick look at the hotel's directory of services and glanced questioningly at Arthur.

"Yes, it does, Deputy Minister. On the roof."

"I will send another chopper to get you within fifteen minutes. We can reschedule our meeting."

"Absolutely not. Business is business. Barry and I will meet with you but we will have an associate go to the scene. Thank you for this."

"Anything for my friends."

Especially friends that had helped him get ten million dollars out of China and invested in North America. Not to mention helping to get his daughter into Julliard.

Arthur made another call.

"I just ordered a Peking duck for myself. Want to join?" queried Chuck on the other end.

"Cancel it. Need you up on hotel's helipad in fifteen minutes. Hell has struck. Can't find Rayna, Henry or Tex but there's a camera feed of a mini-war zone."

"I wasn't hungry anyway."

FORTY-SIX

TEARS FROM HEAVEN

The fifty-year-old monk, caked in blood and lying face down on the ground, stirred. He had lived in the Hundred Hand Monastery ever since he was boy and never stepped foot outside its grounds. His whole life had been dedicated to studying the scriptures, praying, meditating, sweeping the dust away from the corridors and halls, washing dishes and tending the vegetable gardens.

The now sallow-faced man of faith was content with his simple life full of inner peace and tranquility. He had never eaten meat, he had never had an argument with his fellow monks and he never made an effort to speak with the monastery's infrequent outside visitors.

His life was uneventful. Until...

Where am I? Why am I lying down?

Disoriented, he tried to sit up but his body would not respond. Then he noticed blood on his orange robe. *That's strange. Why am I bleeding? What is that sound?*

Then he remembered. *I was in the Great Hall and then I heard a huge explosion. And then I ran out to inves-*

tigate. Another explosion just a few feet from me... And why is the light so bright?

He shut his eyes hard but, even with that, light blazed through his eyelids. It was painful... and wonderful.

Because closing his eyes had no effect, the monk opened his eyes again. He looked to his side to see a cell phone. Although no one at the monastery had one, he knew what it was because every single one of the temple's infrequent visitors had one. He couldn't understand why. Was there anybody so important that he or she couldn't wait an hour or two before someone talked to them?

Then he mused on the possibilities. *Maybe the cell phone is here because it is supposed to be here. I should try to make a call.* He had never even held any kind of electronic device but remembered seeing the visitors use the phone. If they could, so could he.

Dazed, the monk reached to the phone but his arm refused to cooperate. He turned his head to look and discovered the reason: where his arm should be was a bleeding stump. He was in such shock he didn't notice the pain that wracked his body.

He looked around to see where his arm was. He didn't find it.

Then another oddity. The intensity of light that had been glaring so much began to wane... In fact, it was starting to get dark. This was particularly unusual because it was only mid-afternoon when the sun should be beating hard.

He turned his head to the celestial heavens to see if something had happened to the sun. No, it was still there but then he realized he was soaking wet—rain was whipping down on him. Funny how he didn't feel the water droplets, either.

He took another look at the girl and now saw the water beating on her, too. He himself was insignificant but she? She was young and had a life ahead of her.

And then he realized why it was raining so hard.

Even the heavens are crying. With a cry that was barely a whisper, he closed his eyes for the last time.

FORTY-SEVEN

RESCUE OR RECOVERY

This Deputy Minister Zhong must have a lot of pull, thought Chuck as he boarded the helicopter. Chuck, a former Navy SEAL, had ridden in some pretty fast choppers, including the Boeing CH-47 Chinook and the Seattle firm's AH-64 Apache, but the Chinese-made Changhe Z-18 chopper used extensively by China's military was not exactly chump change. *Pretty all right.*

The bird Chuck was riding in was almost a mini-hospital outfitted with a cardiac monitor, respirator, defibrillator, pulse oximeters, oxygen, suction units and a whole lot more, including a weapons arsenal that was enough to outfit a Special Ops team of six.

I like these guys. Chuck's Chinese was non-existent so he was happy when Gee, the chopper's pilot, greeted him with, "Hey, bro. Let's roll."

"You got it, man." It took no time for the veteran Chuck to strap himself in.

Scant minutes later, the chopper was airborne and

speeding toward its destination at a hundred-and-forty miles per hour.

In the distant horizon, Chuck and Gee saw ominous dark clouds. Each had the same thought. *Oh, shit!*

ALMOST AN HOUR LATER, as they approached the Hundred Hands Monastery, the threat of a downpour was fulfilled. The slashing rain made visibility a nightmare, and dangerous for flying at top speed. Chuck was impressed by the pilot's ability to handle the jerky bird.

Over the clatter of the blades, rotors screaming and rain hammering the windows, Chuck yelled, "You're pretty good at this. A lot of bad weather flying?"

Gee replied somberly. "AirWar Strikes: Black Hawk Rising. I'm level 55."

You got to be kidding. AirWar Strikes was one of the biggest selling video game franchises. To hit level 55 meant Gee must have played one hell of a lot of games. "Me?" bragged Chuck, pointing to himself. "Level 105."

The two fist-bumped. Anything under two hundred was pretty good.

Thunder boomed and streaks of lightning crossed the darkened skyline. Chuck looked behind and saw blue running lights and flashing Xenon—the air ambulance that Deputy Minister Zhong ordered had arrived, too.

"I can't see anymore. The instruments tell me that it's somewhere below. I've got to land on instinct so it's going to be slow," yelled Gee.

"Time is one thing we don't have, Gee," called Chuck

as he seized the microphone. "Big Bird to China Sky. Is that you behind us?"

"Yeah. Can you see?"

"Barely. But hey, hey, hidey no, this no my first rodeo."

Chuck chortled at the funny mixture of pidgin English and American slang.

Craning his neck to look below, Chuck called out, "We haven't been able to make any contact with our people or anyone else down there."

"No worries. We got Doctors Steve and Harry, two of the best emergency physicians."

A confident voice with much better English took over. "Gee, if you keep that up, Harry and I are gonna have to treat you for dinner."

"That's the plan, Steve. What do you think?"

"If it's just gunshot wounds that aren't too deep or haven't hit any dangerous spots, we can handle that on the ground and stay until the weather improves. But, if things are complicated, we need to get back to the hospital right away."

"You got it." Chuck looked down out the window and saw the ground in sight—the pilot was landing just outside the monastery entrance. "Okay, kiddies, it's show time. Go! Go!"

Chuck unbuckled himself. He grabbed an assault rifle and a few grenades, then jumped as the chopper moved gently down the last few feet toward the ground.

Using his cell phone as a GPS tracker, Chuck headed toward the copse. Pushing aside the bushes, he found Tex's still body.

He glanced back and saw the AERT chopper landing and a six-person team jumping out.

"One of you here!" called Chuck. "The others into the monastery with me."

The thirtyish lithe and athletic Steve carrying his portable medical kit bag rushed to the greenery where Chuck was. The physician dropped to his knees and put his hand to check for a pulse. "He's gone," he announced, shaking his head.

"We'll deal with Tex later then. Let's see what they've found inside. I'm Chuck."

"I'm Steve. Glad to meet you."

After a moment of silent respect, Chuck and Steve bolted to the monastery to join the rest of the emergency response team.

What confronted their senses as they entered was a scene of devastation—bodies, body parts, buildings in various states of destruction all over. Blood, rubble, debris... While it was new to Steve, for Chuck it was an all-too-familiar sight. Somalia. Iraq. Afghanistan. Ethiopia. And that didn't include the battles he saw as a member of Fidelitas.

Another grotesque, blood-soaked field of slaughter, proving yet again that mankind had hardly evolved from primitive savagery.

It was tough going. The rain had not let up. Being drenched was not the problem, but it made assessment and diagnosis a whole lot harder. With the skies darkening even more, visibility was becoming an issue. And, even though the weather was temperate, everyone felt a dark chill as they checked pulses, faces, bodies...

Half of the first dozen examined were alive. Dazed, unconscious, bleeding, bruised, broken bones, burned... but definitely to be counted among the living. The other six, not so fortunate. Three were dead due to gunshot wounds, the others from bleeding to death. The most gruesome sight was a prostrate monk with one arm missing. A trail of blood of almost twenty yards followed him —his arm was at the beginning of the trail.

As one of the paramedics called for more medical support, Chuck scanned the premises but the cell phone tracker was having problems—where the hell was Rayna?

He noticed an oddly shaped clump in the distance. If the unknown object was human, it would not have been monks from the monastery because there were no orange-colored robes. Chuck moved quickly toward it and saw that one human was draped over another. He raced the last few steps and his heart quickened. Was it?

Yes! Chuck saw Rayna's face. As he gently lifted the body of a middle-aged man off Rayna, he recognized him too. "Over here! It's Rayna and her father!"

The battle-hardened Chuck couldn't hold back his joy when he found a pulse on Rayna's wrist. "She's alive!"

As Steve and Harry scampered to Chuck, the big black man explained, "This is who we came for. The girl is Rayna and the older man is her father, Henry."

Both physicians dove into their medical kits to take out stethoscopes, ambubags, CPR masks, blood pressure kits and more. Chuck watched paramedics hold umbrellas to cover the physicians as Steve checked Rayna and Harry examined Henry.

Even though Rayna had a pulse, it was weak. Steve tore off Rayna's blouse, then shouted, "We have to blitz now. There's a flicker of a heartbeat but there's a bullet lodged just below her heart."

As paramedics raced to bring over a stretcher, Steve continued to examine Rayna, grimacing as he held the stethoscope to her chest. She was cold, sweating, breathing was shallow and irregular. "We need to get real lucky to have a chance," said Steve. "Her blood loss is severe. Systolic blood pressure is low, heart beats at a hundred and thirty per minute, and her skin feels clammy. We need to get her to the hospital ASAP for emergency surgery."

"She'll pull through," declared Chuck. "She's ex-Special Forces."

"Everyone dies, Chuck, even the tough guys." Steve and the paramedics began preparing Rayna for transport.

"What about Henry?" asked Chuck.

"Can't take a chance on transportation," barked Harry. "He was shot in both lungs and they are filling up with blood. He's deteriorating rapidly and won't make it to the hospital. I've got to operate here!"

"Surgery? Here? Are you crazy?" thought Chuck.

As if reading his mind, Harry yelled, "It's the only chance he's got."

"Have you done this before?"

"Not in these circumstances," admitted Harry. "But removing bullets is one of the easiest surgeries to perform."

Not exactly reassuring words, but there was no alternative. Henry would die before he got close to a hospital.

The paramedics carefully positioned Henry onto a stretcher, then gently and expertly carried him to the part of the covered entrance of the Prayer Hall that managed to survive the grenade attack.

"Damn. Damn." As Harry removed Henry's shirt, he began to sweat—there was a sucking sound coming from one of the chest wounds as Henry breathed. That meant the injury had penetrated the rib cage so air passed freely in and out of the chest cavity. That meant Henry wasn't breathing properly.

"What?" yelled Chuck as he helped the paramedics lift Rayna onto the stretcher.

"He's got a sucking chest wound so air is getting into his body but not getting out. His lungs are collapsing so his body is not getting enough oxygen. I've got to plug up the holes quickly."

But first Harry had to get the bullets out. It was a good thing Henry was unconscious because this would hurt like hell if he wasn't.

Chuck wasn't going to have a firsthand look because he and Steve were with the paramedics who were carrying Rayna toward the entrance and the chopper.

BOOM! An unexploded grenade detonated when one of the paramedics stepped onto it. As if in slow motion, Chuck watched as pieces of the dead medic filled the air. As the other paramedic fell to the ground, the force of the explosions threw Rayna, still lying on the stretcher, into the air.

Chuck dove down with outstretched arms. With sheer luck and willpower, he managed to grab the front handles of the stretcher an inch before it hit terra firma.

Chuck looked to the sky and emptied his lungs with a long exhale. Twenty thousand plus hours of physical training paid off in this fraction of a second. Chuck steadied the stretcher so there was no hard impact when it touched the ground.

There was no time to celebrate or mourn. With one paramedic dead and the other woozy, Chuck and Steve lifted the stretcher and started carrying it out.

By now, the monastery was abuzz. In addition to the medical staff that came via the helicopters, a full swarm of security police and military had arrived, shouting orders, waving rifles and carrying more medical supplies.

Two minutes later, the unconscious Rayna was gently placed on board the AERT helicopter.

With engines and rotors whining, the helicopter frantically poured on the power and wheeled up to the sky. With turbulence rocking the ship, Gee held steady.

The pilot spotted a little hole in the dark clouds and navigated directly through it and then, a sight for the ages —clear open sky.

Turbulence ended, Steve could finally release his hold on Rayna and made a call.

"Operating room. How may I assist you?"

"Hey, Cindy, it's Steve. Harry and I have got two patients coming via helipad. At least one of them, maybe both, will need to go directly to the OR. We'll be on the rooftop in less than an hour."

"We'll be ready for you."

Steve clicked off his cell. The copter banked into a tight turn, then streaked to its destination.

FORTY-EIGHT

TRIALS

In the square in front of the Pyongyang train station, General Park and the Mandarin were both dressed in smart suits, silk ties and Raybans covering their eyes. They looked like all the other businessmen seeking anonymity hanging out there while they waited for women in their thirties and forties to approach and ask if they wanted to buy some flowers or needed temporary lodging with full amenities, code for, "Want to hire me for an hour or two?"

While Park would have been content to pay these "older women" to satisfy his carnal desires, the Mandarin wanted someone younger, in her teens or at most in her early twenties. In the end, Bora, the pimp or "love broker" as he liked to call himself, arranged for two women who met both men's criteria to spend three hours in a completely private room.

"Why don't you join us?" asked the Mandarin.

Bora eyed his customers suspiciously. "Why?"

"If they don't perform the way you said they would, you are going to take their place."

"I don't swing that way."

"Suit yourself." The Mandarin motioned to the general and the two turned around to walk away.

"Wait!" called the young man. "I'll guarantee they'll perform."

BORA LED them to the back entrance of a business hotel a block away. The Mandarin understood the need for caution. Smaller offenses than prostitution or pimping had sent perpetrators to isolated prison camps where they could expect starvation, rape and torture, assuming they lived. Making sure no one was watching, Bora used his private key and the five descended a darkened stairwell to the basement. He led them down the hall and opened the door to a numberless room.

It was a small space, big enough to hold two old twin beds, a small wooden table and a functional washroom, but little else.

"Make these men happy," ordered Bora.

"How do you want it and who's getting who?" queried Nari, the older woman.

"We'll take turns with each of you," stated the Mandarin. "But, before we start, I want to get you in the mood."

He nodded at General Park who took out four little plastic bags of white powder.

This was the first time since the deal was being negotiated that either women gave a hint of interest in events to come. They both recognized the white powder contents as crystal meth. However...

"It doesn't look like enough," complained Nari. "I get more than that when I have tea with my girlfriends."

"This is one hundred percent pure. Five milligrams is more than enough."

"This is great. I don't even have to pay!" shouted Yoon, the college student. She grabbed the pouch from Park and immediately snorted the entire contents.

"Whatever." Her older partner took her bag and took a long, slow snort. "Can I have more? This isn't enough to do anything."

"Just wait. It'll hit soon enough." The general turned to Bora. "You want some, too?"

As if he needed to ask. Park didn't bother to wait for a response but simply handed a bag to Bora. The young man whipped out a glass pipe and filled its bowl with the white powder. He flicked a lighter and put the flame under the bowl. Putting his nose over the bowl, he inhaled the gaseous smoke deeply.

The rush hit him within seconds. A tidal wave of euphoria swept over Bora. "Oh, man!" panted the now sweating young man.

"Just wait," said the general.

"Now!" bellowed Bora. He rushed ferociously at Park, swinging wildly. The general sidestepped the blows and landed a punch of his own to Bora's mid-section.

Nari and Yoon began giggling and pointing at Bora.

"Kill him," laughed Nari. "He deserves it!" She

kicked his head, knocking him out. Off-balance, she fell to the floor.

Yoon took off her top and her bra. "It's so hot in here. Not like all the other times."

The semi-nude young girl didn't look at all appealing. The blood vessels in her eyes expanded to crimson rivulets, a curl of white foam formed at her mouth. She plastered her small breasts on the Mandarin. "Make me, take me," she gasped as she tried to thrust her tongue down the Mandarin's.

"No!" ranted Park, pulling the girl off the Mandarin before her tongue touched his best customer's lips. Yoon flopped to the ground.

"I'm so hot," cried the girl, her whole body drenched in sweat.

The general pulled the Mandarin to the door and the two watched in cold, studied fascination as the three alternated between howling, convulsing and biting at each other.

Then cries of pain as if the flames of hell had been shot up their rectums. Quivering, shivering, spasming… then stillness.

"Proof enough?" asked Park as he opened the door.

The Mandarin nodded. "We have a deal. Let's get to work."

In four hours, the next shift would enter the room to find the dead trio. It would be assumed that Bora and the two women for some perverted reason decided to be a threesome. Unfortunately, they overdosed while getting ready for ecstasy.

They at least got that part right.

The hotel would empty the dead trio's pockets and purses of any money they had, then get the basement room cleaned up and ready for use again within an hour.

FORTY-NINE

EYE SPY

The small auditorium in the State Administration for Trade and Commerce Building was full of bureaucrats in suits, television cameras, radio and internet news reporters. They were all watching the latest in Deputy Minister Zhong Li's business triumphs—another joint cooperation deal with the West. This was with Fidelitas, a "major North American investment firm," which was represented by two senior officials: Arthur Yang from the Hong Kong branch and Barry Rogers from San Francisco. Together, China and Fidelitas "would develop and explore new markets for Chinese products, in addition to the products that Fidelitas already distributes."

There were many thousands of these kinds of treaties signed with companies from all over the world, but most of them were for the benefit of no one except the bureaucrats who signed them. Most Westerners, governments, private and public companies had no clue at how to do business with China. They didn't have the patience, they didn't understand the intricacies of Chinese deal making, and they didn't understand that, with the Chinese, there was not a "win win" attitude toward business but that of a "take no prisoners" approach. Of course, the Chinese did everything with a smile and a legion of bureaucrats at every meeting. This made the visitors warm and fuzzy and gave them the false understanding that they had accomplished something.

The biggest mistake that Westerners made in trying to do business with the Chinese was that they didn't understand the importance of "Face Time." Not the video telephony product developed by Apple, but "face time" as in spending hours upon hours in socializing, drinking and having meals together. Only with this actual physical time spent with potential partners would real business opportunities be allowed to emerge. The signing of the treaty was just the beginning but, without face time, there was little going forward.

Arthur understood that well. It was a wonder that he had been able to maintain a trim physique after all the twelve-course Chinese banquets he had eaten at or that he had any brain cells left with all the scotch, *baiju* (a favorite Chinese alcohol) or cognac he'd drunk. Without that, though, he would never have gotten to do some of the exceptional deals that he had with the Chinese government, industrialists or criminals.

Deputy Minister Zhong's ten million in North American real estate was pretty small potatoes compared to some of the other deals Arthur had brokered. Almost too small, but Zhong's influence and contacts were exceptional. He was more than happy to point out enemies of the state as well as introduce Fidelitas to some "wealthy people who needed help." All this for a fee, of course.

The gathered audience gave a standing ovation and applauded after Barry, Arthur and Deputy Minister Zhong finished the signing. Not that anyone could see it, but Zhong held up a copy of the signed treaty for all the media to take pictures of. After that, there was another half hour of photo taking that Barry, Arthur and Zhong used as a photo op with the ministry staff.

Signing ceremony complete, Zhong completely understood that, while Barry was going to join him for dinner, Arthur needed to excuse himself to attend to the situation that developed at Hundred Hands.

One person, maybe the only person, who watched the live streaming of the event, was Mary. Sitting in her office and watching the festivities, she carefully noted the praise that Zhong heaped on Arthur. While she didn't recognize most of the companies that Zhong mentioned, two especially piqued her interest: Hansheng Industries and Northern Star Developments. These two firms were like the Mandarin's; seemingly legit on the outside, they made their real money with a host of illegal activities. Furthermore, both of them had a larger scope than the Mandarin's. Zhong had further mentioned that Hansheng was currently working with Fidelitas on a "major project."

Mary made a call.

"Yes?" asked the Mandarin.

"The Deputy Minister vetted Arthur and he's doing a deal with Hansheng."

"Good job, Mary."

Mary couldn't believe what she had just heard. The Mandarin had never complimented her in all the years that she had worked for him. Until now.

FIFTY

TOUCH AND GO

To Chuck, the chopper transporting Rayna felt like it was going in slow motion, like it was floating over gossamer milky clouds. In reality, it was hurtling at more than a hundred-and- fifty miles an hour. The direct "as the crow flies" journey took less than forty-five minutes before the motorized metal bird landed on the helipad on the roof of Guangzhou Military Hospital, well known in China for its outstanding record of patient outcomes, technological research and surgical teams rivaling the best American healthcare.

Rayna was immediately prepped for surgery in the operation room. There was one minor mercy. Because the bullets had passed through Sting's body before entering hers, they had lost a lot of energy. Not great, but at least they did not penetrate her chest wall and damage the lungs.

However, there was still a hell of a lot of blood loss and it was hard to control the bleeding, especially during the initial turbulence of the flight. During the last few minutes of the flight, her pulse disappeared. Under expert care, the odds for survival were greatly increased. It took the trauma surgeon scant minutes to remove the bullets and Rayna was now prepped for defibrillation shock therapy.

Paddles were placed on her chest and electrical current was delivered. Rayna's body jerked in reaction to the electric stimulus but the EKG did not register any sign of life. The paddles were put back on Rayna's chest and shock was applied again.

Still no registration of heart beat.

A third time and still the same results—nada.

Steve shook his head remorsefully. "I don't think there's any point. She was touch and go at best but there's nothing else we can do."

"No, we can't give up yet," cried Popo's voice. "I can't lose her again."

Chuck, Steve and the medical staff looked to the door to see Arthur hurrying in with Rayna's grandmother. While the signing was going on, Arthur, through Deputy Minister Zhong, had arranged for another chopper to go to Golden Corner to pick up Popo. The elderly woman was frightened to see armed soldiers entering her home. One of the soldiers handed her a cell phone and Arthur explained the situation to her. The old woman didn't understand much except that her precious newfound granddaughter was dying. She accompanied the soldiers to the awaiting helicopter that took her directly to the Military Hospital's roof where Arthur awaited.

"She has lost too much blood and defibrillation has not worked either. It is pointless. You can see for yourself she has flatlined—her heart shows no electrical activity. I am sorry," announced a grim-faced Steve to the entering duo.

"No! No!" wailed Popo, throwing herself on Rayna's bed.

A soldier escorted in an elderly, distinguished-looking Chinese gentleman.

Arthur went to the door and announced, "Gentlemen, this is Dr. Aaron Xi, one of the most progressive practitioners of Traditional Chinese Medicine in Shanghai. I arranged for him to fly here, too."

Progressive was putting it mildly. Radical was a more appropriate term. Xi was often "doctor of last resort." Steve bowed—he knew who Dr. Xi was. "She's dead, Dr. Xi. Even your magic won't work in a case like this."

Dr. Xi gave Steve a withering look. He had heard that statement too many times before. "I don't use magic. But I don't use your definition of medicine, either. I have expanded it."

Arthur pulled authority quietly, "Steve, work with Dr. Xi. You never know what can happen."

Steve resisted an urge to respond and swallowed. "Of course." Steve addressed his staff. "Let's get back to work. Any assistance you can give will be of tremendous value, Dr. Xi."

FIFTY-ONE

YIN YANG

Some of Dr. Xi's treatments were unorthodox at best, at least according to most Western-trained doctors.

But Western medicine had proven itself fallible time and time again. People had awoken after years of being in a coma. Long-suffering cancer patients were inexplicably and suddenly found symptom-free.

What gave Arthur and Barry the determination to continue with treatment, though, were not the miracle stories of others—it was the examples of healing that they witnessed. Both of them had been Fidelitas field operatives. Both of them faced death numerous times. Both of them somehow managed to defeat the odds. Totally irrational... but completely true.

In the Philippines, Arthur witnessed a "psychic surgeon" pressing down and pulling a tumor out of a man's stomach with his bare hands. In Japan, a Fidelitas associate was encouraged to vomit continuously until toxins resembling coffee grounds were puked out—his cancer was cured.

In a small Italian town, Barry accompanied Paulina to the shrine where she prostrated herself for a day. When she got up, a heart condition had disappeared, confirmed by her cardiologist who had initially diagnosed the existence of malignant tumors.

Were these miracles, or alternative therapies that science had yet to understand?

Let the academics and skeptics debate was the attitude that Arthur and Barry took. For them, *what works, works.* They would employ any methods necessary to save their people.

For Barry, Rayna was particularly special. She had been recommended to join Fidelitas by his late son, Jonathan. Jonathan and Rayna co-led Jon's final mission. Jon had saved Rayna's life in a small war-ravaged Iraqi town. Inside a decrepit three-story house, where terrorists had holed up, Rayna and Jon were in the same room as a young suicide bomber. When the bomber pressed the final number on her cell phone to detonate the explosives on her vest, Jon threw himself at her and the two crashed through the window where the bombs detonated in mid-air. Rayna accompanied Jon's body back to San Francisco for the funeral.

Shortly after, Barry recruited her to take the position as an operative that Jon was supposed to have.

WITHIN AN HOUR of Dr. Xi's arrival, Rayna was blood-typed and had two IV drips hanging beside her bed with tubes connecting the bags' contents to her veins via

IV catheter needles. One bag contained blood that was the same type as Rayna's. The other was a special mixture of herbs and medicines created by Dr. Xi. As per Dr. Xi's instructions, her body was also covered with three hundred sharp acupuncture needles that Dr. Xi tapped to increase the *qi* (life energy).

Shortly after treatment began on Rayna, an unconscious Henry was brought into the room. Harry tried his best but the emergency surgery at Hundred Hands failed so, like his daughter, he was medically dead. Barry had asked Dr. Xi to treat him as well so this required yet another trip to the Military Hospital from the temple.

His diagnosis was similar to Rayna's—his *qi* must be restored to proper levels. Dr. Xi's diagnosis concluded that a similar treatment to Rayna's was in order. In a short few minutes, Henry was lying in the bed next to Rayna, his body covered with acupuncture needles and two IV drips sending fluids into his veins.

After her tears had run so much that she could cry no more, Popo remembered her faithful resolve. She refused to sag under the heaviness of despair. Not now. Not after so many years of wondering... and wandering... through the desert of life. Asking *Shangti* (Supreme Deity or God) for forgiveness, she remained steadfast on her knees, praying at Rayna's side while Dr. Xi went back and forth between his two patients. He began tapping the needles, another method of stimulating the energy.

"I will be here for a while." Dr. Xi's fingers danced on the needles in Rayna's body. "There is no way of knowing how long this will take so, if you need to go, you can."

"Someone will contact you if there's a change," stated Steve. While he tried to hide it, Barry and Arthur could sense that the physician didn't hold much hope for a positive outcome.

Barry looked at Arthur. They both knew that their presence was useless. Rayna was in as good hands as she could be. They left the room with Steve.

"I've heard of Dr. Xi's methods working, but I've never actually seen them in action," said Steve. "I must admit the Western doctor in me is somewhat skeptical."

"Steve," replied Arthur, "according to you, both Henry and Rayna are dead. This may be a shot in the dark but it's the only shot we've got."

FIFTY-TWO

GRANDMOTHER'S PLEA

Was it accidental or on purpose or "accidentally on purpose?" No one could really answer that question but what was clear was that there were multiple healing approaches in the hospital room with Rayna and Henry. There was Chinese medicine as practiced by Dr. Xi. There was Western medicine represented by Steve. There was the spiritual, offered by Popo.

Barry and Arthur didn't care. As businessmen, they had learned to hedge their bets. They had brought in Steve and Dr. Xi but were glad to add Popo to the mix. *Whatever works, works.*

INSIDE THE ROOM, Popo buried her face in her hands. *I never thought that I would ever get a chance to see you, Rayna. I didn't even know whether you were alive or not. God, don't take her away now.*

Hours passed with Rayna's kneeling grandmother

keeping up her whispered, almost inaudible, prayer vigil. She had been praying at the little church in Golden Corner for years and God had answered that prayer about Popo seeing her. Now, she was hoping for another miracle.

Dr. Xi was deep in concentration as he periodically adjusted Rayna's needles or strength of tapping. Paramedics and nurses popped in and out to take readings.

After Xi had made his diagnosis, he contacted an aide who brought some of his own personal medicines and herbs from Shanghai. Some of them were immersed in Chinese alcohol to create a medicinal tincture. Others were placed in a mortar where he ground them and placed different combinations in portable metal and glass containers, boiling them in water over a portable burner. After the fluid cooled, he forced some of the fluids down her throat. A special decoction was mixed in with the IV solution.

Rayna lay still on the hospital bed. Eyes opened, unblinking, vacuous, insensate. Or so it seemed.

But, unknown to everyone, Rayna was fully aware— not of her surroundings but of her own feelings. An incredible calm, a serenity. She felt no pain and wondered why she was being intubated. That made no sense to her. She was conscious of being bathed in light of growing brightness. She had no concept of time and didn't know if it were seconds or minutes that the light was with her. But she did know that, as the light grew more intense, the forms of the people in the room faded.

In fact, the room itself seemed to fade, and she felt

like she was submerged in water. Not like water in a bathtub or the ocean or lake but... what was it?

Then inner tears of joy as warmth radiated throughout her being. She was surrounded by the fluid of an amniotic sac.

Rayna was at peace.

Giggling female voices sliced through Rayna's tranquility. She turned her head to discover two women looking through the membranes of the amniotic sac. One of them playfully teased in Chinese, *"Pang Pang.* (Little fat one)." That resulted in a squeal of delight from the other.

The cloudy membrane of the sac transformed to transparency. There was Vivian, her mother, and a teenage girl. To Rayna, they were the most beautiful women in the world. The two began to sing.

> Yě dì de huā,,   Chuān zhe měi lì de yī
>   shang
> Tiān kōng de niǎo er,
> Cóng lái bu wèi shēng huó máng
> Cǐ' ài de tiān fù,
> Tiān tiān doū kàn gù
> Tā gèng ài shì shàng rén,
> Wèi tā men yù bèi yǒng shēng de lù

> *Flowers of the field*
> *So beautifully displayed.*

Songbirds freely singing
Innocently, unafraid
Gracious, Heavenly Father
Always watching me
You shine to all the world
For now, for eternity

RAYNA KNEW that Vivian had sung the song to her since she was a baby but now, as she heard the teenager sing, she realized that she had always known the song—the teenager had sung it to her when she was in the young girl's womb.

The amniotic sac dissolved. Rayna's two mothers were kneeling beside her as Rayna sat up. She held Vivian's hands and looked at the other woman.

"*Mama?*" asked Rayna to the young girl, barely moving her lips.

"*Duì. Wǒ shì nǐ de qīnshēng mǔqīn, Ling* (Yes, I am your birth mother, Ling)," soothed the girl tenderly, stroking and touching her daughter's wounds, pushing her fingers into the bullet holes. There were tears in her eyes and tenderness filled her face.

Rayna looked at Ling, then turned to Vivian. "I will be with you soon."

"Rayna, it's not your time yet," disagreed Vivian.

Both mothers looked heavenwards, pleading to an unseen being. "Did you hear? It's not her time yet."

It's not her time yet echoed repeatedly as the two women began to fade from view.

Rayna wanted to scream, "No!" but her lips would not move.

The bright light returned, engulfing Vivian and Ling in it. As the light grew brighter, the bodies of Rayna's two mothers melded into its glow.

Just when Rayna's eyes pleaded for relief from the bright intense light, it disappeared, leaving Rayna back on the hospital bed.

IN THE HOSPITAL ROOM, no one had noticed anything unusual for the last five minutes. Dr. Xi was attending to Henry, tapping the needles on his body while Popo had not moved from her kneeling prayer position.

Steve came in for his hourly check and glanced at the ECG machine attached to Rayna.

Something was terribly wrong—or amazingly right. The graph displayed a regular sinus rhythm of eighty-four beats per minute. The P wave, PR interval, QRS complex, ST segment, WT interval and T wave—all of these were what one could expect of a healthy, active eighteen-year-old male. "What the?"

Steve's outburst broke the concentration of Dr. Xi and Popo who looked at the ER physician. "What is it?"

"Look!" called Steve, pointing at the ECG. "It's normal. No. It's more than normal. It's..." The physician struggled to force out the next few words. "It's a miracle... I don't know what else to call it."

"There are layers to the universe you need to learn,

Dr. Steve," said Dr. Xi. "But I must admit that I didn't expect recovery this quickly."

"I didn't expect one at all," admitted Steve quietly.

"It was *Shangti* (God)," says Popo. "Who else can make the blind see or raise the dead?"

Even the most ardent of atheists would find it hard to argue that some kind of supernatural intervention had taken place.

Suddenly, a cough. "Can I get a drink of water?" rasped the voice risen from the dead.

"Rayna!" They all turned to see Rayna sitting up.

"Get her water," barked Steve to the nurse who had entered the room. "And call Arthur and Barry."

The nurse scurried out.

Rayna glanced around the room and saw her unconscious father. "How is he?"

"Not good," exhaled Steve.

She looked at Steve, Popo and Dr. Xi. "You've got to do for him what you did for me."

"Of course, Rayna, but first...." Popo gave her granddaughter a giant hug. "Thank you, *Shangti*. Thank you, God."

BARRY, Chuck and Arthur entered the room. Joy, happiness and relief filled their faces. They had only known Rayna for a few months but, during that period, her charm, vulnerability and warmth had captured their hearts.

"Hello, stranger," greeted Barry.

"I hope you've got eighteen-year-old scotch in that paper bag," said Rayna to Chuck.

"What else?" smiled Chuck as pulled out the bottle of amber Scottish liquid gold and four shot glasses.

As Chuck unscrewed the bottle top and poured shots, Rayna announced, "I'm ready to go back to work."

Barry shook his head. "Nonsense. With your injuries, you need bed rest for at least a week. I'll take your place."

Rayna lifted the gown off her torso. "What injuries?" she asked, showing off her body without wounds, stitches or blemish.

Oh. My. God...

"I hope you're an early morning person, Rayna," said Arthur. "We've got a 4:45 meeting tomorrow."

Rayna's jaw dropped. "Barry, maybe I am still sick."

"Right."

FIFTY-THREE

NEGOTIATION?

It was still dark when Mary arrived at her office on the fiftieth floor at 4:15 a.m. While she had worked many hundreds of late nights, this was the first time she ever got here so early to catch dawn rising over the city's horizon. There was no sign of the Mandarin, but she knew there was no point in trying to contact him. He would make his own appearance somehow.

At 4:36, she received a call from the concierge at the front desk in the lobby.

"There are two people to meet with you and your boss."

"Please allow them up."

"Yes, Ms. Wu."

MARY WAS ANTICIPATING Arthur and Rayna's arrival at the elevator. What she wasn't anticipating was to see Rayna dressed in a navy blue scoop neck silk dress that revealed a hint of cleavage. Mary's chest tightened as she inhaled Rayna's light fragrance with a face that glowed from an early morning run. Trying not to stare at Rayna's ebony hair blow-dried to perfection and sensual almond brown eyes, she led her two guests down the hall, trying to focus on the business at hand. "My boss will be joining us via conference call." *I hope.*

"Oh, where is he?" asked Rayna.

"I have no idea. He is extremely security-conscious and meets with very few people. He could be anywhere from Amsterdam to Singapore."

Arriving, Mary opened the door to the surprisingly small office. There were only two rooms: the reception area and a larger corner office. There were no pictures on the walls and no personal mementos on the desks. Mary led them into the bigger room.

"Nice tight operation," complimented Arthur, shooting Rayna a quick glance, who gave a nod of recognition. *Everything is farmed out.*

"Thank you. May I offer you some hot water or tea?"

"No, we're fine. Thank you."

From the way Mary sat down, it seemed obvious that she felt entirely comfortable in her boss's chair. What she didn't realize was that Arthur and Rayna knew exactly why she sat in her boss's chair. There was a hidden camera pointing at them, undetectable to anyone who was not familiar with clandestine operations.

At precisely 4:45, the office phone rang and Mary put it on speakerphone.

"Mandarin, please meet Arthur Yang and Rayna Tan from Fidelitas."

"Pleased to meet you," replied Arthur cordially. "What may we assist you with?"

"This is in strict confidence. Even if we do not agree to work together, can I trust that you won't tell anyone?"

"No, you can't," stated Arthur firmly.

The Fidelitas executive allowed the discomfort to grow by remaining silent for several moments, then he said, "We will ignore that you have insulted us by not revealing your name nor being here in person, but remember this. We are here because you know we can help you. In order for me to answer your questions, I will have to tell you my ideas. If you choose not to work with me, you could go to someone else to implement them and that is something that will not happen. If you choose, we can end the meeting now."

THE FUMING Mandarin was in the room at the Paekdusan Hotel with General Park listening in on the conversation. The military officer looked at the Mandarin and nodded, giving the thumbs up. *This guy is good.* What Arthur said about stealing his ideas was exactly what the Mandarin had planned to do.

The Mandarin gritted his teeth. He was always the one playing hardball. To be at the other end of the stick was an unfamiliar experience. But he had no choice. "I understand. Shall I begin?"

"That's why we are here."

"The United States needs to be taught a lesson. They allowed my son to die of a drug overdose. As payback, I am going to take one million of their children. I need someone to help me get a new drug, N115, into America. The drug is lethal in small doses. Five milligrams will cause death and there is no antidote. I need help with distribution. Can you handle this?"

"Of course we can, but first a few questions. How much are you willing to spend?"

"Twenty-five million dollars."

Arthur picked up the paperweight from the desk and glared at the tiny camera lens that was camouflaged in it. "I'm tired of you wasting my time. Fifty million is my fee alone. What are you prepared to spend?"

An angry beat passed. "A hundred and fifty million."

"Getting closer but we can discuss it later." Arthur nodded and put the paperweight back on the desk. "How big a shipment are we talking about?"

"Ten kilos in fine white powder."

"Where are you planning to strike?"

"Los Angeles. That's where my son was close to," stated the Mandarin tersely.

"When do you want to do this?"

"Manufacturing will be finished in a week. Then we can hook up with a pharmaceutical company and smuggle our stuff in with theirs."

"Who do you plan to use to do the distribution?" Arthur asked, making notes on his iPad.

"The Russians, Mexicans and the Italians, of course."

"And who are you hoping to eliminate?"

"Anyone and everyone."

"I see. So, if you've got it all figured out, what do you need us for?"

"I need some help. The person I was planning to do this with is no longer available."

"You mean Danny from China Red?" Arthur said calmly.

Even though he couldn't see the Mandarin, Arthur could feel his shockwaves as surprise of Arthur's knowledge filled the air.

"Yes, how did you know?"

"I don't like competition," said Arthur as casually as if he were ordering the breakfast special at Denny's.

"You? I thought..."

"Oh, come on. Do you really think someone like Danny was going to get taken out by some cheap trick? Your choice of that two-bit dealer is typical of all that is wrong with your plan. It shows ignorance and a complete lack of understanding of the American situation."

Mary squirmed. She had bought the line and had convinced the Mandarin of it, too.

"This is the last advice I will give you for free. Save your money. You have zero chance of success with your plan. You might be able to kill a few thousand people with your idea but, as soon as America discovers the problem, every agency will crack down big time. As lethal as your drug may be, what's the point when it's pulled out of circulation? And you say there's no antidote? If it's new, how do you know that it's not easily found or developed? But your biggest problems are your distributors and targets. Your distributors will get the easy marks— illegal immigrants and ghetto dogs. So what? These are undesirables. Eliminating them would only benefit the United States. The American taxpayer would no longer have to pay for their welfare payments, jail time, housing and food. It would save the U.S. billions every year."

Arthur and Rayna did not have to be there in person with the Mandarin to feel his shock.

"And one more thing. Ten kilos is nowhere near enough. Fifty is better. Twenty-five will be okay. You have to allow that some people will take multiple doses, some is just going to be wasted, some you'll have to throw away because it will only be a matter of time before you are found out... Even if you attack hard and fast."

Arthur nodded at Rayna and the two stood up, readying to go.

"Wait. What do you propose?"

"If you want to continue this conversation, I want five million dollars deposited into my account by 11:30. If it is, we will be back at noon."

Arthur scribbled something on a piece of paper and handed it to Mary. "Deposit the funds there."

With that, Arthur and Rayna walked out of the room.

———

OUTSIDE THE BUILDING and safely on the street, Rayna asked Arthur, "How did you know who it was that the Mandarin was partnering with?"

"A lucky guess. Danny's death was headline sensationalist news. But, even if wasn't him, the Mandarin would never be able to verify that it wasn't us."

You've got to be good to be lucky and there was no doubt that Arthur was damned good.

Arthur called Julio. The CenCom intel head had

listened in on the whole conversation through a virtually untraceable and untrackable bug planted into Arthur's left earlobe.

"Did you find out anything, Julio?"

"Nothing yet and I'm not sure I will. Wherever he was calling from, it had firewalls, security systems and IP re-routers up the yin yang. As far as we could determine, he could have been in any one of a million places."

"Yes, but not every one of them has the sophistication to make a synthetic drug or the facility for the kind of volume the Mandarin wants," asserted Rayna. "That's got to narrow it down."

"Yeah. That narrows it down to a thousand and I gotta start trying to figure out where it is."

"So we have until noon to come up with a plan. Are you up to it, Rayna?"

"If you're asking me if I'm ready to hop in the sack with Mary, the answer is no but *what works, works* and I'm a working girl."

Rayna winked at Arthur. "Let's start brainstorming."

THE MANDARIN WAS DUMFOUNDED, flabbergasted. Arthur had managed to point out the critical flaws in the Mandarin's plan with just the sketchiest of information. He knew what Mary thought but then again, sometimes his executive assistant did not think with her brain, especially when there was a girl as captivating as Rayna involved. He turned to General Park. "What did you think? You helped come up with the plan."

Park hated to admit it but Arthur was right on every count. As the original plan was to have Park play a bigger part in the vendetta, after Arthur's one minute summary, he knew that Arthur offered a much better chance of success than he did. "Go with Arthur, Mandarin. I'll stick to the manufacturing."

"I thought as much. Put the money into his account, Mary. We'll get back together at noon."

FIFTY-FOUR

PRIORITIES

At precisely 11:57 a.m., Arthur and Rayna sat down again in the Mandarin's office for another conference call.

"You got the money, right?" asked Mary.

"That's why we're here," stated Arthur.

"What do you have for me?" opened the Mandarin, eschewing chit chat.

"You need to begin as soon as possible. Every day you delay gives your enemy a chance to find out what is going on. It also gives whoever you are working with the opportunity to reveal to the United States what your plans are. That would give them advance warning."

"I would never do that," mouthed Park to the Mandarin.

"And don't think that someone wouldn't do this. He could make a fortune on one phone call. In war, you have no friends so, the sooner we start, the less chance of a leak occurring."

"I agree. Continue."

"You don't need to have a million deaths but you do

need to make the deaths meaningful. What do I mean by that? You have to target middle and upper middle and upper class types, the ones who go to Disneyland, shop at Costco, buy modern cars and most importantly, pay taxes —the nice, decent people who contribute to society or would eventually make positive contributions—regular working people and students. If you remember, there were two thousand seven hundred and fifty-three victims on 9-11."

"That's not enough."

"We can aim for a million but anything over six thousand and you can claim that you not only more than doubled the 9-11 total but you have struck terror into America forever, especially if you follow this next suggestion."

"Yes?"

"Los Angeles, San Francisco, New York, Chicago, Seattle, San Jose, and Houston all have non-stop commercial flights from Beijing. Rather than risk all eggs with Los Angeles, spread out the targets. We will have flights to all of these destinations leave on the same day. This reduces the risk substantially. If you focus on Los Angeles only, you have a higher risk of getting caught. By spreading it to multiple locations, you have a much better chance of success in at least one of the areas. Remember, your enemy is not just those who live in Los Angeles. It is all of America that allowed your son's death to happen. Follow my blueprint and you will have your revenge."

"What will you charge for this?"

"Two hundred million dollars. We would require an

additional fifty million dollars by the end of this meeting if you want to begin."

Mary, General Park and the Mandarin reeled. This was more than triple what any of them thought it would cost.

"What guarantees do I have?"

"None. Just our reputations and our past work, which you no doubt have already checked out."

A hint of a grin crossed Arthur's countenance. He could imagine seeing the Mandarin's teeth grinding in cursed thought.

"Would you accept...?"

"Mandarin, this is not a flea market operation for haggling," interrupted Arthur. "I will not accept anything less for my fees. The only way to reduce costs is to allow my colleague, Rayna, to handle the entire operation without my direct involvement. This would save you thirty-five million dollars. She is more than capable and I will offer this. If she is killed or otherwise unable to fulfill the mission, I will take over."

"I don't like to deal with inexperienced people. They make mistakes."

"I may not have Arthur's breadth of experience," interjected Rayna angrily, "but this job is not a problem for me. I don't care if you prefer to go with Arthur but don't insult me by saying I can't perform."

"Do you let all your employees speak to your clients like that?" snapped the Mandarin.

"Only if they're right, and Rayna's right. She has already seen part of your operation and has a strategy that will work perfectly. Tell them, Rayna."

"Mary took me to see the factory where handbags are made. Fashion is notoriously fickle, updating and changing constantly. No one would think there was anything unusual about shipping hundreds of bags on short notice to fulfill new orders. We would hide the drugs along with the shipments to the merchandisers in America. With the sticker price of your handbags, only those brokers, importers and retailers with upscale clients would be interested—the target market. From wholesale to retail is a fairly easy step. Let's face it. Most salesclerks do not make a lot of money. It would be fairly easy for us to identify two hundred that would like to make some easy money. By the time they knew what they were involved in, the operation would be over. This is essentially a surgical strike conducted with military precision."

It was a brilliant and perfectly executable plan if the right players were in place.

"You are sure you can deliver?"

"The weakest link in this operation is you, Mandarin. I would suggest that you delegate a major portion of this to Mary, who understands perfectly the bags and purses we would need. Like Arthur, you might be consulted on a higher level strategic basis, but you could leave the essentials to us."

Silence. Then, "May I talk to Mary privately?"

Arthur answered, "Of course, but keep this in mind. If I walk out of this office without a decision, I will put all of my American contacts on full alert. If I do that, you might as well abort the project because it will be dead in the water."

With that, he and Rayna stepped into the waiting room and closed the door.

The Mandarin was in a foul mood. He hated not being the one in control. He unleashed on Mary.

"Why did you take her to the factory?"

"Mandarin, we have been discussing expanding into the United States for a very long time. She definitely knows her stuff and would be a valuable partner."

General Park cut to the chase. "Mandarin, this is not about ego nor is this about money. It is about your son, your legacy... The Mandarin's Vendetta. Let's have some young girls, eat some food that'll burn your mouth off and then you can go back to Linfu tonight. Let Mary handle it."

The Mandarin blew out a long gasp of air. "Call them back in."

Mary opened the door. "Please come in."

Arthur and Rayna stepped in. This time, instead of sitting down, they stood at the door to listen to the Mandarin,

"I accept your offer and we will work with Rayna. If Rayna can come back at 2:00, the extra fifty million dollars will be in your account."

———

RAYNA STEPPED off the elevator at precisely at 1:57 and walked to Mary's office. Jun the watchdog was standing guard as Rayna entered.

The Fidelitas operative smiled. "We can begin. First

of all, we need to check the status of the drugs to be shipped. Are they ready for pick up?"

"Soon. The Mandarin is working on it now."

"Soon as in one hour, one day or one week?"

"I... he... he didn't tell me."

"Mary, this is basic. Can you contact him to find out?"

Mary hesitated, then shook her head. "He never tells me his schedule and I never know where he is. Can we do something ahead of time to prepare?"

Rayna pondered, then scrunched her face. "I'd rather have all the pieces in place before we do anything, but we don't have any choice if we want to come close to making a deadline. Let's go back to the factory. We can pick out thirty-five bags to be overnighted to our Beijing distribution center. Shall we go?"

"Of course. I'll let the Mandarin know what we're doing."

Rayna waited patiently for Mary to send off the text.

"Done." Mary added coyly." Now we can go. While we're there, we could visit other floors and you could pick out some clothes for yourself."

"The thought never crossed my mind." Rayna gave Mary a stern look, then burst out laughing. "I love it!"

FIFTY-FIVE

PLASTIC

As the elevator descended, Jun stood at its front with his eyes glued to the door. At the rear were Rayna and Mary. Rayna's hidden fingers reached beside and gently tapped on Mary's tush and whispered in her ear, "Mary, can we make a stop at the Oceania before we head out?"

Focusing straight ahead as if ignoring Rayna, Mary replied, "I thought you said that we don't have enough time."

"We don't. That's why I want to do it now," murmured Rayna softly but loud enough for Jun to hear. Rayna put her head on Mary's shoulder and squeezed her bum cheek. "Do you know when I first wanted you?"

Mary felt her breath disappearing. "No. When?"

"In the factory when you stayed behind to do it with one of those skanks that work there. That should have been me, not that little hoe."

Rayna gave Mary an insider's glance. *Yes, I figured that out.*

Rayna blew into Mary's ear, then backed away as the elevator door opened.

Mary turned to Jun and announced, "We're going to stop at the Oceania."

"Yes, Mary."

Inwardly, Rayna breathed a sigh of relief. Thoroughly and completely heterosexual, she had never in her life tried to come on to or appeal to a woman, let alone a person twenty years older than herself. Maybe all those school plays she had been part of did pay off with some acting chops.

Her cell phone vibrated, indicating a text message arrived. *There is no info at all on N115.*

THE OUTWARDLY CALM Jun took deep silent breaths to control his own raging hormones as he walked back to the door of Rayna's Oceania suite. He had just spent ten minutes methodically searching the room for any kind of weapons, unusually sharp materials or hidden persons.

"It's clear," announced the big man.

"Sorry to do that, Rayna," apologized Mary. "Jun has kept me alive so many times that I always trust his instincts."

"I totally understand," said Rayna as she sexily strolled to the table where a bottle of champagne awaited beside a bouquet of scarlet roses in her suite.

As she walked, her dress dropped to the floor. Mary's

jaw dropped. She thought that Rayna in a bikini at the presentation was already scorching hot but to see the ex-Special Forces operative in a turquoise G-string and skimpy lace bra... her body was already quivering in anticipation.

Rayna turned around—the front of the lace bra exposed her nipples. "Oops. Now was that accidental or on purpose?" teased Rayna as she slowly placed her hands to cover her booby tips. She then bent down to the floor, allowing Mary—and Jun—to see the silky smooth skin of her butt. Standing back up, Rayna curled her index finger, beckoning Mary to come to the table.

Mary, obviously no neophyte at eliciting and titillating, removed her French designer outfit slowly and sensually. She tossed the jacket to the floor and wiggled her hips as she stepped to Rayna. Standing in front of Rayna, she allowed the Fidelitas operative to unbutton her blouse while she pulled down the zipper of her skirt.

Top and bottom fell to the floor simultaneously.

Rayna pulled Mary's body close to hers. She reached over and unclasped Mary's bra, then lifted the older woman up and pulled off her panties.

Carefully placing Mary back down, Rayna noted a body of artificial "beauty." It would take a knowing eye, but there were faint scars and outlines of a tummy tuck. As Rayna gazed into Mary's eyes and pressed her lips against hers, she saw that Mary's face did not express the rapture she was feeling. Mary's skin was wrinkle free but also had a little rigidity... not enough to have that ghastly frozen face of those women who overdid it with Botox but enough to be a little too firm. Mary's breasts were a thing of beauty. Perfect and perky like those of a teenager but again, evidence of improperly done surgery with some scarring. As Rayna massaged them, she could feel the implants. Looking into Mary's eyes, Rayna noted the tiny, faint marks that indicated surgery on her eyelids. Her natural self had "slit-eyes" so she, of course, opted to have beautiful almond eyes.

"You are perfect," cooed Rayna as she gently ran her fingers over the tips of Mary's breasts, the hard points of desire.

"Oh, that's not entirely me. I've had the best surgeons do a bit of work," admitted Mary.

"If you didn't tell me, I'd never have known." Rayna's fingers flickered down Mary's body to the vee of her aching loins.

"I just feel the need to be completely open with you."

"Honesty is the last thing on my mind," giggled Rayna. As Rayna lifted herself, she cupped her hands under her breasts, then pulled on her bra strap. After letting Mary have a glimpse, she let go and the strap snapped back. Mary reached for the bra to pull it off but Rayna snatched her hand.

"Now, Rayna. I want you now."

Rayna lifted Mary's hand and licked it. Then Rayna motioned her head at Jun. "I'm not very good with audiences. Especially when I do nasty, terrible things that should not be done to man or beast." She took Mary by the hand and led her inside her room.

Five seconds later, Jun heard Led Zeppelin's signature tune, "Stairway to Heaven," blaring from behind the doors. He walked to the room and tried the door. It was locked. He thought of knocking the door down but was not willing to risk the wrath of Mary being interrupted when she was in her "moment."

He exhaled and allowed himself to dream. Maybe he could get a turn with Rayna too before they left.

FIFTY-SIX

ACTIVE PERSUASION

With the soaring vocals of Robert Plant's tenor pondering for meaning in a world of ambiguity, Rayna let go of Mary's hand, then whipped off her panties and bra.

Mary gasped—she had never seen perfection until now. Mesmerized, her eyes devoured Rayna's body. An exotic beauty. Glorious luscious full breasts that rose above her chest. Ecstasy thrilled her spine as Rayna took her head and placed it between her twin peaks. While her hands wandered over Rayna's body, her mouth traveled down to Rayna's navel, slipping her tongue into Rayna's belly button.

Mary was shaking as Rayna pulled her head up. Rayna's hands caressed the older woman's body. With Rayna's hands sliding up to the crest of her breasts, Mary shuddered with electricity. Rayna knew the fine line between pain and rapture, knowing that the crossing of the boundary would heighten the experience even more.

As Mary's heart pounded like it would explode, Rayna's body language transformed. She aggressively pushed Mary off, then sauntered to the music sound system and turned the volume to an ear-splitting decibel level.

With her sexual confidence radiating heat like a supernova, Rayna squeezed Mary's hand, then led her into the bathroom. Rayna poured bubble bath into the tub, then turned the water on. The Oceania was one of those hotels with a rapid fill system.

As the oversized tub filled, steam rose off the surface of the water. Rayna inhaled deeply, then stepped in and sank into the sea of bubbles. She then jumped up. Seeing Rayna's wet hair hanging over her breasts and water droplets glistening on her body, Mary couldn't take it anymore.

"Please, Rayna. Now."

Rayna pulled Mary's body tight into hers and plunged her tongue into Mary's greedy mouth. Rayna sucked hard then jumped up, wrapping her legs around Mary. It was euphoria. No one had ever dominated Mary the way Rayna had.

With Rayna on top, the two fell into the two feet of water. Rayna's legs locked tight, squeezing Mary around the stomach.

After twenty seconds submerged in the water, Mary wanted to scream to release the tension but Rayna's lips would not release.

Then Mary felt the pain of bones breaking. Rayna had squeezed too hard.

Mary tried to push Rayna off but the Fidelitas operative was too strong. Mary was going to drown. Didn't Rayna know what she was doing?

Suddenly, Rayna released her legs, and put her hand over Mary's mouth. "Where is your boss and what is his name?" She lifted her hand off Mary's mouth.

Mary tried to scream but Rayna quickly pushed the older woman's head into the water again, this time holding Mary's mouth open so that water flowed inside.

Rayna pulled Mary's head up again. As Mary coughed and gurgled, Rayna asked, "I can do this for the next half hour before Jun would think anything is wrong. Again, where is your boss and what is his name?"

Mary coughed, then yelled, "J..." Before she could complete saying Jun's name, Rayna pushed her head back into the tub of bubbles.

This time, Rayna waited a full twenty seconds before pulling Mary's head out of the water.

"His name is Deng," Mary gasped as she struggled to breathe.

"Where is he?"

"I don't know. He didn't tell me. Now, please. Let me..."

But before she could complete her plea, Rayna pushed her head down into the water again. When movement had almost stilled, Rayna yanked her head up again. "Where is he?"

The executive assistant whimpered, "He will be in Linfu tonight."

For the final time, Mary's head was shoved under the water. This time, Rayna waited for the end of Jimmy Paige's soaring guitar solo before letting go. Mary's body was already limp as Roger Plant sang the a cappella last line of the song.

Rayna screamed in the throes of ecstatic climax, "No, no. Yes, yes. I love you. I love you. I LOVE YOU! AAAH!" While her imitation of Mary's accent was poor, the screaming and ear-shattering volume of music would prevent Jun from figuring out that it wasn't his boss lady in the throes of wild orgasm.

Rayna then pulled herself up out of the water and turned on the shower. She wrapped a towel around her body, left the bathroom, locking and closing the door, then tiptoed to the door of her bedroom.

She unlocked the door and, as she suspected, saw Jun standing there with his head pressed to the door. The hormonally-berserk bodyguard quickly straightened up and tried to be professional as he forced out, "Where's Mary?"

Rayna's fingers made an encore performance on the large bulge between Jun's pant legs. "She's in the shower," said Rayna slowly, pointing to the bathroom where the sound of water pounded down.

Jun's body started gushing sweat, the muscles in his neck bulged like cord and his face turned scarlet as Rayna's finger movements turned from ballet to dirty dancing. She pulled herself closer, her hips undulating against his body.

He forced out in a gasp, "We have a job to do."

"Yes, we do and we have seven minutes before we have to go. You could join her. Or..." the towel dropped off her sleek, taut body, "...you can join me."

Jun unbuckled his pants and they fell to the floor—he was commando. No underwear. Just his thick stick pointing out.

"Oh..." cooed Rayna as she eased slowly to her knees, fondling Jun's throbbing merchandise, first with one hand, then two.

Jun emitted a quick series of small groans, panting.

"Oh, you are a man, a real man," murmured Rayna as she wrapped both hands around his shaft. Then, with a sudden grip, she bent his penis hard, fracturing it.

There was a weird cracking sound. Jun's penis went flaccid as he screamed, "AAH!"

Rayna leapt up, crooked an elbow and jammed downward at his face. But Jun, used to pain, was hardly incapacitated and rolled over a millisecond before Rayna's elbow arrived. She hit the floor hard, and was shocked for a brief moment. It was all the time Jun needed to lumber on top of her. He put his mitts around her throat and started crushing her windpipe.

Rayna was flailing. For all her martial arts and physical fitness training, thousands of hours in a gym, there was no way she could escape the clenched grip of a hundred-and-ninety pound bruiser of pure muscle... unless...

The unexpected defeats the impossible. The expected in her situation was for her to try and pull off Jun's hands. The unexpected?

Rayna went limp. Sensing victory, Jun relaxed his grip. That heartbeat reprieve was enough for Rayna to bang her forehead against his, then ram a thumb with a pointed thumbnail into his eye.

Jun backed off screaming as Rayna's thumbnail slashed the eyeball and then she ground her thumb into the socket hard. She thrust her left knee against his tortured groin and pulled Jun's body in tight—it was the most painful thing he had ever experienced.

But damned if he was going to be beaten by a woman. He pulled his right arm back and hurled a straight fist at Rayna's head. She tilted to the side but couldn't completely avoid the blow—it hit her on the side of the temple. Not enough to knock her out, but enough to make her woozy.

Both wounded warriors struggled to their feet. Yes, they were both injured but, battle veterans that they were, they knew that pain was just part of the territory for the lives they had chosen for themselves.

Rayna snapped out a side kick. Jun turned just enough so that her foot landed on his meaty upper thigh inside of his groin. He latched on to it and twisted. Rayna followed the arc of the turn by doing a standing somersault.

In mid-air, with her face pointed toward the ground, she pinpointed two fingers at Jun's good eye. He side-stepped, releasing his hold on her. Another knee slammed his balls into his stomach and Jun reeled back, howling.

Enough of this. While there might be some honor in hand-to-hand combat, Jun had had enough. He ripped a gun from his pocket and snapped off a series of shots at Rayna.

Rayna took random running steps to avoid the bullets and ducked behind a sofa. Most sofas are no match for a speeding bullet, but the ultra-thick, padded sofas of a luxury hotel suite were up to the challenge. Jun wasted his rounds, then angrily tossed the gun aside and stormed back at her, roaring wildly.

Rayna made her move. She dashed to the table and pushed it over. The vase holding the flowers toppled and broke. She picked up several of the glass fragments, expertly heaving them at her assailant.

Jun advanced toward his prey, nimbly avoiding the onslaught of sharp, translucent shards. Out of glass fragments, Rayna appeared helpless as Jun charged at her, knocking her to the floor.

Smirking smugly, he was about to put his hands around Rayna's neck again to choke her when Rayna reached over and snatched Mary's designer handbag. Before Jun could react, she yanked the metal chain strap off and wrapped it around his neck, pulling as hard as she could with her hands while kicking at his groin with her feet.

Jun struggled, but it was no contest. Lightheadedness, then darkness swallowed the muscled criminal.

The naked Amazon had defeated the armed enforcer.

Rayna walked to the door that separated her room from China HQ.

PART FOUR
ENDGAME

FIFTY-SEVEN

MOVING FORWARD

Arthur, Barry and Chuck had no clue what had been going on next door. When Rayna entered *au naturel,* the men were speechless.

But not Rayna. She walked directly to the washroom door, stopped, then turned to face her gawkers. "The weasel's name is Deng. He'll be in Linfu in the evening. There are also a couple of dead people in my room." Without waiting for a response, she turned, closed the door and headed directly to the shower.

The three amigos hopped to Rayna's room and shook their heads.

"Damn fool for trying to mess with my girl," stated Chuck as he got down on his knees to examine what Rayna had done to Jun's eyes.

"And there's a drowned rat in here," said Barry, coming out of the bathroom.

Arthur called in for a team of three to sweep her room and clean up the situation while Barry transmitted all the data from Jun and Mary's cell phones to Julio at

CenCom. Similar individuals were sent to Mary and Jun's apartments, as well as to the Mandarin's office.

TWENTY-SEVEN MINUTES LATER, the group of high level Fidelitas operatives met in China HQ. Julio and his wife Helena participated by video conference.

The smiling Helena waved at Rayna, *Hi,* then began, "We took the data from Mary's cell phone and tracked it as best we could. The calls came from somewhere in Pyongyang, the capital of North Korea. The last communication we had was at 2:00 when Arthur was also at the meeting. Since then, there have been no other calls."

"Mary told me Deng was working on delivery 'soon,'" interjected Rayna. "We can probably assume that Pyongyang is where the N115 is being manufactured. But then she said Deng would be in Linfu tonight."

"The China side of the North Korean border," mused Arthur. "Do you think they're done making the product and are bringing it over the border? Did you get a sense, Rayna?"

The Asian woman shook her head. "Why don't you call our North Korean contacts?"

"Because we don't have any," sighed Arthur. "Fidelitas has done zero work there and no one from the Hermit Kingdom has approached us. In other words, to find the Mandarin and his source of drugs, we would be flying blind into a morass of government and military obfuscation, denial and half-truths."

The group digested this information. This was so not

good. The Mandarin was bad enough, but to have North Korea involved? Economic mismanagement and natural disasters led to millions of starving citizens who continued to rely on foreign aid to eat. Since the end of WWII, the mysterious hermit nation had been ruled with an iron fist. Human rights were non-existent with rumors of public execution, slave labor, prison camps and hundreds of thousands in detention facilities. The country, led by a dynasty of ruthless men characterized by extravagant excess and quirky unpredictable personalities, sent out dangerous mixed signals. The Supreme Leader's whims and dictates were backed up by unethical government officials purported to have the world's highest rate of corruption, and a huge military that pervaded the life of every single inhabitant in the country.

Arthur looked at the video monitor. "Helena and Julio, have you gone through the guest lists of Linfu hotels to see if any persons named Deng are registered?"

"Yes, we are doing that now but I'm not hopeful. Someone like the Mandarin who is a maniac about hiding info about himself has likely either paid cash so there is no record or used a pseudonym."

"Not to mention Deng is one of the most common surnames in China," added Helena.

"Well, it seems that the first thing we have to do is get some weapons and send a group of us to Linfu," said Chuck. Chuck mimed a machine gun spitting out its pellets of death.

"That won't work, Chuck. Too risky," advised Julio. "There are no private airfields so you'd have to use the

Linfu airport. Because it's small and there's nothing else to do, half the time security goes overboard either to get a bribe or to escape boredom. Either way, we'd never get weapons in. But we do need to send someone there."

"I've booked your flight, Rayna," announced Helena. "You leave in an hour."

"What about me? Rayna needs back up," said Chuck. "We can't send her in alone."

Arthur disagreed. "Chuck, a big, hulking black man towering over a sea of Asians? You'd be as conspicuous as a red rose in a garden of daffodils. Barry's the same deal and unfortunately, I still have limited mobility from the gunshot wounds."

"Not to mention that Deng saw Arthur and Barry on his spycam when they were in his office," added Julio. "Rayna's got to go in solo."

"So I'm going to a place with no intel, no cover and no weapons?" mumbled Rayna.

Barry, who had spoken very little, chimed the immortal words. "Don't forget, 'And no plan.'"

FIFTY-EIGHT
EVERYONE HAS A SECRET

Rayna was stuck going to Linfu in economy. Not that she was a snob and didn't want to mix with the masses. No, she'd done that all her life and hardly considered herself a member of the elite class. The problem was that, with only a remote chance she could get a secure Internet connection, she wouldn't be able to liaise with Julio and Helena—or to get any updates on her father's condition.

She found herself in the middle seat between two late middle-aged Chinese women who fancied themselves as cougars who had just taken a "girls bonding trip" to Guangzhou. Rayna had barely buckled in before she felt a migraine coming on. In addition to crying the blues about skinflint husbands, there was incessant nattering between them about the young studs that each of them had treated themselves to on their last night. Rayna offered to exchange seats so they could sit beside each other instead of leaning over Rayna to talk.

They looked at her as if she were crazy.

"What? I want see outside the window," responded one.

"Are you crazy? I have to have an aisle seat so I can go to the bathroom without climbing over anybody," replied the other.

Naturally, neither looked out the window or used the bathroom during the five-hour flight. Rayna wished she could escape until the conversation switched to another popular women's topic.

"Your new boobs are fantastic."

"I just love them. No scars, nothing. The doctors in Guangzhou are the best!"

"For sure. I don't know how they do it, but when I had my tummy tuck last year, you couldn't see any marks or anything. I told everyone that I did ten thousand sit-ups!"

Rayna's ears perked. *No scarring?* When their gales of laughter died down, Rayna asked, "I have a friend who got some surgery but she couldn't get rid of all the ugly marks. There were still lines and blotches. She has enough money to get the best in the world. I couldn't figure it out."

"Where were they?"

Rayna pointed to the areas around her breasts and just above the midriff.

One of the women snickered. "You are very pretty but you are dumb. Where you pointed has nothing to do with the surgery. They don't cut there."

"Oh! What can cause that then?"

. . .

FOR THE REST of the flight, Rayna had an in-depth course in the pros and cons, the successes and botched jobs of cosmetic surgery. Ice broken, the trio began chatting girl talk about men, clothing and shoes for the rest of the trip. After the plane landed, her new friends, Anna and Lily, offered Rayna to "help with anything" she needed in Linfu and gave her their phone numbers.

When the plane landed, she quickly thanked them, then dashed away to call Julio and Helena. As she punched the numbers into her phone, she took a quick look at the airport— austere, small and grungy. Not a place to want to hang out in.

"Hello, Mario's Pizza. Can I take your order please?"

"Julio, anything new on Deng?"

"Sorry, Rayna. We're coming up with doughnuts. We've found half a dozen different persons with the surname of Deng registered at various hotels but none of them seem remotely possible."

"How about the N115?"

"Well, nobody knows anything about it or maybe there's fifty possibilities. There are rumors but nothing concrete."

"Okay. Did our team take any photos of Mary when they cleaned up? If so, can you bring them up?"

"Sure, will do. Any particular reason?"

"This might be just a shot in the dark, but he might have some unusual sexual preferences."

"Yeah?" interjected Helena skeptically. "Him and every other being with a stick between their legs."

"Yeah, and I'm thinking that he might have had a relationship with Mary." "I thought she was gay."

"She might have swung both ways—she was fanatically loyal to Deng and might have been in love or lust with him, too. When we were together, she not only craved sexual satisfaction but wanted a strong dominating person or it wouldn't be enough. She was also one of the most plastic people I've met. Not in personality, but because she had more plastic surgery and artificial enhancements than anyone else I've ever met."

"So your theory is that she was doing this for Deng?"

"No, my theory isn't that she was doing this for Deng but because of Deng. When I saw Mary's body, I noticed some unusual scarring. I thought that whoever she hired for the surgery just did a lousy job. Maybe I'm wrong. Maybe the physical abuse that Mary suffered was so extensive, that was about as good a job of patching her up as could be done. She could afford the best so the skin defects make no sense."

Helena drew in a long breath of air, then exhaled loudly. "I've got the photos of Mary's body up right now and yes, I can see that your theory is plausible. Not saying it's right, but it hangs together."

"Have you dug up anything for me in the way of weapons?" "Not anybody we can trust just yet," admitted Julio.

Rayna saw a porter pushing a cart with Lily's luggage toward the door. She ended the call with Julio, then rushed up to her.

"Hi, Rayna! You want to join me? I can give you a ride in my husband's limo to wherever you want to go," offered Lily.

"That would be great and, actually, I'm wondering if

you can help me with something else," said Rayna with strained concern.

"Oh, what's the matter?"

"I'll tell you inside the car," whispered Rayna.

INSIDE LILY'S LIMO, Rayna took a breath and confided, "I'm not really who you think I am."

"You mean you're not a hooker coming here to make some money?" asked Lily, furrowing her brow.

Rayna looked at Lily with surprise. "Am I that obvious? You figured that out."

"You don't need to be obvious. No one, especially a girl as pretty as you, ever comes to Linfu except to make money. And, no offense, but from the way you talk, the way you are, there's only one way you can earn some. You're not exactly a genius, you know."

Rayna fought back mock tears. "Yeah, I know but what works, works. A girl's got to make a living somehow."

Lily put her arm around Rayna. "What's happening, Rayna? You can tell me everything."

Rayna could sense Lily's vicarious excitement with how she imagined Rayna's life.

"I'm worried about my client. Just before I left, I found out he can be rough. He paid the girl good but now she can't work for a month. I... I don't know what to do."

"Don't do it then."

Rayna choked out the words. "My pimp won't let me.

The client is a Guangzhou businessman and girls like me are his hobby."

"Girls like you?"

Rayna swallowed and stretched out each word. "I do special... things... I'm the best so I cost more. A lot more. The client is here in Linfu, bored with the local girls and doesn't want a Korean."

Lily nodded in empathy. "We should castrate all of them." She tapped the driver on the shoulder. "Give me my other bag."

The driver reached into the glove compartment and took out a handbag. He reached over and handed it to Lily in the back seat.

Lily opened the handbag up and pulled out a pocket pistol. Rayna stifled a gasp. In disbelief, she asked, "You own a Sig Sauer P238?" The P238 was one of the most popular small handguns in the United States, definitely not a lady's weapon.

Lily handed it to Rayna. "Of course. A lady needs real protection. You keep this. If it's small, he won't notice so much. Don't worry. I've got a dozen of them."

"You are amazing."

Lily didn't flinch or acknowledge the compliment. "Keep it close and be ready to use it. Where are you staying?"

"That's another problem. I'm waiting for his call. My pimp said to wait for a call from Deng or the Mandarin. He's in a hotel."

"There are only two hotels that a respectable Guangzhou businessman stays in. The Hennessy or the Linfu Plaza. The Hennessy has the best food and entertainment. The Linfu Plaza isn't as fancy, but a lot of Chinese stay there because North Koreans prefer to do business there."

Bingo! Thank you, Lily. "Lily, thank you so much for all you've done for me. I don't want to trouble you anymore. Just drop me off anywhere. I'll wait for Deng's call."

"Are you sure? I'm happy to stay with you."

"No, no. I'll be okay but I'm not... You don't want to be anywhere close."

Lily shot Rayna a puzzled glance and saw the fiery determination on Rayna's face. *She doesn't need me.* Lily instructed the driver to pull over to the curb in front of a department store.

Rayna got out and waved goodbye as Lily's car drove off. After the car disappeared from sight, Rayna pulled out her cell and sent a text. *Hey, Julio, can you go through the guest list at the Linfu Plaza? I think Deng is there.*

IT WAS ONLY a minute before Rayna got a call from Julio. "Okay, I'm looking at the Linfu Plaza now. Two hundred and fifty rooms. Presently forty percent occupied. Are you sure? There's the Hennessy Hotel, which is a lot more upscale with a sixty percent occupancy."

"Focus on the Plaza. See who's there by themselves from Guangzhou and checked in today or will check in later."

"Yeah, yeah. Give me some time."

Helena burst into the conversation. "I just found this.

A hooker, age thirty-two, was admitted to Linfu General Hospital yesterday five days ago with overt sexual trauma. She died within an hour of admittance. Sodomized. Hands, breasts, butt and thighs severely bruised... "

"Hands?" asked Rayna. "If her hands are bruised, maybe she tried to fend him off."

"Or maybe he's got some bruises on his body. They've already cremated her so there's no way to check anything else." Helena continued. "Her body was found in a construction site two blocks from the Linfu Plaza Hotel. The building being constructed is owned by Sunmoon Holdings, a company with headquarters in Pyongyang."

"Okay, okay," said Julio. "There are twenty-seven possible candidates currently staying at the Linfu Plaza. None of them are named Deng or are from Guangzhou."

"That doesn't mean anything. Any of them on the contact list of Mary's cell phone?" asked Rayna.

"No. Twenty of them have been there for two to three nights and the rest checked in or will be checking in today. I'm sending the list to you now."

"Book me a room, Julio. I'm on my way there now. And send me any information you can about the murdered girl."

"Will do. And get back to us when you check in."

"Of course."

Rayna thumbed her cell off, then stepped into the department store. Half an hour later, she had racked up a bill of three thousand dollars on two outfits, not an easy thing to do in this non-cosmopolitan town. The admiring salesclerk marveled, "You look dressed to kill."

FIFTY-NINE

SEARCHING

Half an hour later, Rayna was in her room at the Linfu Plaza back in conversation with Helena. Definitely not the Oceania, it was more Holiday Inn than Ritz Carlton. "Rayna, I've tried to get more info but not having any luck. It seems a lot pay cash, use their own phones or have their own packages for Internet use. If you're Chinese, you don't want anyone to know you're doing business with the Koreans. If you're Korean, you don't want anyone to know you're doing business with the Chinese."

"You got anything I can use?"

"Got room numbers for twenty of the possibilities."

"It might take me hours or even longer to check them out individually," mumbled Rayna, shaking her head.

"He's been calling Mary's cell for hours," reported Helena.

"He's probably freaked or pissed or both that she's not picking up. Hm. Where is he?"

"I can't figure that out."

"That indicates he might still be in North Korea because of telecommunication weirdness?" It was more of a question than statement.

Helena laughed. "Love your use of technical terms. Yeah, something like that. Why don't you sit in the bar and see who approaches you?"

"I already checked out that possibility. The competition is too fierce. I'm over the hill. I have wrinkles. I need botox."

"Are you kidding? Who the hell have you been talking to, girly girl? Never mind. The guy you're looking out for may have bruising or hematomas. If he's at the Linfu Plaza, sooner or later, he's got to go through the lobby."

"You call that a plan?" quipped Rayna sarcastically.

"Hey, it's a stakeout. It would be great to be proactive, kick down doors, then bust chops but sometimes you got to sit and wait and see what happens but I'm all ears if you've got another suggestion."

Rayna cooed seductively, "Hey, I'm thirsty... "

"You are so bad. I like it."

WHERE THE HELL WAS MARY? The Mandarin had been tied up the whole day with Park, pushing the chemists as hard as he could. When he wasn't doing that, he was on the phone trying to figure out what the hell was going on with Mary and Rayna. When he didn't hear from them, he tried Jun but there was no answer there, either.

And traveling from Pyongyang to China, cell phone coverage was its usual totally crappy self and he couldn't get through even to their phones. Now, back in Linfu, he wanted to know what the hell was going on.

He wanted an update, but Mary was still incommunicado. He wasn't worried that she might run off with the dough—he owned her and could do anything he wanted. And then he remembered. *Damn her. She forgot to charge her phone again. She is so damned irresponsible. I will definitely have to teach her a lesson. Did she and Rayna get the bags off to Beijing?*

And then a disturbing thought dawned. He knew that while she would never be satisfied by any man but him, she had a weakness for strong women. *What if Mary had done a side deal with the girl and the two had skipped out with his money?*

"Get me to the Linfu Plaza. Now," ordered the Mandarin to Park's chauffeur as the modest vehicle crossed over the Sino-Korean Harmony Bridge connecting the two countries.

"Yes, sir."

RAYNA DIDN'T REALLY NEED to worry about competition from the other girls in the bar. In the twelve minutes she had been sitting at her table, she had been propositioned three times by customers after they had looked over her overly eager, overly made-up and underly dressed "rivals." Her stomach churned for three reasons: She felt helpless that she couldn't do anything for the girls who had no other means of support; none of the men who approached her seemed like potential candidates for the Mandarin; and she hadn't a clue what Deng looked like.

She also felt vulnerable. After all the effort of getting a weapon from Lily, she had to give it up. There was no way to hide it under her barely-there black dress with a libidinous thigh-slit and plunging V-neck.

Then a possibility entered the hotel lobby. A muscular older middle-aged man with a scar down his face whose body language broadcast he was about to explode.

It was show time.

Rayna's body was a knot. Some called that fear or even cowardice. Rayna knew that was what kept her alive —always expecting the worst and realizing that was just the beginning. Donning her sunglasses, she briskly stepped toward the man who was entering the elevator. She squeezed in just as the elevator was closing, pushing him toward the back of the lift.

On automatic pilot, the man took a roundhouse swing in the direction of the head of the person who shoved him.

Rayna caught his arm. "Relax."

The man turned around and recognized Rayna immediately. "You're bikini girl."

"And you're Deng."

"You're supposed to be coordinating our shipment. Why are you here and where is Mary?" snarled Deng.

"Same place as Jun." Rayna flipped open her cell phone, revealing a picture of Mary's drowned corpse and of the naked Rayna in a picture of conquest and humiliation of Jun, a man twice her size.

"You should thank me. I had to kill them. As soon as the money transfer was completed, they were going to take your money and run. Mary asked me to go with them but you are our client, not her."

"The bastards. I made them. I MADE THEM! How the hell did you find me?"

"Obviously, I'm very persuasive," shrugged Rayna. "But that's not important right now. I'm here so we can coordinate the shipments. Show me the N115 and I can put my team in motion in two days."

The Mandarin bit his lip. "There's been a change. My Pyongyang manufacturers made a modification to the formula. It is now N117. It takes far less to kill and we can take full delivery tomorrow."

He just saved his life—at least for now. I've got to find out where the stuff is. Rayna's voice turned to ice. "We gave you our price based on certain parameters. We cannot do business with you changing the rules after we've started. So what are we going to do now?"

"Come to my room. I can be very entertaining."

Visions of the brutalized dead hooker and Mary's abnormal scarring leapt to Rayna's mind. She grabbed his head with her hands, thrust her tongue down his throat, sucked the air out of his lungs, then released him.

"Business first. You need to tell me everything."

SIXTY

NEED TO KNOW

In the glowing orange sky flecked with purple, with the setting sun reflecting into the sparkling waves of the Yalu river, it was a stunning Linfu sunset. Rayna and Deng strolled along the charming walkway with the luscious forest abuzz with the cooing, giggling and moaning of clandestine lovers.

"I didn't take you for being the romantic type," said Rayna as Deng stopped in a quiet, isolated portion of the bank.

Deng's face steeled. "This is where delivery will take place. At strategic points along the river."

Her inner radar working in overdrive, there was a note of ominous concern in Rayna's voice as she studied the emotionless expression that stretched across the Mandarin's face. "At the hotel, you told me it was being made in Pyongyang. I assumed we were picking it up from there."

"The General prefers not to reveal where the factory is."

The General? The North Korean military are involved? "I'm not asking this to be nosey but I do need to know if we'll be dealing with the Supreme Leader or any of his military cronies. That changes our approach... but not our price."

"No, no. It's a private affair. The man I'm dealing with is an independent broker. He's got North Korea's best chemists working on our product."

"So if we're not picking it up, how are we going to get it?"

The Mandarin turned to the Yalu River and pointed. "This river is shallow and goes on for ten miles. Sometime tomorrow morning, manufacturing will be finished and we will have the merchandise shipped to the other side of the river. The general is arranging to have seventy-five women crossing different parts of the river. Each one of them will be carrying a little Ziplock bag. Some of them will contain N117, some will contain crystal meth, some will contain flour."

"Obviously not here. It's too wide. Where?"

Rayna heard a faint familiar noise—the cocking and pulling of the trigger on a gun—and dropped hard and rolled to her side. There was a thud and puff of dirt rising from where the bullet handed.

Looking up, she saw Deng cold, methodical... He had the barrel of a .22 caliber gun, fitted with a long silencer, aimed directly at her. Had she not lowered herself, the bullet would have gone directly into the middle of the back of her head, likely exploding and decapitating her.

He's figured me out! I asked too many questions.

The predator was moving in on its prey.

Standing stark against the orange horizon, the Mandarin spat in Rayna's direction, then unleashed more silent fire.

Rayna rolled over, one direction, then the other. The random movements didn't allow Deng a clear target and bullets ricocheted off the ground, missing their prey by millimeters. Out of the corner of her eye, she saw a rock explode into granular particles as bullets slammed into it.

On the ground, she did a sideswipe of the Mandarin's legs. He quickly jumped, missing the brunt of Rayna's kick. Still poised to fire, he shot again while in the air. Rayna quickly turned and dodged the sizzling lead. The bullet bypassed her and seared the river's water as it entered.

Rayna looked desperately for anything to defend herself with. A small rock, barely the size of the extinct silver dollar, lay by her hand. She picked it up and, with pinpoint precision, launched it at the Mandarin's face.

He angled his face so that the stone embedded into his cheek. Blood spurted out but there was no serious damage. It was, however, a minor distraction. Rayna dove at the Mandarin's legs and he toppled awkwardly.

Rayna ripped the gun from his hand and tossed it into the water.

"That was stupid. Getting it and shooting me was your only chance of survival," snapped her foe as he pulled another gun from his pocket.

There was a microsecond for Rayna to decide her plan of attack... or retreat. She ruled out retreat because an assassin of the Mandarin's caliber would not miss from pointblank range. There was no way she could compete with him in any kind of street brawl.

That left her one choice for survival—the martial arts training she'd received ever since she was a child. It had to be fast, and it had to be accurate.

Rayna lunged at the Mandarin with both arms whirling like windmills on steroids. Not expecting the blitzkrieg attack, he put his hands in front of his face to prevent the tiger claws of Rayna's hands from ripping out his eyes.

Rayna reached to pull the gun from the Mandarin's hand but he yanked it back, countering with a vicious left hook.

With her feet firmly planted, Rayna deftly moved her upper body to the right then, demonstrating incredible flexibility, she threw a side kick into the Mandarin's chest, knocking him down.

Rayna fell on top of him, arm slugging him in the throat, then gouging at any part of his body she could. The Mandarin countered by using the .22 as a bludgeon. Rayna ignored the pounding she was taking. She reached her arm back and drove her fingers toward the Mandarin's eyes. As her arm descended, the Mandarin's head rocked up and bit her on the forearm, piercing the skin.

Blood spurted out as Rayna yanked her arm back before his incisors tore into her flesh. For the Mandarin, he had his small victory—his eyeball was still in its socket. He tossed her off, landing a blow to her midsection.

Fighting through the agony, Rayna crooked her elbow

and landed it squarely on his nose. There was a horrible cracking sound as his nose was pushed into his head.

Both combatants stumbled to their feet, warily watching each other

Roaring, the Mandarin aimed at Rayna and fired. But, as he shot, another side kick from Rayna hit his hand. The bullet shifted direction and grazed the ear of the ex-Special Forces operative. Like its brother, this miniature rocket found a grave in the Yalu River.

With blood dripping from her wounded ear, Rayna summoned every last bit of strength as she threw twisting hammer punches at the Mandarin's mid-section. He withstood them all like Muhammad Ali absorbing the heaviest blows Joe Frazier could throw at him in the *Thrilla from Manila*.

Rayna was tiring, but so was Deng—the barrage of blows weakened him, too. Time for a counter-assault.

The Mandarin barreled at her, clipping her arm with a jackhammer blow but Rayna sidestepped the full frontal assault. He whipped around and threw a devastating sidekick at her. Her reflexes dulled, Rayna was not quick enough to avoid his foot colliding with her head. She managed to stay erect but staggered backward.

Standing three feet apart, both were panting and sweating, two exhausted wounded warriors. Rayna's mind was working overtime. There was no way she could continue like this. She had to end it soon or she would be finished. She used the only possible weapon she could think of—his male ego.

"Mary died happy because half an hour with me was worth more than a thousand nights with you. All you did was hurt her, abuse her until she bled, whereas I thrilled her with these."

Rayna ripped her blouse off and tore the cups off her strapless bra. It may have been the sight of Rayna's delectable breasts or maybe it was just the shock of Rayna's action but, whatever it was, it was enough to distract the Mandarin for a microsecond. Time enough, though, for Rayna to yank the handgun from him and shoot him in the leg.

The Mandarin would not allow himself to scream but dropped to his knees.

Rayna booted him hard. As he lay in agony on the ground, Rayna twisted her foot into his bleeding thigh.

"Where is the factory?"

The Mandarin gritted his teeth and grunted but refused to talk.

Rayna, aiming the Mandarin's weapon at his head, crouched and took the cell phone out of the Mandarin's pocket. She thumbed a familiar number.

"Hello, Mario's Pizza. Can I take your order please?"

"Julio, if I keep this phone on, can you pull all the data and recent phone calls off it and get me addresses and locations?"

"Boom. It's done. What do you need to know?"

"Any recent addresses in Pyongyang?"

"Just one. Seems like a lot of calls were made there today."

"Thanks, Julio. Will you have any more need for this phone?"

"It would be nice but not necessary."

"I'll take that as a 'no.' I'll call again in a bit."

Rayna stroked the gun as she inched closer to this purveyor of human tragedy. "So it doesn't matter if you feel like talking or not. I've got what I need."

The Mandarin locked a menacing stare on his foe. "It doesn't matter about me. I will still have my revenge on America for the death of my son. I've given orders to proceed with a different plan if I am not heard from. You cannot stop me."

"Says who?"

Rayna coldly pumped a hole into the side of Deng's head and watched as life spurted out of him. She wiped the gun down, then put it in his hand. She then flipped through the images on his phone until she found a picture of Jackson. She placed the phone in the Mandarin's other hand.

Not that anyone would check that hard but it would be pretty obvious to the authorities when they arrived that Mr. Deng from Guangzhou had committed suicide because of his son's drug overdose.

Rayna fished around in the Mandarin's pockets. Sure enough, there was another cell phone there.

SIXTY-ONE
FLYING SOLO

Fidelitas' goal for this China trip was to exact payback for those responsible for the Zongtian school disaster. With the Mandarin's death, that had been largely accomplished.

But before anyone could pat themselves on the back, there was another matter to take care of: finding and destroying the N117 in Pyongyang.

Tonight.

And Rayna had only the skimpiest of information to work with.

But at least Julio was able to provide an address for her.

Rayna had to continue to fly solo.

Not to mention she was weaponless. She would have liked a few bricks of C4 and an AK47 but she didn't have the gun that Lily gave her anymore.

Lily. Lily?

Rayna took the Mandarin's cell and made a call.

"Hello?" sounded a familiar voice.

"Hi, Lily, it's Rayna."

"Oh, thank God you're alive. Did you use the little present I gave you?"

"No, as things turned out, he decided to behave but I'm wondering where you got it. I'm looking to get another kind of protection."

There was a brief pause in the conversation as Lily thoughtfully made light clicking sounds with her tongue.

"Lily?"

"Yes, I'm here. I'll need to take you where you want to go. She won't deal with anyone without an intro-duction."

"Thanks. Lily, can I ask why you're willing to help me?"

"Of course. Once upon a time, I was like you... a working girl. We have to look out for each other... I'll be at the Linfu Plaza in twenty minutes."

"Perfect."

TWENTY MINUTES WAS ENOUGH for Rayna to get back to the hotel, change into comfortable functional clothes, primp herself a bit, and liberate a dozen books of matches from the lounge.

She met Lily at the hotel door and hopped into her limo. "Thanks, Lily. I appreciate this."

"No problem. Anything for my little sister."

After several blocks of Chinese and North Korean enterprises, the limo turned down a narrow dark alley. Not a whole lot of places open except for bars and massage parlors. The vehicle pulled to the side in front of a dimly lit shop with a sign that read, "Used Appliances."

An elderly woman was waiting in front and opened the vehicle door. After Lily and Rayna stepped out onto the curb, the cautious senior ushered them into her store, then locked the door. The store was full of washing machines, fridges, microwaves—none that looked as if they worked.

"Hello, Lily," said the shopkeeper.

"Hi, Mama. Rayna, this is my mother, Anna. Mama, Rayna needs some things."

"What kind of 'things?'"

Rayna looked back and forth between Lily and her mother. The eyes, the long fingers ... there were definitely resemblances. *I wonder how much I look like Ling.* "I was looking for some high intensity flares that can generate some heat quickly. Maybe twenty of them that I can carry with me?"

"Rayna, if that's what you wanted, I could have taken you to a hardware store. What do you really need and why?" asked Lily. No longer the airhead cougar, Lily looked a formidable businesswoman.

There are times to tell the truth and there are times to tell a lie. Rayna's normal instinct was to lie, but there was zero time to bullshit.

"Lily, I'm not who you think I am. I'm not a hooker and I didn't come here to earn a few bucks."

"I knew that but I could see you didn't want to tell me so I played along with it. What do you need and, if you feel like telling me, why?"

Rayna had nothing to lose by telling all—she really

didn't have any options. Using flares might have worked with pinpoint shots at the chemicals in the manufacturing facility but that seemed like a long shot.

"I need portable IEDs. And/or grenades. And/or C4... I am going to blow up a meth lab in Pyongyang but it's not meth I'm destroying. It's a new synthetic drug that kills with very small doses."

Lily and her mother looked at each other, then burst out laughing.

"I always told Lily, if you tell a lie, make it the biggest one you can but I've never heard such a crazy story from a hooker."

Rayna stepped to a clunker of a washing machine. She stooped down and grabbed its bottom. She slowly stood up, extending her right arm out, lifting the washing machine to shoulder level. She held it still without wavering for three seconds before placing it gently back in position.

"Elite fitness. Canadian Special Forces. Do you want to see me shoot?"

"No, no," gaped Anna. "I believe you. I don't have what you're asking for but I do have something that will suit your purposes. Give me a moment."

As Anna went to the back of the store, the puzzled Rayna turned to Lily and asked, "What is going on? I don't get it."

Lily snickered. "My mother is a businesswoman. Weapons are her specialty and she sells mainly to North Korean businessmen and officials."

"Because they're illegal there."

"Exactly. But people still want them."

Mama carried in a cardboard box. "Here you go." She opened it up and inside were half-pound bricks of *Belgium's Finest White Chocolate.* "Be careful with these. It's my own brand of plastic explosive. The blast sets off at high heat. All you need to do is set fire to the paper. Each brick will be enough to blast an area within a six-foot diameter. Heat waves will be over a thousand degrees."

"That's ingenious," nodded Rayna with admiration.

"It is a best seller for those who want to pay for it. How many do you want? They are five thousand dollars each and I only take cash."

"Have you got twenty?"

Lily was shocked. "You carry that much with you?"

"You never know when you'll need it. Can you wrap them in Ziploc or plastic bags?"

Lily shook her head. "That's not a good idea. It makes them stand out if you are checked."

"Yes, but I have to cross the Yalu River, then steal a car to get to Pyongyang."

"That's how you're planning to get there? That's stupid, crazy and dangerous."

"How would you get there then?"

HALF AN HOUR LATER, Lily's limo dropped Rayna off on a stretch of highway outside of Linfu that was lined with canteen kitchens. Every one of the truck stops had a number of long- and short-haul vehicles parked outside.

"Good luck. And be careful," cautioned Lily.

"Thanks for everything." Rayna stepped outside with

her new backpack. She looked to see which of the road-side restaurants had the most trucks outside and stepped toward it.

Arriving, she entered. Her senses were assaulted with the stench of cheap booze, greasy food and kimchi, the fiery Korean fermented spiced dishes of vegetables.

Rayna looked around, her eyes shifting as she studied the room. Anna told her to pick a table with girls. They were either "mules" for drugs or North Korean government-sponsored waitresses. Both would likely be hitching rides with truckers back to the big city.

Rayna approached one table where a trucker sat with a couple of twenty-something young things. "Do you have room for one more?" asked Rayna. "I'm going to Pyongyang."

"I'm full," said the trucker.

Rayna reached into her pocket and pulled out an American twenty dollar bill. "I don't mind staying in the back as long as there's something to lie on."

The trucker took the twenty and beamed as he stuffed the bill into his jeans. "I'll take you for free for ten minutes alone."

"The ride will be enough."

SIXTY-TWO

NOXIOUS

At the border checkpoint, the truck and its passengers were cursorily searched but there was nothing out of the ordinary. One of the guards on duty hoped Rayna might offer him one of her chocolate bars as a bribe but she stood her ground, saying that those were treats for some of the millions of malnourished orphans. Clearing inspection, all were ushered through. Rayna knew she was just imagining it but, as the truck crossed the boundary from China into North Korea, she felt an insidious evil penetrating her soul.

As if ignoring Rayna's fantasies, the truck traveled quietly without incident for the next hour and a half. It was almost 4 a.m. by the time it arrived in Pyongyang at the industrial park where the drug factory was housed.

THE UNREMARKABLE, small three-story building in Pyongyang's industrial area had been shuttered for more than five years. When it first opened at the turn of the new millennium, it was to great fanfare. After all, the North Korean pharmaceutical company Geongang Products claimed to have developed a super drug that was the cure for MERS and SARS, combining Korean ginseng, trace minerals, and rare earth elements. However, it turned out to be false hoopla, so typical of the extravagant claims made by the Supreme Leader. The state-of-the-art factory closed down.

However, the facility continued to generate enormous profits. It became a leading manufacturer of crystal meth. For this, North Korea's claim of purity in production was absolutely true. The meth produced out of this building was sold throughout North Korea, China and Asia until pressure from the Chinese government, which was dealing with an addiction crisis, again caused the factory to close its doors.

At least officially. Unofficially, business continued without a hiccup, the main difference being that the chemists, instead of being hired by the state, were now freelancers who worked for the contractors that hired them.

As with so many other well-known drugs, the creation of N115 was an accident. A chemist, who had worked for three days straight without sleeping, made an incorrect formulation of crystal meth, with the result being the deaths of several of his co-workers.

The chemist's boss, rather than getting angry and firing him, chose to hire him to refine the product.

That boss was General Park Daesoon. It took Park less than three days to find his first client for the new deadly chemical.

The assembled team of lab workers were working frantically to fulfill the Mandarin's huge order of the deadly synthetic drug.

"YOU SURE THIS is the right place?" asked the driver.

"Yes. My uncle works here and we will go the orphanage after he gets off work. Thank you very much," said Rayna.

The driver waved goodbye and Rayna carefully walked around the building, studying every possibility, hoping to glean some clue to help her formulate a plan. Although she could not see inside, there were lights on every floor.

Then she rounded the building to the back and quickly flattened herself on the pot-holed asphalt. She saw two vehicles: a panel truck and a military transport van. There were three soldiers standing around at the loading bay smoking. Rayna recognized the aroma—it was around her all the time in Afghanistan. Marijuana. She inhaled gratefully. If she was going to have to take action, there was a good chance that these three jokers would not present a problem. She spotted remnants of half a dozen joints lying by the dumpster.

There were several stacks of empty wooden pallets closer to the loading bay. She could get a better look if she could squeeze through the space between the stacks. She removed her backpack and wriggled in.

Kneeling, Rayna crawled through the crack between two of the piles—the musty smell told her they might have been sitting there for years. She craned her neck to get a better look at the panel truck—its back door was open. Inside, there were a few small cardboard boxes, piled haphazardly.

She surmised the truck was to carry the N117 and the military van was for protection. The cargo was only fifty kilograms but, with a hundred million dollars at stake, there better be some kind of back up.

And then the world went black.

SIXTY-THREE

SURROUNDED BY DEATH

When Rayna woke up, her hands were tied in front of her and she was lying on the ground. Where, she didn't know. All she knew was the back of her head was throbbing. She was having a hard time focusing—her heartbeat was racing and she felt really hot. Her mouth was dry and had a chalky taste. And then, she was giddy, laughing... Incredibly happy, she wished she could feel like this forever.

And then, a flash of lucidity. She saw that she was next to an open box that contained bags of white powder, one of which had a hole in it. She realized what had happened—someone had forced crystal meth into her mouth and she was experiencing a rush.

Because of her dead ex-fiancee Tanner, a singer/drug dealer in New York, she knew the symptoms. She loved Tanner when he was like this and she hated him when he was like this. It was artificial love. She also knew that sometime in the next half hour or so, the high was going to end and she was going to start coming down.

Would willpower work in battling the mind-altering effects of the drugs? Yes, no, maybe so but, even if she were able to, there was still the matter of the three rounds of heavy-duty braided nylon cord wrapped around her wrists and ankles.

Rayna forced herself to evaluate her environs. Trying to keep her movements undetected, she slowly rolled onto her back. As she did, she saw that the room was dimly lit, the walls were made of concrete and the ceiling was about twenty feet high. *I'm inside the warehouse in the loading area.*

She blinked hard and clenched her fists. There was an unbearable growing smell of diesel exhaust and the sound of a large engine that threatened to explode her eardrums. She shook her head violently but that didn't ease the anguish. Counter-intuitively, she told herself, "Relax." She inhaled slowly, taking a dozen seconds to fill her lungs. Then she exhaled, again drawing out the time as long as she could.

It worked. Inside the loading bay, she saw a large truck backing in. With men shouting in Korean, she figured they were giving directions, guiding the driver who was having a difficult time. She rolled onto her stomach silently to get a better look. The two-ton truck stopped and the driver got out—he was Chinese. (While many find it difficult to distinguish the ethnicities or origins of Asians, that is not difficult for many Asians. It was imperative for anyone working covertly in the Orient.)

The truck's back door was unlatched and its accordion door pushed up. Three men began unloading the cargo. There were two sizes of boxes. One was more rectangular, the other square. In the poor light, Rayna strained hard to see what was written on either of the boxes. It was undistinguishable until one of the men carrying a rectangular box passed briefly under a glowing low wattage bulb. In that flash of a second, Rayna saw the Chinese characters 麻黄素.

Ephedrine. The other square boxes must be full of phenyl acetone.

The key ingredients for making meth, ice...

The driver spoke in Mandarin to the shippers. Rayna could see that they were having a hard time communicating. *No wonder he was having a hard time parking. He doesn't understand Korean.*

One of the shippers made a call.

Five silent minutes passed as the men continued to unload the truck.

Then a man about the same age as her father appeared. Stern, stout and wearing the uniform of a North Korean General.

He barked at the Chinese driver in Mandarin. "Why didn't the Mandarin send the regular guys who speak Korean?"

"We do all his top jobs in China, General Park."

Rayna and the general did the same thing--looked over the two men that the Mandarin sent. Obviously, enforcers with experience, just in case there was a problem.

"Okay. Let's load up the truck." The military officer then motioned his head toward Rayna. "And let's send them to Yodok."

Rayna's head jolted. There were two things in Park's last short comment that surprised her. He said, "Them." Plural. That meant there was more than just her. The other word was "Yodok." This was for prisoners who were deemed "enemies of the state." Prisoners here were given the harshest treatment and living conditions, if they were allowed to live at all. Unsubstantiated rumors of systematic torture, rape and organ harvesting abounded.

———

A SOLDIER CARRYING a rifle with its bayonet pointed at two grim-faced North Korean prisoners whose hands were also tied, approached her. The soldier's bayonet poked them toward a military van and motioned them to get inside. The three prisoners complied. The two North Koreans sat on a bench that ran lengthwise in the back of the van. Rayna and the soldier sat on the other side of the van on a bench that faced the Koreans. A metal barrier with a thick glass window separated the prisoner containment area and the front of the truck where another soldier drove with Park in the passenger seat.

Rayna watched the truck carrying the N117 pull out of the parking area. Five seconds later, the military vehicle left the drug factory, too.

There was tense silence for five minutes. Rayna turned her head to look out the front window and saw that the truck was two hundred feet ahead. She saw her guard glaring at her. She spoke to the soldier in a friendly tone. "You're ugly. Uglier than my ex-boyfriend's dog. Maybe you are a dog."

Rayna flashed a broad smile. "And you are stupid. Really stupid."

The soldier's angry expression melted away.

"He doesn't understand English," said one of Rayna's fellow prisoners.

"That's what I was hoping for," advised Rayna, smile still plastered on her face at her captor. "Do you want to get out of this?"

"Of course. But there's no way," claimed her other prison mate. "They caught us... I'm Minjoon and he's my brother Woojin... we found out they were ramping up production for the last few days and wanted to steal some of their drugs. We need money for food and we don't have any other way to get any."

"Don't underestimate the situation. Trust that I know what I'm doing."

Minjoon and Woojin nodded.

"When I count to three, I want you to scream as loudly as you can and then duck. One. Two. Three!"

The young men started howling. As per Rayna's instructions, they fell off their bench to the floor. The soldier did exactly as Rayna anticipated he would. He looked at the prisoners on the floor and prepared to shoot.

That gave Rayna the opportunity she wanted. She lunged at the soldier and butted him in the head. Yelling, he dropped the bayonet. She quickly cut her bonds free, then grabbed the soldier's balls and squeezed as hard as she could, incapacitating him.

Park, noticing the commotion in the back, ordered

the window down and whipped around to fire. Rayna hoisted the pained soldier in front of her as a shield and angry bullets lodged in his neck. Blood gushed from a punctured vein. Rayna pushed the dead soldier at the general, knocking him to the side.

"Get out," screamed Rayna as she made like Supergirl launching herself through the barrier's window to the front cab.

No argument there. Minjoon and Woojin leapt out, taking the bayonet with them to cut their own bonds.

Rayna launched a right hook to Park's head, knocking him out.

A left elbow met the driver's jaw. He flinched, allowing Rayna to grab the steering wheel and pull herself into the front.

The driver, regaining his composure, started hammering at Rayna's arm. As Rayna swung the wheel back and forth to avoid his fists, the truck swerved violently to the left and right.

Rayna slammed on the brakes and gripped the wheel tightly. The driver's momentum carried him forward, and his head collided with the windshield. Rayna reached over quickly and opened the driver's door, then pushed the soldier out. The truck carrying the N117 was now about a thousand feet ahead of her. Rayna killed the headlights in the military vehicle and put pedal to the metal.

SIXTY-FOUR

TERMINATED

The driver of the panel truck turned to his partner. "Hey, do you hear that? Kind of a rumbling."

"There's nothing. Let me sleep. I'll take over at the border."

As his partner closed his eyes and leaned against the window, using it as a pillow, the driver looked in his rear view mirror.

Aiyah! A woman was jumping out of a military transport vehicle at a hundred-and-fifty miles per hour, less than twenty feet behind.

That was the last thing he ever saw as the vehicle collided with the truck. The synthetic drugs ignited almost instantly, incinerating everything inside both vehicles.

AT THE SIDE of the road, Rayna caught a glimpse of the incendiary explosion as she rolled on the ground. She came to a stop and took a glance to confirm that yes, the truck carrying the Mandarin's deadly cargo was destroyed, along with all participants and witnesses.

She then started running back to the meth factory. Bypassing Minjoon and Woojin, she shouted, "Come with me."

The two got up and joined her in the run.

"What do you need us for?" asked Woojin.

"I like your voices," replied Rayna. "They work well."

"Yeah?"

"Yeah."

After fifteen minutes, they arrived back at the meth factory. Rayna went to the spot where she was initially knocked out. *Good.* Her knapsack was still there. She turned to her new accomplices. "Move to the right twenty feet. When I get to the entrance, I want you two to start shouting as loudly as possible."

"You kinda like shouting, don't you?"

Rayna snickered. "Only if it's a good joke." She turned serious. "Then go back onto the road we were running along. I'll pick you up."

"With what?"

Rayna pointed to a parked car. "That."

"Do you have keys?"

"Don't need them. Get ready." Rayna picked up her knapsack and advanced with quiet stealth to the loading bay entrance. She pulled out half a dozen "candy bars."

Suddenly, there came the loud, anguished howls of two tortured souls from Hell wailing their fate of eternal damnation.

The workers inside the loading bay looked curiously in the direction of the sound.

Perfect. The distraction allowed Rayna to enter unnoticed in the opposite direction of the sound. A cat couldn't have been quieter. Rayna ripped the paper off three of the candy bars simultaneously and threw them at the boxes of *phenyl acetone.* Tearing the wrappers off the other three bars, she threw them at the boxes of ephedrine.

She ran like hell toward the entrance, but not before picking up a box of meth.

She dashed to the parked car, smashed the driver's window, opened the door and threw the box into the back. As she hot-wired the car, she heard BOOM! BOOM! BOOM, a constant series of explosions.

The car belched to life and Rayna was off. She caught up to Minjoon and Woojin. They jumped in. Rayna drove to the entrance of the industrial park when Minjoon blurted, "Stop. Can we take a look?"

Rayna laughed. "That's a hell of an idea." She pulled to the side.

The three got out and basked in the glow of countless shafts of color piecing the night to a symphony of turbulent clamor. Red and orange flames, created by the illicit pharmaceuticals exploding, swept through the factory. There was enough ephedrine and phenyl acetone to take down the building on the loading bay alone, but dazzling eruptions of fire on every floor proved this was one helluva big operation.

It was a stupendous, breath-taking spectacle of power... and devastation.

The Mandarin's Vendetta was over.

WITH CARS so uncommon for ordinary citizens in North Korea, Rayna dropped Minjoon and Woojin at Woojin's home a mile away. Meth in North Korea was legal and socially acceptable at anything from soirees to afternoon tea. There was enough pure meth in the one box to keep the two and their families fed for years.

Despite the danger, Minjoon insisted on driving Rayna to the Yalu River across from Linfu.

Rayna was too tired to argue. "Thanks," was all she could muster. She slept for the hour-and-a-half drive. When Minjoon woke her up, his parting words were, "I never ever thought that a Chinese would be the one to save me, let alone a woman."

Rayna smiled as she shook his hand. "We can be useful sometimes. Good luck."

A minute later she, like fifty others that morning, was wading across the Yalu River.

"HELLO, Mario's Pizza. Can I take your order please?"

"Hi, Julio, I'm done. I'm at the Linfu Plaza Hotel. I'm going to take a shower, then catch a plane to Guangzhou and then I'm going to the hospital."

"I've got a little task for you before that."

"Give me a break, Julio." Rayna inhaled. "I want to check in on my dad. Make sure he's okay."

"Even if he wasn't, is there anything you could do?"

Rayna was so angry she wanted to crawl through the airwaves and strangle Julio. It was only professionalism that stopped her from screaming at her colleague. "You're right."

Arthur's voice sounded. "Rayna, you don't have to do this job... but I think you'll want to."

Yeah, right.

SIXTY-FIVE
DEVIL'S PRAYER

Ponytail and Sting were pretty rotten brothers. Instead of mourning the loss of Johnny, their attitude was, "Live by the sword, die by the sword."

The two worked around the clock for a few days to change the color of the Mercedes.

"Man, we're good," bragged Sting as he surveyed their handiwork. No longer ebony black, the car was now brushed silver.

"We're the best," agreed his older brother. "Now, let's see who bites."

Besides changing the car's color, there was another reason Ponytail took a couple of days off before letting the word out about the availability of the Mercedes and the temple's artifacts—he wanted to make sure there wasn't going to be negative publicity or sensationalist news about the attack at the Hundred Hands Monastery. If there were, they'd have to wait until the buzz died down before trying to sell their loot.

Ponytail was an atheist but still prayed that there was

no bad karma for attacking a religious site. He was shocked and amazed that there wasn't the slightest mention at all from any source about the barbarous thefts. *Maybe there's something to this God business after all.*

Or maybe not. Barry and Arthur had asked Deputy Minister Zhong to suppress any news about the rescue or the attack on the monastery. Their request was accompanied by a new Audi SUV. Upon acceptance, Zhong asked, "What attack?"

The long-haired criminal decided to let the word out about the Mercedes Maybach. He couldn't believe the response—in an hour, he had five inquiries, more in that short time than from any other vehicle he had offered for sale. Of course, he didn't know that Julio had written a program to flag the mention of the car on any of the legal or illegal websites in China.

All parts of China wanted the car. Shanghai. Beijing. Xian. He put those queries onto the back burner when he got a text from someone in Guangzhou. A series of texts was furiously exchanged.

Finally, a deal was concluded for $750,000 cash, assuming the car was in as good a condition as Ponytail claimed.

"Go for it, bro," were Sting's parting words.

SIXTY-SIX

ILLICIT

Ponytail pulled the silver Mercedes Maybach into the Oceania's circular driveway. An older Chinese man approached. Accompanying him was a large black man carrying a flight bag. Ponytail got out of the car as the two men stopped in front of him. The black man cautiously opened the bag for Ponytail to peer inside.

Yes, there were stacks of used one hundred dollar bills inside. Ponytail's eyebrows shot up and his eyes glinted with anticipation. The black man zipped the bag shut.

"I only go with you," said Ponytail to Arthur.

"He's my assistant," protested Arthur. "He has to come."

"Then we have no arrangement. I have other offers."

As Ponytail got back into the car, Arthur called, "Wait!"

Ponytail paused.

"We won't need you, Chuck. I'll call you when I'm ready."

"Yes, sir."

As Arthur started inspecting the vehicle, Ponytail gave a running commentary. "Mercedes Maybach. Perfect condition. Brushed jet silver. This year's model. Less than 2,000 kilometers. Twelve cylinders, over 500 horsepower. Classic Mercedes architecture. Soft, tempered nappa leather in the interior."

"Stop," barked Arthur. "I know what this car is about. I already have one. It's my mistress that I have to get it for. She is so damned expensive. Cars, clothes and antiques. That's all she cares about."

Ponytail's ears perked up. "What kind of antiques?"

"Anything Chinese. Ming Dynasty. Buddhist collection. Taoist. Wine cups. Bowls. The rarer the better. Do you know two weeks ago, she got me to spend twenty-five thousand bucks on some dumb horse? Twenty-five thousand? And I'm so stupid, I'll get her anything she wants."

"You must really love her."

"Are you crazy? If I want love, I'll get a dog. I do it because there is no one else in the world who is as good in bed as she is. And three years later, I still feel the same way. Anyway, forget about that. I hope she'll be happy with just this damned car. Can I drive it now?"

"Do you want her to think you're a real hero?" asked Ponytail.

"I think this is going to cost me money," bristled Arthur.

"It will but it will be worth it. I've got some rare historic items that will make you a god."

"I want to bring my appraiser."

"The black guy?"

Arthur snickered. "Not a chance. Chuck's muscle. Barry's the snob who knows everything."

───────────

ARTHUR, Barry and Ponytail drove the Mercedes to an industrial park with rows of carbon copy warehouses. Each one was built of concrete, fifty feet wide, a hundred feet long and had two entrances. One door led to the warehouse office. The other was a loading entrance wide enough to accommodate a large van. Perfect for the small business entrepreneur who needed limited storage. It was largely deserted, with the owners off cutting deals at who knew where.

"Drive to the end of the row," ordered Ponytail. "So. How's the drive, Arthur?"

"The drive is fine. What I don't like is you telling me where to go," complained Arthur as he braked the car to a stop. "Once you've seen one warehouse, you've seen them all."

"Not this one. Like I said, I'm going to make you a star."

The three men got out. Ponytail opened the loading door and flicked on the light. He led Arthur behind a wall of boxes and grinned. "Am I great or am I great?"

Carefully laid out on large bookcases was the booty taken from the monastery. Antique vases, bowls, cups, Buddha statuettes, everything Ponytail, Johnny and Sting could get their hands on from the Hundred Hands Monastery plus items from other robberies.

Identity confirmed.

Skepticism crossed Arthur's face. He looked to Barry. "Is this stuff real? I've seen lots of fakes."

"These are real, Arthur," nodded Barry, picking up a vase and examining its markings. "These are pretty esoteric items. Never seen anything like them before. My guess is that they're from some obscure monastery." Barry looked over to Arthur and Ponytail. "These are mid-level, meaning you could get anywhere from $10,000 to $75,000 per piece, if you knew the right buyers."

"I do," smirked Ponytail, his oversize ego filling the warehouse. "Done this before. I know that this is worth at least a million and a half to the right buyers."

"But do you want to spend the time tracking them down and risk getting caught in the process?"

"They're real. Check this out." Ponytail lifted a tarp that held a three-foot figurine of a Hundred Hand Buddha. "Another three million bucks gets you everything. I could get twice that if I waited, but hey, money isn't everything. I just want a quick sale."

"Way too much. I'll give you ten thousand."

Thus began the process of negotiation. Ask for a ridiculous price and counter with a ridiculous price. As soon as Ponytail mentioned three million, Arthur knew there was going to be a deal. Same for Ponytail. As soon as Arthur made a counter, he knew there was a deal to be had.

The only question was how much. After two hours of arguing, yelling, insulting and bickering, a final price was agreed upon. Arthur knew this extended process was necessary. If the negotiation went smoothly, Ponytail would be suspicious.

"You are a bandit," sneered Arthur, shaking Pony-tail's hand.

"That I am. Just get me the money."

Arthur made a phone call. "I need another half million in cash. I'll pick it up on my way to the restaurant. Get us a private room at the Emperor's Delight."

Back in San Francisco, Julio made a call to Chuck. "We found him. Things are going to kick into high gear."

SIXTY-SEVEN

RETRIBUTION

The Emperor's Delight was "the" elite Guangzhou restaurant. It would be impossible not to spend at least five hundred dollars per person on a meal and even more in this private dining room.

On the far wall, easily half a million dollars was spent on the nine hundred and fifty bottles of scotch, wine and Chinese liquor on display. On the wall to the left was a large Chinese watercolor painting of ethereal mountain peaks rising above the clouds painted by renowned Zhang Chun. On the right were several small side cabinets containing fresh dishes and cutlery to replace the ones at the table after each dish was served.

A waitress wearing a red *cheongsam*, a body-hugging Chinese silk dress with a slit at the side, a high collar, and embroidered with Phoenix tails led Arthur, Barry, Sting and Ponytail to their table in the elegant room.

"What would you like to drink?" asked the girl. "We have..."

"Something expensive. We're not paying," bellowed Sting.

"Of course." The waitress pointed to the liquor cabinet to a bottle of cognac with a gold ring around its neck. "Would you like the Louis XIII? Three thousand dollars a bottle."

"Good enough for me," chortled Ponytail's younger brother.

The waitress went to the wall and picked out the bottle containing the deep amber liquid. She placed it on the table, bowed deeply, then left, closing the door after her.

"Now, time to pay up," demanded Ponytail.

Arthur put a large padded bag on the table. "To confirm, four hundred thousand dollars for the car and six hundred for the monastery relics."

"Unless you want to give us a tip for good service," guffawed Ponytail as he filled four glasses to the brim. Sting snatched a glass. Grimacing, he drained it, exacting every last drop before shaking his head. "That is good shit." He poured himself another glass.

Ponytail roared, "Hey, you're the driver so don't drink too much."

"Let these guys pay for a night at the Oceania for us, too," laughed Sting, his bright eyes glistening with greed.

Arthur pushed the bag to Ponytail who excitedly poured the contents of the bag onto the dining table. "Good thing we got a big table," he grinned as he and Sting started counting the numerous wads of cash.

"There are ten thousand American dollars of used one hundred bills in each bundle."

Arthur watched patiently as the two brothers counted the stash, riffing through each one.

Twenty minutes later, Ponytail finished counting the last of the stacks. "Ninety-seven, ninety-eight, ninety-nine, a hundred."

"*Ganbei*! (Bottoms up!)" Ponytail and Sting lifted their glasses and clinked.

Sting was going to pour another round but the bottle was empty. "Hey, we need more."

"Definitely." Arthur opened the door to the room and shouted out, "*Foo Woo Ren* (Service Person)! Another bottle, please."

Within seconds, a different Chinese waitress entered the room. Like the earlier server, this one wore a clinging cheongsam that emphasized every curve of her svelte figure. She went directly to the liquor cabinet and pulled out another bottle of Louis XIII.

Arthur locked the door as the waitress carried the bottle to the table.

"Do you remember me?" the waitress said.

Ponytail's and Sting's faces drained of color. This was the girl in the monastery that Ponytail had shot and left for dead.

"Bitch!" As quick as Ponytail and Sting were to draw their guns from their pockets, the ridiculously expensive alcohol had slowed their reflexes. Rayna calmly pulled her weapon out from behind her dress.

The cold steel of Rayna's soulless pistol stared her attackers in their fear-filled faces.

Ponytail and Sting raised their hands in the air. Every

trace of bravado disappeared as Ponytail uttered two words.

"You win."

"I know," agreed Rayna.

Two silent bullets and justice had been served.

Rayna turned to Arthur. "I'd like to see my father now."

"Of course."

SIXTY-EIGHT
ALIVE

Flashback - Fifteen Years Ago

Twelve-year-old Rayna lay unconscious on the parking lot just outside the Granville Island Theater where her clothes were covered with her own vomit. Lying beside her and equally catatonic was her best friend Heather. The two had gone there with school friends to attend the album launch of the band of Heather's oldest brother, the Smilin' Buddhas. Gary was not only the lead singer, he happened to be the cutest guy in the world, or so thought Heather's pre-pubescent friends.

The band came on at 10:30 and the music was totally awesome with Gary's vocals soaring into the stratosphere. Everyone danced and everybody partied. As it was a private function, no one checked for ID so, when the drinks started flowing at 10:45, well... there was no one checking to see if there was anybody underage or not.

Rayna promised to be home by 11:30 but, when she didn't arrive, Vivian, Rayna's protective helicopter mom, started calling her cell every five minutes. Henry tried to calm his wife down but, when 12:15 rolled around, he agreed to go with Vivian to the theater to check out what was going on.

"She's going to die! Maybe she's dead already!" wailed Vivian in the car.

"I'm sure everything is fine. The music is probably too loud for her to hear the phone," said Henry, trying to convince himself as well as Vivian as he climbed behind the wheel and drove down to the Vancouver hot spot.

When they arrived at the theater, they were lucky to get a parking spot by the door. And yes, the music was loud and the party was in full swing, but there was no sign of Rayna or Heather anywhere. Not in the bathrooms, not backstage... not under any of the tables. Seeing drunken underage partygoers got Henry frantic, too.

He and Vivian went outside to search around the theater.

"I told you she was too young! But you, you... it's all your fault!" blamed Vivian.

"Don't worry, Vivian."

But Rayna was nowhere to be seen either in the front or back of the building or its neighbors. Had Rayna been abducted? Was she being raped?

Then, scouring the parking lots, they spotted Rayna and Heather lying on the ground. Both of the young girls were unconscious with ugly, smelly pools of vomit around them and on their clothes.

"Omigod, Henry. They're drunk! They're drunk!" cried Vivian as the two parents dashed over.

Henry leaned over to check their pulses and breathing. All seemed normal.

Heather quivered—she was cold. Henry took off his sweater and put it around her. She opened her eyes and groaned, "Hi, Mr. Tan. Um, we.... Uh..."

Then Rayna sat up and retched—there was nothing else to come out except horrible yellow bile.

"Rayna, how could you do this?" cried Vivian. "You must never, ever do this again. Do you understand?"

But Rayna was too sick to respond. She grunted as her glassy eyes rolled upward.

"I could kill you, Henry, for allowing this. She is never going out again. Never. You got it?"

"Shut up, Vivian!"

His outburst shocked Vivian and even the inebriated young girl twitched. Henry had never been so resolute or told Vivian to shut up before.

"Rayna is going to make a lot of mistakes in her life that are much worse than this. If you don't allow her to make them, this will only get worse. Be thankful that we are around to help pick her up this time. If you keep acting like this every time it happens, she isn't going to tell us anything and we'll never know what the problem is."

"You are an idiot, Henry. God doesn't want her to get drunk."

"But God is infinitely understanding and forgiving. And stop throwing God's name around every time she does something you don't like."

That evening marked a new beginning for Rayna. Even though she was too sick to move, she learned one thing: her dad would always be in her corner, no matter what happened.

When she told her parents that she was no longer going to go to church because it was "full of hypocrites," it was Henry who assuaged Vivian and told her that Rayna had to find her own path.

When she told her parents she was going to enlist in the armed forces instead of becoming a teacher or accountant like her cousins, it was Henry who spent extra time with Vivian, helping her cope with Rayna's decision to want to defend her country, even in the most dangerous of situations.

And when Rayna fell in love with Tanner, a singer in New York, it was Henry who defended Rayna's right to fall in love with someone they both disapproved of.

And, when Vivian died a year ago while Rayna was unable to be contacted because she was on a secret mission, it was Henry who went to Syria for one day to hold his daughter in his arms and tell her, "I know you feel guilty about not being at Mom's funeral, Rayna. Don't deny it. You feel guilty because you think you hate her for what you think she did to you... She wouldn't let you go to sleepovers, she gave you a hard time about your drinking and the guys you dated. You think you hate her because of that but you don't. Why do I say that? Because you also know she was the one who stayed up all night to hold your hand and wipe down your forehead so you would feel better that first time you got drunk with Heather. She never ever said, "I told you so" when you broke up with some of those guys that both of you knew were wrong for you. You say you hate her but I know you don't. More

importantly, she knows you don't. And, even if you didn't
say goodbye in person, she knows you say so in spirit."

That night, after her father flew back home, Rayna
watched Terms of Endearment and cried the whole time.

PRESENT DAY

POPO WAS STILL on her knees with her hands folded in prayer, but the elderly woman had fallen asleep. Rayna kissed her, then sat down on the chair beside her father's hospital bed. She pulled out a souvenir from tonight's escapade at the restaurant—a bottle of limited edition eighteen-year-old single malt scotch.

She unscrewed the lid and put the bottle directly to her mouth, slugging down an eighth of the bottle. With her body unsuccessful at unwinding from its coiled tension, she took another deep pull. Feeling the jolt from the liquid ambrosia, she closed her eyes and leaned her head back as far as she could.

"I thought I told you not to drink so much," growled Henry quietly.

Rayna's eyes filled with tears. "I never was a very good listener." She got up and went to her father's bed where he had fallen asleep again. She cradled his head and touched his stubbly face, something she had never seen before. Her father was always meticulous in his grooming.

Rayna was becoming unglued. This time she was more ladylike. She poured the scotch into a glass before downing it. *This is the life I have chosen. It won't end because... because I don't want it to end. But survival? Is there more than this? Maybe yes, maybe no. What will I be like in ten years... assuming I live that long? But there is one thing I'm grateful for.*

Dad is alive.

And that thought brought a smile to her soul.

EPILOGUE

Tiansahn was a sleepy farming village in southwest China. There were about fifty tumbledown homes, half of which were empty. The families who used to live in them had all been part of the great moth-to-light-like mass migration to the big cities. Those that remained were too old, too stubborn or too sick to travel. They lived in one-room houses with old clay or brick walls, and tile roofs that were decrepit fifty years ago. They still did their laundry and bathing in the river, bathrooms were foul-smelling outhouses, a communal well supplied the drinking water, and open fires were the preferred method of cooking. Somehow, they all managed to eat by working their small plots of land and growing chickens, ducks and the occasional pig.

Yet, despite the poverty, the town had its private charms. A choir of croaking frogs or the chirping of mating swallows soothed the heart. A huge banyan tree covering almost three hundred square yards provided shady relief from the scorching sun. And, amazingly, there was the ubiquitous Internet because some nameless bureaucrat deemed Tiansahn worthy of electricity despite its small population.

One of the little houses was the home where Ling was brought up and where she lived with her grandparents. However, when all the savings ran out when her grandfather got ill, Ling felt she had to go to Guangzhou to earn some money. When Henry brought her back, for the first time since she left, the elderly couple was ecstatic to see her again. They celebrated by killing one of Grandfather's prize chickens, the main course of a grand feast. Like many Chinese, they preferred chicken to be "almost cooked," with blood still visible.

Normally, the grandmother cooked just enough for a single meal but, because she wanted to impress and thank Henry, there was way too much to eat. However, because they did not own a refrigerator, the food was left out. In the hot weather, the bacteria in the chicken began to multiply. When the family ate the poultry, all of them got sick.

While Ling was young and strong enough to withstand the onslaught of this variation of bird flu, her grandparents were suffering. They lay on the dirt floor, alternating between the chills and sweating with heat.

Ling was freaked out. There was no money left. And Henry and Rayna had not shown up. Were they liars? Had they abandoned her?

"Ling."

The young girl turned to the door to see Henry and

Rayna entering, carrying foodstuffs and presents. She burst into tears. "I thought you weren't coming back," she cried, wrapping her arms around Rayna.

Rayna stroked Ling's hair, soothing her. "That wouldn't happen, Ling, but we had some problems to sort out."

Ling glanced at her grandparents. "They've been like this since the day after you left. Can you do something?"

"We'll bring them to a hospital."

"The closest one is three hours away. They might not last that long," wailed the hysterical girl.

"We'll see what we can do," said a familiar voice.

All glanced to the door to see Arthur and the doctor who had attended to Rayna at the military hospital.

"Hello, everybody. I'm Arthur and this is my son, Steve," greeted the Fidelitas board member. "Ling, Henry told me he was worried about your grandfather so I asked him if he would come along and check him out."

"You're very kind," said Henry.

"No, I'm actually a self-centered jerk but... " He smiled at Rayna. "But I wanted a chance to come and ask you out for dinner and a show."

This broken-down dirt house full of disease was hardly a romantic hotspot but...

"That's the most stereotype date in the universe," pouted Rayna.

"Yes, but with our dads looking on, I'm not going to ask you to come to my place where we can copulate like minks... especially if your minister father might damn me to hell if we got caught."

All laughed.

I like this guy. He's got a sense of humor.

Dear Reader:

I hope you enjoyed this book. Many of the descriptions come from personal experience. The model for Golden Corner was my mom's home village with her. It was a sleepy hamlet during WWII and it was a thriving metropolis when I took her for a visit, fifty years later.

I've spent a lot of time in China's big cities putting together projects and sadly, witnessed the corruption on a firsthand basis. But it is still a fascinating country...

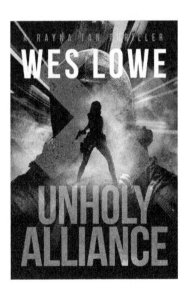

Rayna's next adventure, *Unholy Alliance,* brings us back to America where two groups that normally hate each other, Nazis and Jihadists, come together to destroy a ceremony of their common enemy: the Jews.

It's a chilling and plausible action thriller that keeps us on our toes... and looking over our shoulders.

For more information, visit www.weslowebooks.com

GET EXCLUSIVE STORIES

I enjoy connecting with my readers - it really makes writing worthwhile to me.

With so many books available, I'm so glad you discovered mine. If you'd like to read more, why don't you sign up for my newsletter?

You'll get two stories that are available exclusively to my newsletter group and you'll be first to hear of new releases and any special promotions I'm running.

To subscribe, visit www.weslowebooks.com

BOOKS BY WES LOWE

THE NOAH REID ACTION THRILLER SERIES

Fury Unleashed
Venomous
Manipulate
Forbidden Cargo
The Dragon Deception

THE RAYNA TAN ACTION THRILLER SERIES

American Terrorist
The Mandarin's Vendetta
Unholy Alliance

Visit www.weslowebooks.com or more info or

if you are a member of KINDLE UNLIMITED, you can borrow the ebooks for free.

ABOUT THE AUTHOR

Wes Lowe began as pianist and composer for film & tv, including four seasons on Sesame St. Expanding to writing and directing, his books have appeared on numerous best seller lists, and his films are recognized with international awards and nominations.

Lowe's novels focus on crime action thrillers. Contemporary worlds infused with mysticism. Breathless, brain-twisting plots. High-stakes suspense. Relentless, warp-speed action. Intertwining cultures. Colliding and colluding worlds.

Thrillers that grip the soul.

Printed in Great Britain
by Amazon